I0780210

WAITING ON AUTUMN

Waiting on Autumn

VINCENT JAMES

Copyright © 2025 by Vincent James

All rights reserved. No part of this book may be reproduced in any manner whatsoever without written permission except in the case of brief quotations embodied in critical articles and reviews.

Cover Art: Trudi Castle

First Printing, 2025

~ 1 ~

"People don't want to accept how short our lives really are, and that is truly scary," a stranger at the bar explained to her friend. "They have published these studies on how time seems to pass more quickly as you get older. My understanding is that they claim it's related to how our perception of time has changed once we are older because we have accumulated more years of life to make a day seem much shorter than it seemed to be when we were children. That kind of makes sense to me, but I think there are many other variables involved. For example, I believe our minds give us the opportunity to explore so many other worlds when we are kids. As kids, we connect with and value other people, different places, animals, and even inanimate objects on this deeper level that most of us lose completely by the time we become adults. I believe time passes more quickly when we are adults than when we were kids because most of us stop exploring and we settle for barely breathing. Doesn't it feel like that's all we are doing right now? We're sitting here at this bar while we are drinking ourselves numb and pretending to enjoy ourselves before we go to a party we don't really want to go to. Doesn't it feel like we are simply taking up time and space?"

Autumn felt it was beneath her to listen to other conversations in public. Yet almost every time she went out somewhere, she found herself engaging in this very activity despite the fact that she absolutely hated it when somebody else did it to her.

"At any moment you can die, get a terminal illness, lose a loved one, lose your job, lose your mind, or settle for a life you never wanted," the stranger continued. "At any moment these things can happen. That's why people turn to drugs, alcohol, social media, video games, and other addictions. They want to numb themselves to life, pretend it isn't happening, or fantasize about living someone else's life. They do these things so they don't have to think about their lives... why? Because life is scary. The most successful people in the world know and embrace that life is scary, whether they are conscious of it or not. They are willing to take risks, willing to live fully, and don't settle, even though life is scary. That's true confidence. They don't live the boring insecure lives that we do. They don't have to drink like we do to feel like they're on top of the world—"

Autumn couldn't hold back any longer: "Then why are so many successful people just as insecure and immature as everybody else? Why do they distract themselves with scrolling on their phones? Why do they still drink too much and do drugs? Why do they lack the leadership skills and knowledge to make the world a better place like we apparently do, despite clearly having the resources to make a huge difference for all of us?" Autumn's volume when she was interrupting them had sounded much higher than she had intended.

At first, the stranger briefly pretended to ignore Autumn and continued to face the friend she was speaking to. The friend was sitting at the bar on the other side of the stranger from where Autumn was sitting. The stranger had her back to Autumn and was blocking much of Autumn's line of sight for her to be able to see the stranger's friend. Autumn was therefore unable to see the expressions on their faces, but she knew they had heard her based on both the sudden silence and the tense energy she felt coming from the stranger's direction.

The stranger and her friend were wearing beautiful backless mini dresses that each individually looked more expensive than the cost of Autumn's entire wardrobe. They looked like they had only stopped there for a happy hour drink before they were going to go to a far more expensive venue.

Autumn imagined they were probably going to the type of party she would never be invited to.

After nodding at one another, the stranger and her friend sat up from their barstools and looked back briefly at Autumn quietly with disdain before they proceeded to take their cocktails from the bar and move to an empty table outside on the patio.

Autumn looked down at the bar awkwardly, wondering why she still occasionally felt compelled to jump into conversations like that and expect people to let her into them when most of the time she would get responses like that one.

"What are you doing here..." The familiar and always perturbed-looking bartender started to ask as he approached her from serving customers on the other side of the bar. He looked unusually mystified and genuinely confused: "...when you are already here?"

"Don't you remember today is my birthday?" Autumn asked while looking at him with glassy bloodshot eyes that reflected a complicated mix of sadness, anger, and burnout, "I can't believe people still forgot this one... Ugh, I'm 40!"

"Yeah... but you're... already here," the bartender said cautiously in a way that suggested his own thoughts were interrupting his words.

"Nooo, I just got here," Autumn replied, looking at him impatiently.

It was mid-October, but it was unusually mild that day for that time of year and the temperature was around 65 degrees. The restaurant management had opened the bar area's window-paned garage-like doors up to its outside patio. On cold days, the garage-like doors covered a portion of the large rectangular bar that protruded out onto the patio. Autumn was sitting at the inside part of the bar that was directly across from these opened doors. The patio space was almost as large as the interior of the restaurant, and it also included several tables and chairs. Autumn was able to view the entire patio area from where she was sitting. She observed that it was way too crowded for her to sit in. The stranger and her friend had filled the last empty table that was on the patio.

It had been sunny all day, which was also unusual for mid-October. She noted a sprawling sunset augmented by large cumulus clouds spread endlessly throughout the sky beyond the patio. The glass door beside the bar that exited out onto the patio was propped open along with the opened garage-like doors. There was a small, almost inconsequential, but perfect breeze that floated into the restaurant. The breeze was muted enough to feel mildly refreshing without being a nuisance.

Autumn could not remember her birthday ever being this nice weather-wise except one year when she went to Hawaii by herself and watched couples holding hands and making out on the beach while she drank either a Blue Hawaii or a Mai Tai (neither of which she really liked, but when she was in her late 20s she was still trying much harder to fit in anywhere she went).

"No, you're here," the bartender repeated as he stepped aside from standing directly across the bar from Autumn.

As the bartender stepped aside, she couldn't believe her eyes as she saw a clone of herself sitting in the chair directly across from her in the part of the bar that was situated within the outdoor patio area.

This other version of her had been completely obscured by the bartender when she had initially looked outside.

The other version of her was wearing the exact same clothes and hairstyle. She had the same long dark hair with red highlights that stretched to just below her shoulders. She was also wearing the same long sleeve black off-the-shoulder top with the same dark gray button-down sweater over it. She was also wearing the same jeans. Autumn was the only person she knew of at work who wore jeans and as far as she knew, she was the only one who could get away with it.

There were differences, however.

This other version of her was wearing less makeup but still looked a lot better, as though the makeup had been strategically and expertly applied with a "less is more" approach. This was the opposite of Autumn, who had a well-known reputation of over-applying makeup dating back to high school. The other version of herself didn't have the same subtle dark circles under her eyes despite the minimal use of makeup.

She did have the same black hair tie around her right wrist that spent much more time on Autumn's wrist than it ever did in her hair.

She then recognized how her other-self was surrounded within the crowd by some of her current coworkers and other various acquaintances from different arenas of her life (that she still pretended were her friends).

Unable to continue to look at them, she returned her focus to the beautiful, colorful sunset behind them. But instead of enjoying the sunset, she felt her entire body freeze into a semi-catatonic state as though she had just been administered a powerful numbing agent that placed her in a state of paralysis (and somehow didn't impact her mind). She sensed her mouth had already opened a little bit in awe at the sight of herself. She wondered if she had really died and drifted outside of her own body. But she quickly realized that wouldn't make sense because her other-self was clearly alive and even in her own frozen state, she sensed she was still breathing.

"Uhh, are you okay?" The bartender asked in his usual tone of smug but calm detachment (as though he himself had quickly reconciled the fact there were two different versions of her at the bar). "You look like you could use a drink."

And at that moment, Autumn hoped that maybe she really was in some kind of out-of-body spiritual state in which she was still able to have her own seat at the bar and could experience her happy-hour birthday party alone without feeling the pressure of surrounding herself with people that she barely liked on a major milestone birthday.

She could let her other-self handle the responsibility.

"So, are you her twin or something?" The bartender asked.

"Yes," Autumn lied, realizing she was still able to speak.

The bartender did another double take of Autumn and her lookalike as the pint glass he was filling from a nearby beer tap started overflowing all over his hand. The beer then started spilling over to the floor.

"Bartender," the other version of herself called from across the bar right as the bartender caught himself and released the tap handle, "um, we're all going to need another round here."

Upon hearing someone else speak in her own voice, Autumn couldn't help but look at herself in amazement as her other-self ordered more drinks. She never did that for her co-workers (or anyone else) in her life.

Witnessing how this second version of herself behaved differently than her had an odd, calming effect on her mind. She thought about how she had lived so much of her life feeling like she was somehow outside of her own body watching the different phases of her life unfold from a detached perspective: *Maybe this doesn't feel so weird after all.*

"Will do," The bartender replied as he set aside the overflowing pint glass underneath the tap and wiped off his hand with a towel. He then paused briefly and looked back at Autumn strangely for a moment before proceeding to work on the other drink orders without handing Autumn her beer.

The familiarity of being forgotten seemed to lift her body out of its semi-catatonic state.

She quietly returned to observing the ambiance of her surroundings as she usually would have when she was there, as if to take her mind off the fact she had a doppelganger nearby. The bar and restaurant areas were filled with orange and black string lights along with various fancy looking fall-themed decorations. There was an undefinable energy in October that she had felt for as long as she could remember. She experienced this feeling at no other time of the year. One of the few things she could appreciate about her parents was that they named her after the season she was born in and loved more than any other. In October, it was like her identity could be on full display. She also appreciated that October included a holiday like Halloween where she could paradoxically both further express who she was and hide who she was at the same time by dressing up in costumes and wearing masks.

The bartender himself was a doe-eyed man who appeared about 10 years older than he looked, so he looked like he was Autumn's age. He was the type of person who always looked emotionally wounded, even when he smiled. If you didn't hear him openly discuss looking forward to going to the dive bars he frequented after his shifts ended, you got the sense from his appearance that he frequently did just that. The bartender's arms were covered in tattoos that seemed to reference various movies and video games that Autumn was unfamiliar with since she had lost touch with trends in pop culture when she was around his actual age. He had a slightly overgrown beard that he kept maintained just enough to remain a bartender at a high-end restaurant without losing his job. Autumn had noticed that unlike the other restaurant employees, he was allowed to wear short sleeves that exposed his tattoos.

She eventually noticed that the bartender had finally set down a pint of the exact type of beer she usually ordered in front of her (the previously overflowing one). She had initially planned to order something different, like a cocktail or a glass of wine, since it was a milestone birthday. But after contemplating it for several seconds she took a long, wistful swig as she thought about how 40 already sadly resembled her 30s: *I already hate 40.*

"Umm, you're in my spot," a voice sounding exactly like her own said from a few inches away from her right ear.

She turned and saw her other-self standing behind her with a resting-bitch-face that looked like a mirror image of the same facial expression that she sensed was also pasted on her own face at that moment.

She didn't remember herself saying "um" as much as her second-self seemed to use it.

Autumn quietly obliged to the request as she would with any other stranger at the bar who thought she was in the way. She moved dutifully to the next empty stool over with the sad comfort of doing so that only a person who had been asked a similar question many, many times throughout their lives would have had. After Autumn had moved over, she watched as the other version of herself sat next to her, holding a pint of the same type of beer she was drinking: an amber. She couldn't help but notice that while they shared the same clothing, hair style, eye color, height, weight, and general physical characteristics, that this other version of herself looked so much more confident and at ease than she had ever imagined herself being in her lifetime. Because of that aura of confidence, this other version of her appeared somehow more beautiful than the best photo she had ever kept of herself (and occasionally looked at whenever she felt down about her aging appearance).

"Who are you?" Autumn asked as they made eye contact once her doppelganger was seated.

"You know how you always wanted to quit your job, travel the world, make passive income, and live in your own little world doing whatever you want with minimal responsibility? Well, now you can," her other-self answered with the tone of an advertisement.

"Really?" Autumn asked after a mix of confusion and consideration of what was said. She was both mesmerized and offended by what her body-double was saying.

"I am you, but better..." her doppelganger added with a casual, matter-of-fact tone that one would use when making a cold observational judgment off to the side to a close friend.

"Better?"

"I have to be better. I was made to be better. I was made specifically to replace you. Actually, I already have," her 2.0-version explained as she took a sip of her beer. "I am you at 40 if you took better care of yourself. I am you if you ate fruits and veggies instead of junk food. I am you if you drank more water and exercised. I am you if you knew how to buy better clothes and used a better hair dye for your highlights. I am you if you had a better relationship with your parents and the other people who have come in and out of your life. Most of all, I am you if you didn't live in that ridiculous fantasy world you've spent most of your life in since you were a kid. In fact, you might as well go there now. There is no need for you to be here."

"But this is my birthday party..."

"My birthday party."

Autumn looked at her in stunned silence. She felt like she should be angry. But instead, she felt a weird sense of relief that didn't totally feel right, since she was still freaked out.

"This is what you always wanted," her body-double indicated as if she had been able to directly read Autumn's thoughts, "you don't need any further explanation than that. You are no longer needed here. Let it all go."

"Let it all go?!" Autumn asked. "But I don't even know you."

"I am you..." Her doppelganger reiterated.

"Ha, but better?!"

"So much better..."

Her second-self then turned to her with her nearly full glass of beer and started gulping it down while maintaining side-eye contact with her throughout the process. Her other version was able to pound the beer seamlessly without any struggle and Autumn could only watch in astonishment, knowing that she wasn't capable of such a feat even when she was in college. After her other-self had finished the beer, she slammed the empty glass safely onto the countertop of bar with a triumphant smirk.

"I can handle my alcohol better than you can."

"I can see that," Autumn said. "Are you sure that makes you better?"

Autumn was surprised the glass didn't shatter and that none of the bartenders seemed to be bothered by the loud noise it made when the other version of herself slammed the beer glass on the bar.

"What's the true value of the human heart when most of life is comprised of pain and most people you meet are engaged in some form of escapism to avoid that pain or at least mask it as much as possible? Isn't that what you've done since you were a kid? Escape from life? Find ways to numb yourself from reality like coming here for your sad happy-hours? You of all people should know that there is no value in human emotion and all that propaganda they feed you about love is to distract you from reaching full self-actualization as an individual. What do you need love for? What the world needs is more detachment. We get too involved in each other's business. If you ask me, the root of fear is really love. What would we be afraid of if we did not love ourselves or love others? If you are able to detach from everything, but remain grounded in reality, you can succeed without having to go on your fantastical endeavors into the other world you created for yourself to avoid this one. But unfortunately, you are also human. You are still human whether you like it or not and humans can't help but continue to have hope and continue to love. You may keep it buried deep down inside of you, but as long as you're alive, they are still there. That's why you have failed. That's why you need me."

"I have always been detached in this world," Autumn declared in a defensive and derisive tone, "hence the value of 'the other world' you are referencing that I have ingeniously accessed since I was a kid. That's what has made me more successful in this world as an adult than I ever could have anticipated. A copy of me that seems to know everything else about my life should know better."

"A copy?!" her body-double repeated incredulously. "A copy?!"

Autumn looked at her second-self coldly.

"There's a difference between you and me. I'm the direct answer to you being a failure. I'm here because you are 40 and you are a failure. Let's make that clear. You haven't been successful. Your family wants nothing to do with you. You have no real friends. You don't like your job anymore. Your coworkers only talk to you and act nice to you because they have to deal with you almost every day. You're 40 and you've done nothing with your life. I'm only 4 days old, and I'm celebrating your birthday for you because I can already do it better than you can. I'm not some kind of messed up late bloomer like you. I am not all highly sensitive like you. I already know what I'm doing and you still have no idea who you are."

"Another one for you?" The bartender asked as he approached them.

"You know it," her other-self replied with a confidently friendly tone that would imply she had known the bartender for years, "you know how I roll."

The bartender looked at them both with peculiarity and with some hesitation before picking up her doppelganger's glass to refill it.

"Only four days?" Autumn asked with intentionally short and vague wording now that the bartender was within earshot.

"I'm programmed to know everything. Anything extra that I feel like I've needed to 'relearn' by experiencing firsthand, well, I had already accomplished all of that by the halfway point of day 2."

"Programmed, huh?" The bartender asked as he placed a re-filled glass of amber in front of her 2.0-version.

"Oh, you know we've all been programmed in a way," her second-self responded before laughing inauthentically in the same way that Autumn was known to do with people she pretended she liked.

The bartender looked at her other-self blankly as he scratched the back of his head before moving on to new customers who had sat at the bar a few seats away from them.

"Programmed?!" Autumn asked again once he had walked away.

"I'm you..." her doppelganger said with a brief smirk before continuing, "...developed by AI."

"AI?!" Autumn laughed.

The AI version of herself seemed unfazed that she had this kind of humorous reaction to it.

"So you're not real then. I'm real. You're some inferior copy of me that doesn't always make sense because you are flawed despite having superior superficial characteristics like your appearance and the way you initially present yourself to people," Autumn continued as she struggled to keep a straight face.

"I'm specifically designed to be superior to you," AI Autumn contended with a straight face. "I'm here to replace you and now you are free to go to your little imaginary faraway lands and pretend to be a confident person in them."

"I am. A confident. Person," Autumn stammered as she found it much harder to say it out loud than she expected.

AI Autumn broke its serious expression and started laughing hysterically as though it had witnessed the funniest thing it had ever seen.

Autumn observed it oddly for several seconds as though she was still trying to believe there was a full humanoid AI replica of herself laughing at her before taking a short, awkward sip of her beer.

"How are you able to appear so human and do human things?" Autumn asked.

"My development included the use of modified human DNA to replicate and simulate human functions and behavior but with all undesirable traits removed and replaced," AI Autumn explained.

"What do you mean undesirable traits?"

"You know how we all are digesting information all the time on blue screens but not retaining most of it because the constant staring at those screens along with the incessant scrolling on social media gives us brain fog? I'll put it this way— I don't get the brain fog."

Autumn looked perplexed, and it was more by what she was seeing than what was being said. She realized she still was not doing a good job of hiding it.

"I'll admit that fantasy world you spend most of your time in is amazing, but it's all in your mind and only a few people in this world know how to access it the way you do. You've wasted your life visiting it every day. What you do in that world has no impact on 99% of the people in this world who think you are either crazy or still forever lost in your childhood..." AI Autumn continued.

Autumn remained silent, pulling her beer glass closer to herself as a child would pull a favorite stuffed-animal closer when in duress.

"You ever think about how you don't know for sure if other people's minds and bodies are capable of experiencing the same emotions exactly the same way you do or if everyone experiences the same emotions in a very different and unique, slightly nuanced way like snowflakes are different? You and I aren't snowflakes. I initially experience emotions exactly the same way you do, but I have removed the undesirable ways you react to experiencing them," AI Autumn added.

Autumn continued to look at it with an increasingly complex expression that suggested she still couldn't grapple with the idea that this other version of herself existed. It was clear she was continuously being flooded with experiencing the mixed emotions she had been feeling from the moment she first saw AI Autumn and that it all seemed impossible for her to accept.

"So you have my DNA?" Autumn finally asked after a long pause.

"Your DNA." AI Autumn confirmed.

"How?"

AI Autumn remained expressionless as it glared at her in silence. It eventually picked up its beer and took a long sip of it before turning to walk away.

"You seem to drink a lot more than I do," Autumn said from behind it as it started to walk away from her without turning back to acknowledge her comment.

~ 3 ~

Autumn's relationship with her parents was almost non-existent.

Her parents were the kind of parents who had only one unplanned kid and subsequently did the absolute bare minimum in their roles as parents, mostly out of guilt. They otherwise pursued career-driven lives as though they had never had a kid. Autumn's parents took this approach to a further extreme in that they continued to prioritize friends, in addition to work, over parenthood. When they weren't working extra hours, they frequently hosted parties and engaged in date nights and other activities with other couples that included extravagant vacations to other countries.

None of these activities ever included Autumn.

Autumn and her parents had become more estranged after they forced Autumn to finally move out of their house when she was 35.

Autumn managed to get away with living there rent-free for so long by taking advantage of that guilt her parents had over not being more hands-on with her upbringing and due to the fact that they were frequently out of the country for extended periods of time on their vacations. Her parents had retired wealthy at the same time, and they had almost immediately started spending the majority of their retirement together traveling to other countries for several months at a time.

Her parents had eventually considered her a disappointment after they had spent the first fourteen years of her life boasting to their friends about her high level of intelligence while frequently pointing out her rapid progression in early childhood development, her good report card grades (always earning A's and B's though certainly capable of straight A's), and how she was always so well-behaved compared to other kids her age (especially when she was a baby). But Autumn's astounding resume as a quiet intelligent child who stayed out of trouble ended up being a double-edged sword. Her parents took her for granted and failed to observe the signs that she had as a young child that she was heading down a different path. Even back then, she wasn't working to her full potential in elementary school and middle school because she spent nearly all her time outside of school in as her parents would say: "her own little world." By her freshman year of high school, Autumn had lost the ability to make new friends (she had struggled through elementary school and middle school with keeping them but making them hadn't been as much of an issue). While she was in high school, her parents became concerned about her but made no real effort to address it formally out of fear that it would embarrass the family. They never directly addressed any of their concerns privately with Autumn either. Instead, they occasionally speculated about their daughter's behavior in conversations with only their closest, most-trusted friends and various conditions were mentioned to them (ADHD, Borderline Personality Disorder, Asperger's, Generalized Anxiety Disorder, Schizophrenia, Major Depressive Disorder, Bipolar Disorder, Acquired Dyslexia, and the possibility Autumn may be a Highly Sensitive Person were all considered). Eventually, her parents determined that the speculation about Autumn's condition was causing a strain in their marriage, and they decided to drop the subject entirely as if it had never been discussed.

By the time Autumn was 18 and in college, there was virtually no communication between her and her parents despite the fact they still technically lived in the same house. Within the domain of their very large home, Autumn had her own bathroom, kitchen area, driveway, and side entrance. Her parents had a cleaning service take care of the rest of their home, but Autumn was expected to take care of her own area of the house. Communication was restricted primarily through Autumn looking at their social media posts and seeing the pictures they took on their vacations while occasionally "liking" these posts without commenting on them. But about once every 3 to 4 months, Autumn would receive a text message from either of them (sometimes they seemed to take turns) with an update on their travels or a request for her to complete a task (throughout the last two years she lived with them, it was usually a request for her to give them an update on her apartment search).

When Autumn heard her text tone go off right after AI Autumn walked away from her at the bar, she anticipated it was a text message from either her mom or dad wishing her a happy birthday because they usually waited until the evening to send her a birthday text. She rarely received texts or phone calls from anyone. On this occasion, she hoped it was her parents, as she could remember at least two occasions where her parents didn't send her a birthday text until a day or two after her birthday. She took a swig of her beer as she wondered if her parents would text AI Autumn now instead of her.

When she looked at her phone, she saw it was a birthday text from her mom, but it was a longer text than usual (by her mom's standards). She re-read it several times anxiously, taking a longer swig of her beer as she did so:

"Happy Birthday, Autumn. My father was transferred to Rising Ginkgo Hospice Center after being in the hospital since September 3rd. He has been asking about you. Please visit him if you can."

Autumn was shocked, as she had no knowledge of her grandfather's hospitalization. She gradually stopped re-reading the text message as her ability to focus was drowned out by waves of guilt that she hadn't reached out to grandfather more. Her maternal grandfather was her only surviving grandparent and the only one she had ever developed any type of close relationship with. As a kid she only saw her grandpa 1-2 times per year, and as an adult she saw him maybe once every 2 years. They almost never communicated via phone as they both separately disliked talking on the phone in general. Yet, she had always felt a close relationship with him, closer than she ever felt to either of her parents. Whenever she did see him, he would unashamedly demonstrate genuine excitement and enthusiasm to see her and his mood was always brightened by her presence. It was an impact that Autumn had never observed herself having on anyone else. When she was in elementary school and middle school, she had really loved painting landscapes, but with an overly exaggerated abstract quality to them that her parents criticized and her grandpa loved. She called her style of art "autumnscape" (which actually fit, as many of the art pieces had a fall-theme). Her grandpa kept many works of "autumnscape" art up on the walls of his home.

On and off over the years, Autumn had wondered why she didn't have an even closer relationship with her grandpa but would end up reminding herself that he had a cordial, but very distant relationship with her parents. Her grandpa never connected well with her mom and Autumn could sense that he didn't like her dad (though he never directly acknowledged it in any way). Her mom was born when her grandpa was in his late thirties and her birth had been a surprise to both her grandma and grandpa because up until that point, they were under the impression they were unable to have children. Their marriage had also started deteriorating by the time her mother was conceived, and her maternal grandparents divorced when her mom was 7. Both of her grandparents had declined to discuss the divorce and remained close friends, so it was a mystery to both Autumn and her mom as to why they had divorced. Nevertheless, her mom was raised thereafter by her grandma as her grandpa moved out on his own after the divorce was finalized. Autumn's mom never said it explicitly, but she seemed to blame her grandpa for the divorce. Her mom had maintained a distance from her grandpa after her grandma passed away when Autumn was 23.

She felt a strong pull to go to the hospice center to see him right at that moment.

She looked up at her birthday happy-hour group on the patio and saw AI Autumn entertaining her coworkers and "friends" (none of whom had ever seemed to notice that Autumn herself was sitting there staring at them from across the bar). Other than their occasional loud cackles and amplified hisses of laughter, she couldn't hear them over the noise of the crowded restaurant. AI Autumn appeared to be telling them an enthralling story that closely held the group's attention, as they frequently laughed and smiled in AI Autumn's direction.

She decided then and there to leave immediately to go see her grandpa.

As Autumn took out her credit card to pay for the beer, the bartender nodded to her.

"Your twin already took care of it," the bartender said.

*** *** ***

"Awards, trophies, accolades, degrees, diplomas, plaques, badges, and whatever are all just pieces of paper, temporary markers, or shiny things that all expire after 100 years," Autumn overheard her grandpa say as she approached the doorway to his room at the hospice center. "Well, for 99% percent of us, they do. You can collect all the honors you want that you think will mean something to later generations, but most of the time, they won't. All that matters is whether they mean something you right here and now. There is no guarantee your children, grandchildren, or great-grandchildren will respect what you have done or choose to learn about what you have done. Trust me, once you have lived 100 years like I have and have seen all that I've seen, you'll know."

"But you are only 99 years old," Autumn said as she stood at the doorway, "Grandpa, why do older people add a year to their age when they talk about their age like teens and younger college kids do? It seems like everyone in-between subtracts from their age when they tell other people how old they are."

Grandpa turned his head in Autumn's direction and laughed once he recognized her. He then turned back to the nurse he had been speaking to with a broad smile. "This is my favorite granddaughter, Autumn. She's the smartest kid you'll ever meet."

"Grandpa, I'm your only grandkid," Autumn reminded him with an awkward half-hearted fake laugh as Grandpa looked back in her direction, "and I'm here to tell you that you can't die now. You always talked about making it to 100 years old and your birthday is in three weeks. You're so close."

"As long as I made it to yours, I can die a happy man...happy birthday, Autumn. I can't believe you are—" Grandpa stopped short of stating Autumn's age aloud and instead turned to the nurse.

"She may not want me to tell you her age," he laughed.

Autumn walked over to Grandpa. He had been laying in a hospital-type of bed but pulled himself slightly more upright as she approached him. The tired looking but very young nurse with a ponytail that was dyed purple didn't approach Autumn and remained where she stood near the foot of Grandpa's bed. She merely nodded downward to Autumn with a half-smile and looked relieved that she had an incoming excuse to leave the room.

Before he had recognized Autumn, Grandpa had appeared like a hyperactive corpse-like ball of anxiety, fidgeting uncomfortably around, trying in vain to locate a position within his bed where he could find a little more comfort as he interacted with the nurse. But as Autumn approached him, he seemed to suddenly relax, as though her presence was like both a painkiller and a mood-booster. His effort to be his best for her made her think about how time really passes by as quickly as many older people say, and that life was short, even to someone who lived as long as he had been living. The longer you live, the more you realize how life could easily have those moments where it could quickly become like a bad dream but one you couldn't just wake up from on your own. The only way out of that bad dream would be to slowly climb out of it with evolving patience and endurance that not everyone would learn over the course of a lifetime. Grandpa seemed to have learned that skill that she still hadn't learned. He knew how to manage the pain that life had inflicted upon him with any opportunity for love or for humor, especially when he encountered those he loved.

Despite being on what could have been his deathbed, Grandpa still appeared younger than his actual age. He had a full head of gray hair with a few black strands still intact here and there. His thin van dyke beard reflected a similar mix of gray and black hair. He had thinned in some places nearly to the bone and his skin appeared worn and leathery. However, his dark brown eyes, though sunken and tired, still had a kind gleam about them that Autumn had observed in them throughout her life. She reasoned it was the eyes, along with the talkative energy, that still made him seem younger.

"We're all slowly becoming more and more interconnected in the world." Grandpa had returned to the topic of his prior conversation (that appeared to be one-sided) with the nurse. "We are more connected now than we ever were with globalization and technology. But there will be more wars. Probably world wars. I don't agree with most wars, but every now and then, you have to fight a war to save people. In the war I was in, we saved all kinds of people without completely realizing what we were doing. A person like me probably would have been persecuted too in Europe at that time. Back then, we thought that war was more than enough to wake everyone up to how terrible war can truly be. But there will be more moments when humans will have to learn the hard way that we need each other, and many more millions of people will be sacrificed along the way. Even so, we are still gradually becoming more connected. I've seen it throughout all the generations I've witnessed during my time here. I've seen the periods of progress, I've seen the periods of backlash, and then I've seen the return to progress again. Sometimes it takes a fire to forge two separate parts together, like in welding. Sometimes only conflict can help two opposing forces realize that we are all human and that we need to honor each other in order to survive. Unfortunately, it too often takes two opposing forces to go against each other for us to realize that we are all human and love is the only thing that matters. You must find what you love in life, to love this life. As far I know, we may only have one life, so we may only have one opportunity to embrace all the love we can find within it."

The nurse nodded meekly to Grandpa with a forced smile and then excused herself to give them privacy.

"What's up with the nurse?" Autumn asked once she felt the nurse had walked far enough away from the room to be out of earshot since the door to the hallway remained open.

"Burnout. Already hates her job and only graduated five months ago," Grandpa replied. "That's the problem with the world today, everybody only wants to be comfortable. They want to get paid simply for existing and being themselves rather than do any real work and learn about how life really is. I don't understand it. Back in my day, you didn't have all this luxury and convenience around you that apparently gives young people this impression that they do not have to work for anything. Younger people don't seem to want to talk to anyone either. Most of these automated systems they have now so you don't have to talk to people as much don't work most of the time anyway. You ever notice that? They digitized everything and transferred almost all services online, but it's like you still end up needing to talk to an actual real person to get anything done. People desperately want those machines and computers to work to replace as much of what we have to do as possible, but they don't see how you miss that one intangible thing with people. I can't describe that one thing, so I call it 'the thing'. Young people don't have that thing."

"I'll admit I often wish that memories were like something you only store on a digital note or a word document that you could permanently delete from all your digital devices with just one click," Autumn quipped.

Grandpa looked initially like he had a reply in mind, but he instead paused as if to further take in what Autumn had said. As he did so, she looked around the room. The decorations and accommodations had a more luxurious feel than she anticipated. She had driven past the hospice center a few times before and it looked nice on the outside, but she was still somewhat surprised how much nicer it was on the inside. During the few times she had been to a residence or facility for the elderly before, she noted how the exaggerated outward appearance of these places were more or less a mirage of what they were really like on the inside, as if to draw people into them like an apartment complex or a resort often do. Grandpa was on an IV but otherwise it looked like he had his own private hotel room with his own bathroom and a big screen TV that was turned off.

"It's not bad," Grandpa said, noticing as Autumn looked around the room. "You see that?"

Grandpa pointed up at a painting on the other side of the room from where Autumn was standing. Autumn squinted in its direction as she initially didn't recognize it.

"I had your mother bring it here," Grandpa revealed as he weakly took Autumn's hand, "it's like you're here with me all the time."

At first, she thought that Grandpa was randomly pointing out some cheap generic painting by a mediocre artist that the hospice center had contracted with. But she soon recognized that it was an old "autumnscape." It was an unusual one that Autumn had specifically made for Grandpa that depicted a plane flying through dark clouds in a gray-black sky. It didn't have the usual autumnal landscape and bright leaf colors that about 95% of her other paintings had.

"This is still my favorite one," Grandpa observed.

Autumn looked at Grandpa's hand holding hers with a slight smile.

"Grandpa, organizations treated people more like humans back when you were working. You had pensions, unions, company picnics, and more of an overall family-feel in the workplace. Now it's reverted back to the generations before you when people are expected to work crazy hours, productivity is valued more again at the expense of employee satisfaction, and the middle class has returned to being the working class as the rich have gotten richer. It's capitalism on steroids. The difference now is that the younger generations are still standing up to it in their own way, but it's a lot more individualistic in the way they are reacting to it. What I mean by that is rather than banding together like they did in your parents' generation; the younger people now are simply transferring jobs or careers individually as a way of coping with huge domineering organizations."

"I still don't like it," Grandpa concluded after a silent moment of consideration. "It's like no one is loyal to anyone or anything anymore except to themselves. But I appreciate you being upfront with me about how you feel. I always admired that about you. Most people don't have it in them. You have it."

"It?"

"Yes, 'it'..."

Grandpa looked up at her with a strong smile that belied his state of weakness. When she first saw him as she entered the room, he looked younger than 99 but still had the aura of an old man. With that smile, he seemed like he was her age. This observation almost made her think that she should smile more too.

"Happy birthday, Autumn," Grandpa repeated as he ever-so-slightly squeezed her hand, "I'm happy I got to see you grow into the successful woman you've become. I'm so proud of you. I think about that everyday"

"Thank you, Grandpa" Autumn mumbled, gazing down pensively at the floor.

Without making eye contact, she sensed Grandpa still gazing at her intently.

"Well, you know you have to tell me what's wrong sooner rather than later," Grandpa laughed. "I'm a little limited on time here."

Autumn turned her focus to the black mirror-like screen of the TV and wondered how long they had to talk alone before the nurse came back in.

~ 4 ~

"Sometimes I think I was born in the wrong time," Autumn speculated as she still gazed at the black screen as though there was a show or movie to watch on it. "Maybe if I was born when you were, life would've made a lot more sense."

"It wouldn't have," Grandpa stated bluntly.

"Well...what?"

"It wouldn't have," Grandpa repeated with more bass in his voice, "just because you had more people around you back then either telling you how to live or quietly expecting you to be a certain way doesn't mean your life would have made more sense if you had been born back then."

"Really?!"

"Really. If anything, you might be more confused if you lived back then than you are now. I know I was at 40."

"You think you were more confused than I am at 40?"

"Probably...I was still with your grandma, but by that time, I had long known I didn't love her the way a husband should even though I had love for her as a person. I was finally accepting that I was different. I knew my heart wasn't fully in our marriage and she knew it too. I knew if my heart couldn't fully be there in a marriage with her, it couldn't fully be there in a marriage with anyone. That's why I divorced her two years later and never married again. For so many years after that, she talked about how much happier she was when we were together. It was unfortunate that she never opened her heart to anyone else and that was my fault, because she deserved better than what she thought she had with me. She never got to experience it because back then, you were expected to get married only the one time and make it work. I didn't want to ever get married, but I chose her because she was the best option I had, not because I was in love with her. Back then, everyone was expected to get married, period. At the time, I thought I was lucky that she was in love with me but now I realize how unlucky I am to have to still live with the mistake I made all these years later to have married someone who I didn't love the same way. She lived the rest of her life believing we should have stayed married, because I committed the error of marrying her in the first place. She should've had the opportunity to marry someone who would love her in the ways I never could and there were plenty of those guys around her who would have. One guy in particular had loved her since they were both five years old. I heard he never married either. Maybe I ruined his life too."

"Grandpa, you can't think like that," Autumn pleaded with him. She was visibly perplexed that he was opening up to her in this way. "Maybe she wouldn't have it any other way."

"You're right, normally you shouldn't think like that, but you can think like that when you are trying to find peace with everything as you're reflecting on your life on your deathbed."

Autumn silently maintained eye contact with him, unsure how to respond.

"Don't worry, Autumn, I'm long past the point of beating myself up about it. I didn't know any better at the time. Some of the saddest people you'll ever meet are either the people who think they know everything or the people who think they remember everything. There are no experts in the world anymore, and I realize now there never were. There are just people who really are focused on certain subjects and have their own subjective opinion about them. One identified expert on a subject can think completely the opposite of what another so-called expert on the same subject says about the exact same thing that you are seeking their consultation for. That's why more and more people seek second and third opinions from medical doctors, scientists, lawyers, engineers, or any other specialty that requires years of education. People my age complain that there is no one trustworthy anymore, but back then there weren't very many trustworthy people around either. People just didn't know as much about each other and kept more secrets. If anything, back then, we probably trusted each other too much because we didn't know enough about each other." Grandpa gave Autumn's hand another gentle squeeze before releasing it.

"Weren't people more genuine and authentic back then? You know...not as fake?"

"Every generation is full of people who don't act like who they really are, each generation just has a different way of expressing how they do that."

"Yeah," Autumn murmured, unsure of what else to say. She usually had a lot to say to other people in conversations like this, but Grandpa had a way of making her think a lot more during the course of a conversation than anyone else did. It had been that way since she was a little kid. She realized now it was because he seemed to understand her more than the others. She didn't have to say as much.

"You see how a lot of older people struggle more with talking to people or fitting into social settings because we've been through so many bad people by a certain point of our lives that we only want to be left alone. Especially when you tried to fit in or create the life you wanted and felt like you failed every time you tried," Grandpa continued.

"I totally get that," Autumn agreed, "I feel that way right now."

Grandpa laughed: "You feel like you have had all the life experiences of an old person?!"

"Of course," Autumn replied, genuinely laughing along with him this time, "and I want to know what it feels like to be young even more now that I'm older because I'm not sure I ever knew what being young feels like."

"Life doesn't wait for you, but you are always in a position to catch up to it," he reflected. "People don't realize how much we really run on memories. We replay the same events in our heads while inserting our own biases to eventually create our own revisionist history of an event that becomes so twisted that we can no longer remember objectively how it happened. Memories are everything, and they become your reality if you let them. You end up revisiting them so often that they become your new reality more than the actual real world is your reality. Even right now, I feel like I am still trying to catch up to life."

"Do you have any regrets Grandpa?" Autumn asked in an abrupt way that felt like it came out involuntarily. As soon as she asked, she wanted to take it back.

"October 20th, 1943," Grandpa immediately answered. There was a tense pause before he added: "That was the only one. My only true regret. I don't count marrying your grandma because then this world wouldn't have your mother and you."

"When you were in the war?! Is that why you don't really tell us any details about your time in the war?"

"One of the reasons," Grandpa acknowledged. "I also didn't talk about it much because it reminds me how my parents...your great grandparents, and my sisters were in a Japanese internment camp. I found out later your grandma was in one too. If I hadn't been in the Army Air Corps, I know I would've been there too. It's hard to think about, to talk about, and to explain to anyone now, since it was so long ago, but I have a feeling now you will understand. My family counted on me to represent the best in them: to show our loyalty, to remain strong, and stand for our perseverance through the adversity we were going through. I took that role in our family to heart, and I failed them."

The silence in the room after Grandpa had uttered that last line weighed so heavy on the air in the room, that Autumn felt there wasn't sufficient air in it for her to breathe, much less reply.

"I was a bombardier on a B-17 Flying Fortress. We were part of a large bombing formation that got dispersed by horrible weather. Our plane ended up completely on its own after it got separated from the rest of the group by a storm. Up until that point, I had a reputation as one of the best bombardiers, if not the best, in our squadron. I felt a level of confidence going into that run that I still haven't been able to recapture since then. But on this run, we encountered this thick grayish-black misty fog in the sky that was unlike anything I'd ever seen before or since. We had strayed from the rest of our bomber group, but we still eventually discovered an area that looked like our intended target...I released the bombs, and it was a direct hit. Some of the crew started to celebrate but I realized right away that something didn't feel right. I found out later we had accidentally bombed a remote German village located several miles away from the target. Fortunately, the bomb bay jammed, and we didn't release all the bombs we had on that village... We ended up dumping the rest over the English Channel on our way back to England. But that village contained no major military installations, no industrial works, none of that— only civilians that I killed with my bombs."

"But Grandpa, the Germans were still the enemy back then, right?"

"So were the Japanese..."

"There's a difference, you are a Japanese-American."

"To everyone back then, I was only Japanese," Grandpa cried, "I still am."

"You had nothing to prove; a lot of bombing errors were made during the war. Wouldn't it really be on the navigator? I would think the pilot would take partial blame too. You were doing your job based on their directions."

"Everyone would say 'well blame the navigator' or 'blame the pilot', but I know in my heart I went against my own intuition that day. I released the bombs...and enough civilians in the world were already killed or hurt by the war," Grandpa explained with a shaky tone of seemingly inconsolable sadness. "With everything my family was going through and to have them counting on me to show this country we loved it too and would still fight for it, I never thought I'd be one of the people who would kill civilians too."

There was a strained pause in the conversation, as tension swirled through the room. The same nurse from earlier stopped by at the doorway to check on Grandpa and he miraculously changed his whole complexion and countenance, even so far as displaying a reassuring smile.

He returned to his previous body language once the nurse left again.

"October 20th?" Autumn finally asked after the nurse had departed.

"Yes, tomorrow. I was so relieved that you were born on October 19th and not on October 20th," Grandpa said. "Tomorrow, it will be 80 years ago."

"Wow..." Autumn whispered. She was responding as much to the length of time as she was to the fact that Grandpa was continuing to open up to her in this way. He had never given her the impression that October 20th was a difficult anniversary for him, but she also could only remember ever seeing him around this time of year on October 19th. She couldn't imagine being haunted by a memory like that for 80 years.

"I was one of the few men of Japanese heritage to serve as an American airman in the war," Grandpa continued, "I was 19 years old, they thought I was 23. I know I was young. I know it was war. I know the weather was bad. I know they still had air defenses firing at us in the vicinity of the village. We received no disciplinary action for it. One of the other bombers in our group hit the wrong target that day too because of the weather. But I felt like I dishonored my family. I felt like I dishonored our country. I should have known better. I was better than that...I am supposed to be better than that."

"You were 19 and they thought you were 23?"

Grandpa paused before he broke his sad expression and laughed, "I loved airplanes ever since I was a little boy. I lied because I thought it will help me get in the air corps. They said, 'you japs age well' and the rest was history. You know, Autumn, you're the first in the family to know I told them I was older. I probably shouldn't have done that either. I'll tell you, there was nothing like being on a plane back then. It was magical. Being on a plane now is still great, but back then it still felt like the sky was a new frontier. I think what made the B-17 so special was that you had this big crew of people in it helping each other out throughout the journey. We had 13 machine guns on our plane. Everyone did their job to keep the plane in flight, and everyone helped defend the plane too. All types of people from all over were in the plane. It didn't matter whether you liked each other or not or whether you got along or not, because you made it work as a team knowing that you had to in order to survive and to have a successful mission. You were always together, and you needed each other to survive. I experienced a lot of racism in the military, but never while we were up in the sky. Each man had a role that the life of everyone else in that plane was depending on. Everyone had to do their jobs right, and everyone had to work together."

Grandpa looked up at the painting and Autumn looked at it again too. She hadn't imagined a B-17 when she painted it, but she was amazed at how the sky in the painting was similar to Grandpa's description of the weather in his war story.

"The mistake people make when they don't feel like they connect with people is that they only want to connect with people based on how they see the world. They often aren't willing to meet anyone halfway in their worldview to connect with others they can learn from. They aren't as open to understanding a different perspective. History has been a roller-coaster of progressive periods of time intermixed with darker ages where the world devolves rather than moves forward. I didn't want to tell the nurse this earlier, but I'll tell you: I feel like people I meet nowadays are more reactive and untrusting like we are entering a dark age. I hope I'm wrong, and you know me, I always hope, but people are losing the ability to connect with other people. It's part of 'the thing' I was telling you about earlier. We had more open discrimination, racism, and separation in this country back in those days but the people within the same groups still trusted each other. Now people from the same groups don't seem to trust each other either."

Autumn turned to him with a recurring thought she had been having recently that she felt would make a perfect and convenient response: "A lot of people I meet are impossible to communicate with because they are boring, but don't realize that they are. Everybody now is entitled and thinks they are special for whatever reason when really, they are only trying to impress other people by tricking themselves into believing they are impressing themselves by fitting in with the latest trends, knowing the latest technology, and investing in the next great thing regardless of whether it's consistent with their personality or their values. It's like people become eternally lonely because they don't know how to connect with themselves before they can even start to learn how to connect with other people. They are either willing to sacrifice their values and mental health for money and fame or they never learn what their values are to begin with as they still pursue money and fame. I really have no room to judge though, because I realize now, I was right there with them all along by thinking that I was special."

She noted how Grandpa's eyebrows perked up upon her use of the word "lonely," as the word seemed to inadvertently trigger him.

"You think you understand loneliness when you are younger, but there is no greater loneliness than when everyone you loved when you were younger has passed away and you are the only one," Grandpa lamented.

Autumn was shaken by this unexpected reply: "But I'm here, Grandpa."

"Yes, you're here and you know how much I love you, it's not that," Grandpa said softly. "It's hard to describe. There is something special about connecting within the generation you grew up with and spent almost your entire life with while experiencing all the different world events together when you were around the same age. There's a unique understanding there. You may not appreciate it so much now, but you probably will as you get older. There is a kinship there that the generations before can't quite understand nor the generations after. It's an unspoken bond you have with many of the people who understand the world we grew up together in, had children together in, and had grandchildren together in. You won't have it with everyone in your generation, but you do with many of them. You don't always talk about it with them because you don't want to admit to each other how old you all have become, but you feel a connection with them anyway. You may not like very many people in your life right now, Autumn, but you also have more ways of connecting with them than you realize. You just have to be a little more open to them."

It was with that observation from Grandpa that Autumn confirmed to herself that Grandpa was listening to everything she was sharing with him despite his condition, and he was gradually replying to her in his own way. She also now completely realized that she was experiencing the outpouring of everything he wanted to share with someone before he passed away. She now understood that there was this deeper reason as to why he had asked for her and why she had felt such a strong intuitive pull to see him right away despite the strange, unprecedented event she had been experiencing at the bar.

She was amazed at how sharp Grandpa's mind was for his age. It was like a large rock on the seashore that was shaped and molded like a jagged mountain peak through the course of crashing waves, howling winds, and every other possible form of erosion over thousands of years. She again noticed the glow that remained in his eyes despite his ill health. It was a glow that hinted at the youth she imagined him experiencing in his earlier story. She hadn't planned to stay long but she noticed how staying seemed to re-energize what remained within him that had the ability to be rechargeable.

"Your relationship with someone close to you can continue to evolve within your heart and your soul long after you have stopped interacting with them. I feel that way with your grandma. Your mom never understood me, but your grandma did. Your grandma and I stayed close for your mom but we also stayed close because we shared a lot of the same values. Shared values are the number one most important part of any relationship; your shared values are the foundation and the way you keep each other strong. Love is only a part of shared values. I never talked about how my mind was the way it was with your grandma, but she honored our shared values by still accepting me and never speaking of it to anyone else. I never told anyone this before, but on her deathbed, when she asked to speak to me for a moment alone, she told me that she had known that my mind was different from other people for a long time, and she still would've married me and had a child with me anyway. She told me that even though we never got back together like she wanted to; she wouldn't have it any other way. She told me she wouldn't have it any other way, Autumn, and somehow you knew she would have said that. That brought me a lot of sadness when she said that, but it also eventually brought me some peace. I am not totally at peace with it like I was telling you earlier, but it brought me some peace."

Autumn was initially speechless as she absorbed the story and imagined a visual recreation of it unfolding within her mind.

"Your mind was different?" She eventually asked with a raised brow.

"The earlier in life that you accept who you are, the earlier you'll receive the peace of mind you deserve," Grandpa reflected.

Autumn pondered this for a moment. She was curious about what Grandpa specifically meant about how his "mind was different" and inevitably found herself starting to think again about her own search for a better understanding of who she really was.

"Grandpa, how long did it take you to accept who you are?" she asked.

"I never have," Grandpa humbly admitted.

~ 5 ~

Autumn involuntarily took a step back.

She couldn't suppress her surprise by his response.

"But I've seen the peace it brings to people who have accepted themselves. I still haven't given up," Grandpa added as he lifted his head slightly to get a better view of Autumn since she had stepped away.

"But Grandpa..." Autumn mumbled as she stepped forward again to her original position.

"I know... I'm running out of time," Grandpa laughed as he lowered his head back into the pillow, "but if I have learned anything in life, it's..."

"...never too late," they both said in unison before they both laughed.

"So, you've heard me say it before—" Grandpa started to say.

"A few times here and there," Autumn interjected as she continued laughing.

Autumn couldn't remember the last time she had sincerely laughed this much. It had been a long time.

Grandpa laughed a little longer until his facial expression changed in a way that suggested he had reminded himself of something.

"Autumn, you'll have to excuse me for asking you this question because I imagine you've been asked it before, and I hated it when people asked me this question after I got divorced...but I have wondered, do you ever plan on getting married?"

Autumn's default response whenever she was asked this question was "no way" but for Grandpa, she decided to give the impression she had left the door a little more open.

"Probably not, but you never know," Autumn answered with a skeptical tone that she couldn't hide.

Rather than reply to her words, Grandpa replied to her skeptical tone with a skeptical glance back in her direction.

"I still feel so much pressure to be in a relationship," Autumn acknowledged. "A lot of people say they only feel complete when they are with someone they are in love with. But I still feel the most complete when I am my own."

Grandpa smiled abruptly, in the broad kind of way that he didn't seem to anticipate himself.

"When you marry someone before you really understand who you are, you may discover you are a totally different person than you thought you were when you got married. Maybe other people saw that you were different than who you thought you were, but it really doesn't make a difference at all if you don't see it too. All along, I was one of those people who wasn't meant to get married or be in a relationship. It's harder for people like us to be in long-term relationships."

"People like us?" Autumn laughed, but this time with unease.

"People like us, who see the world differently," Grandpa somewhat vaguely clarified. "I always had a feeling you were more like me. I lived most of my life in a time when I couldn't just be me. Now it's easier to find a lot more people like us, but one thing I love about the world is that those of us who are 'the same' are still different. Of all the people who have lived and died on the earth, you're the first one to ever be you and you're the only one who will ever be you. As far as I know, this is the only opportunity you get, and you can't take it for granted. If you finally start embracing who you are when you're 40, then be grateful that you have attained a goal that many people never attain in a lifetime. Some people live into an old age and never learn to embrace who they are, while others either directly or indirectly commit suicide. Not everyone will learn what you feel like you were 'too late' in learning, so it's never 'too late.' Accepting yourself is not a responsibility to be successful in this world, as there are a lot of people who haven't accepted who they are and have been successful. It's not a responsibility, it's a privilege."

"Right now, I wish I could give you that ability to embrace who you are, Grandpa," Autumn stated sincerely.

"You have look deep inside of yourself to determine what you really want in this life. Otherwise, you will always, and I mean always, be miserable. Most people don't realize how life has a way of resetting you back on the path you really want to be on deep down without you knowing it. You think you are taking a step backwards in life, but what life is really doing is pulling you away from the wrong paths for you and putting you back on the right one. You will continue to encounter setbacks, discipline, and punishment while you are on the wrong ones. I shaped my life around regret, and my life mostly punished me for living the rest of my life around one single regret. Though I didn't embrace who I was, I still followed the path life led me on as much as I could. Deep inside, I stayed true to who I was and nearly everyone I knew never seemed to understand what I was doing. I've found that there is a happy medium, a neutrality, a moderation, and a detachment you learn when you've lived this long that enables you to enjoy life without swinging wildly in any direction because you already had your opportunities to be that way when you were younger. The secret to living a long life is allowing your mind to pay attention to the little things your body and soul tell you. It involves being self-aware but not overly self-aware. I haven't embraced who I am, but I learned to listen to who I am."

"I am pretty sure I've done neither." Autumn smirked.

"Often your journey may either take you through your past in order for you to reach your goals in the future or to find a greater peace with your past in the future. We are meant to struggle to learn how to be strong, but not everybody understands that lesson. When we are born, your mother struggles to give birth to you and it's a struggle for the child being born to be removed from the only world in the womb that the child has known up to that point..."

Autumn's feet shuffled side to side uneasily. While she appreciated all that her grandpa was sharing with her, especially the willingness he had to share it all specifically with her, she couldn't help but feel increasingly defensive. She felt overwhelmed by the fact he was dying and by everything he was sharing with her. The desire to leave the room had also emerged as she no longer wanted to continue this arc of the conversation. It was all too much. She felt the urge to go home and pay a visit to "the other world."

Grandpa looked into her eyes intently once he realized she wasn't going to offer a verbal response.

"Fantasy in all of its forms is a mirror that shows you what you really want, should or shouldn't do, and how you really feel," Grandpa advised her as though he had read her mind.

"Fantasy?!" Autumn heard herself ask without thinking about it.

"Sometimes you never fully realize how lost or unhappy you are in life until you see yourself in the mirror or in photos," Grandpa reflected. "You can go through years without really looking at yourself and seeing what other people see every day. You live it every day, but you don't see it. You only see in yourself what you want other people to see. Therefore, you are not allowing yourself access to see who you really are. But you can access who you really are by allowing yourself to accept that you are living in the real world. Part of accepting that you are living in the real world involves accepting that you are always going to deal with some kind of pain. It's up to you on how much you want to distract yourself from the pain you have and subsequently allow it to grow on its own when you aren't paying attention, like pain tends to do. I've known you since the day your mother and father first brought you home from the hospital and you've always kept your head in the clouds, Autumn. You've never allowed yourself to be fully present for either yourself or others— in this world."

Autumn's eyes widened and she looked around the room as though she might find someone standing nearby with cue-cards for Grandpa to read that had a detailed description of how she lived her life behind closed doors when nobody was around her.

"Grandpa... how do you—"

"As you get older, you get more attuned to life around you again like you were as an infant. You're more sensitive to every environment you find yourself in. You're more sensitive to pain, to fear, and to sadness, but you are also given back the gift of being more sensitive and attuned to all forms of love. Thankfully, if you're as fortunate as I have been, you retain your intellect and intuition," Grandpa explained before she could finish.

"It's too late for me, Grandpa," Autumn muttered with tears unexpectedly welling up in her eyes as she said that. "I invested too much into the way I am now. If I was still in my 20s and know what I know now, I'd be doing something completely different and have all the time and energy I would need to pivot into that new life."

"You are afraid of aging when you are in your 30s and 40s because it is around that time when you realize that time is passing more quickly than you ever imagined it would when you were a kid and a young adult. When you're a kid, you're soaking up everything there is to know and learn all around you in the world while exploring every corner of it that is remotely interesting to you. You also explore the places in life that aren't so interesting because you always feel like you have extra time to do so. But then suddenly you get older and slowly but surely, you learn to detach from the things that aren't right for you or are harming you. You pull away from the things in life that you don't want or need because you are becoming aware that life is short. The longer you live, the more you realize how quickly time passes by because you only truly have all the time in the world when you are a kid. I'm sure you have probably heard that before but let me tell you something that you probably haven't heard as much before: As they get older, many people also inadvertently detach from the things they love too, because they think they have no time. It's a natural human instinct. You detach from the things that hurt you, but in doing so, it's easy to also detach from the things that you love. You don't just do it because you feel like you are running out of time, you do it because you realize more and more how complex life really is, and you want to keep it as simple as possible. You might ask yourself: 'Why can't it just be simple?' Most people want a simpler life by the time they are 40, and they don't want to make it any more complicated than it has already become. A lot of people experience a mid-life crisis because they want to revert to simpler times when they were young. But when you are a deeper person, your only option is to know how things are complicated. Autumn, you are going to have to endure the complications to learn how to embrace the simplicities in life without distracting yourself from life altogether. I know a part of you has been distracted, but if you aren't careful, you'll become even more distracted until you learn how to accept reality. The irony is that life is complicated, but the best way to get through it is to keep it simple, but to keep it simple, the right way is a complicated process of learning more about who you are and what you really want in life that isn't simply attained."

Right after Grandpa finished what he was saying, he suddenly looked around the room himself with a look of concern. Autumn soon joined him, but she saw no discernible difference in the room from when she had entered it.

"Grandpa?" Autumn asked as she turned back to him.

"I still see the bursts of flak shooting up around me sometimes in my dreams and sometimes like now when I am awake. I'd see the flak anytime I went on an airplane and looked out a window and sometimes when I was just walking along the sidewalk in the neighborhood," Grandpa whispered. "It seemed like it was always around me, even if it was invisible. It reminds me how I failed."

"Grandpa..." Autumn started.

"It never went away..."

"Grandpa," A familiar voice sarcastically said from some distance behind Autumn's back.

Autumn turned and saw AI Autumn standing in the doorway. Grandpa turned his attention to AI Autumn as well.

As soon as Autumn looked back at Grandpa and saw that he was looking at AI Autumn in hushed amazement, she moved herself quickly in front of his line of sight to the doorway.

"Grandpa, I have to go, but I'll be back," Autumn gasped, "my friend who gave me a ride here from my birthday happy-hour party is ready to go."

"Am I dreaming? She looks...like you," Grandpa mumbled, still gaping in surprise.

"Oh no, she's way better looking than me," Autumn hurriedly remarked as she leaned and gently hugged him while he remained on the bed, "she wore the same clothes as me and had her hair styled to look like mine as a joke on my birthday. We really have to go; I promise I'll be back tomorrow."

Autumn was surprised to see that AI Autumn was no longer standing in the doorway as she turned to leave. She still expected to find it in the hallway waiting to speak to her, but when she entered the hallway, AI Autumn was nowhere to be found.

6

Autumn was sitting up against a massive 700-year-old maple tree that was on top of a grassy hill and was 200 stories high in elevation. The surface area of the summit was only large enough to accommodate the tree and Autumn underneath it. The hill was so steep that it could only either be accessed by helicopter or by the most experienced and dedicated climbers. Despite being a height that was typically designated as a mountain and having an unusual shape that made it so steep, the hill otherwise had the grassy features of an average sized hill. There were dense white clouds several feet underneath the summit that were visible to Autumn for several miles all around her. The sun glinted off these clouds in a way that suggested it was sunrise.

The tree's foliage was so dense over dozens of branches that it more than compensated for the lack of cloud cover above by providing Autumn with ample amount of shade from the sun. The tree's leaves uniformly changed color each minute to a new color before moving on to another color a minute later. The leaves changed from green to yellow to orange to red to purple and then back to green again and so on. A few feet above Autumn's head, the maple tree had horizontal slits in the bark of its trunk that subtly resembled eyes and a mouth and were capable of moving.

The Maple Tree looked down at Autumn with its eye slits and sighed.

"Isn't it time for you to go back to the real world and go to work?" The Maple Tree asked with its mouth slit. The Maple Tree had a voice that sounded like an elderly woman with a thick Canadian accent.

Autumn yawned. "Probably..."

"You've been spending a lot of time here lately, Autumn," The Maple Tree observed. "You don't want to become anti-social in this world too, especially since you talk about how important it is for you to feel important in this world because you have never felt that way in the real world."

"No need to call that world 'the real world' because this is my real world. That world is just the necessary evil I go through to be in this one. That has always been the reality I've faced," Autumn explained. "I've recently found that my life in that world has become so exhausting and boring that I need more rest here. I feel like this is the only place I have anymore where I can clear my mind."

"Do you ever actually clear your mind?" The Maple Tree asked.

Autumn ignored the question as she observed how the colors of The Maple Tree's leaves were now changing at more a rapid pace. They were now changing color every thirty seconds instead of every minute.

"What if after a person you know dies, they have the ability to see exactly how you lived on earth in every moment and have access to knowing how you really thought of them and talked about them?" Autumn asked. "I mean like, what if they were able to review all that information in heaven? I used to think about that a lot."

"The real world, or rather, what the others who visit here call 'the real world', will always make you feel like you're nobody if you don't acknowledge that you're already somebody within yourself. That's why people often delude themselves into believing that other people in their lives think they are more special than those other people really think they are. They don't want to do the hard work within to discover what is real and what is or isn't truly special about themselves on their own," The Maple Tree replied in its usual way that both intrigued and somewhat annoyed Autumn because it never seemed to directly answer her questions.

"That's one of the many reasons why I wish I could stay in this world 24/7," Autumn rationalized, "Over here, I am already special, I don't need to prove anything to myself or anyone else. It's automatic."

"It's not always about having anything to prove," The Maple Tree cautioned, "that's where much of the insecurity comes from in the people I'm describing. Regardless of how much you think you have anything to prove, it's going to come down to whether you can accept yourself for who you are now and where you are at in life. I don't know if having that mentality makes you special but it's a special mentality to have that will draw other self-accepting people to you. You have so much to share with others, but they won't accept you if you don't accept you. You will also find you won't concern yourself so much about what other people think of you when you accept yourself. People are correct when they talk about how much this anxiety about what other people think can be a detriment to your mental health, but they don't talk enough about how much it can also prevent you from using your spiritual gifts. You are what I call one of 'the forest people'. What I mean by that is that you are one of those people who can see the forest through the trees way ahead of almost anyone else. Not everyone will understand you right away even if just for that reason alone, but it's still a gift you can use to guide yourself and others. It's better than not accepting yourself and ending up either alone or only attracting other people who don't accept themselves. You should ideally use your gifts to help people rather than judge them all the time like you've been doing. We all need more positive people around with your insight and with your foresight."

Autumn heard everything that The Maple Tree said but didn't reply as she was increasingly mesmerized by the changing colors of its leaves. The leaves were now changing to a new color every three seconds.

"You ever wonder why the leaves change different colors before they fall off the trees? I love those colors like red, orange, purple, yellow and the mixes of all those different colors."

"Some of them are brown or stay green when they fall," The Maple Tree pointed out.

"Yes, and some of them are brown or stay green," Autumn acknowledged, "but you ever wonder about that?"

"You're asking me this?!" The Maple Tree laughed.

"Well, you are obviously not like most trees," Autumn laughed with that awkward form of laughter that she seemed to occasionally have from not laughing enough, "I wasn't sure if you knew..."

"For many other trees, their leaves change color during the autumn season due to the reduction of chlorophyll upon the onset of colder days that include less exposure to sunlight. These changing conditions enable the other pigments in the leaves to reveal new colors," The Maple Tree explained, "I am obviously a very different kind of maple tree, so my leaves can change color at any time."

"When I was a kid, I wasn't raised in a religious or spiritual household, but I felt a spiritual connection to nature and just based on that, wondered if there was a God or a Creator," Autumn pondered after a long thoughtful pause in their conversation. "I used to envy other kids who had parents with strong spiritual beliefs because it was like they already had that part figured out for them. It was like they already had a foundation to build upon without having to do their own research and inner reflection to determine what their beliefs were. But now I no longer I envy them. I understand now that my spiritual beliefs involve an ongoing quest of intermingled evolution as a human and transcendence as a social being in the service of living my best life in a way where my personal goals also work to the benefit of others and serve as a model to them. I call it 'altruistic reattachment.' I don't think altruistic reattachment is a process anyone has ever fully mastered though, because life is always changing. The changes you experience in life both personally and in the world around you demand that you manage the abilities you have obtained rather than simply believing you have mastered them."

"Since when did you suddenly start caring about other people?" The Maple Tree laughed. "And what does this have to with trees?"

"At every stage of life, it's like there is a threat to be this other person that you think you are supposed to be, rather than just being yourself. There is this threat to be something we are not, because it's easier and more convenient to be that person at that stage of your life and live a lie than to stay true to who you are. I realize now at different stages of our lives we have different and new opportunities to become a fake person if we haven't already become one. Even if we already have become a fake person then we still must evolve to become a new fake person that better fits the new stage of life that we've entered. In other words, just like there is always a new opportunity to live a lie, you also always have a new opportunity with each new stage of your life to stop living a lie if you've been living one for a while. When I think about how the leaves on trees change colors in autumn, it reminds me of these new seasons of our lives when we are presented with that opportunity to either live another lie, or to be free to be ourselves. But no matter what choice you make, you shed your old self just like the trees shed their old leaves. When I was a kid, I thought the leaves showed their 'true colors' when it came time to fall from the trees. In the same way, I believe you have the chance to observe your true self when you are transitioning to a new stage or we'll say, a new season of your life."

"Why do you only choose to be so wise and empathetic in this world?" The Maple Tree asked.

"I don't ever have to explain or defend myself here," Autumn reasoned. "This is the only world where I can contemplate a concept like altruistic reattachment because I'm anything but altruistic in every other environment that I'm in. In those other environments, I simply detach because that's the only way I know how to survive."

The Maple Tree changed the color of its leaves to yellow and remained with that color. The sunlight had more time to reflect off the yellow leaves to make them seem even brighter, almost as if they were part of the sun too but still somehow able to provide shade.

"When you are young, you are energized and ambitious to learn new things. You are always searching, and the process never feels overwhelming despite all the searching that is required to learn. Then most of us at some point in adulthood believe that the searching ends for us, that we have our version of all the answers. But the truth is that you never have all the answers in life, and you are still finding the answers you need right up to the day you die. The searching never ends," The Maple Tree reflected. "I believe there is a balance to doing the things you know will help you in addition to following the advice that other people who are the right people, will provide to help you. It's often a combination of those things. People like to think it's either one way or the other. I really don't think we are expected to find all the answers we need in this lifetime; we are meant to embrace the searching and the finding right up until we die."

Autumn closed her eyes, and as she did so, that final phrase of *"the searching and the finding right up until we die"* echoed through her mind.

*** *** ***

"Autumn, are you... uh, are you okay?" a youthful voice with an English accent that sounded concerned but confused asked from just over her head. The voice sounded vaguely familiar.

As Autumn opened her eyes, she realized she was still sitting alone on a bench in front of the building where she worked, right beside the main front entrance. The bench looked out into a small plaza that contained a massive twelve-tiered fountain that she could hear gurgling and bubbling in the background among the sounds of birds intermixed with sounds of people walking and talking in the plaza. It was sunny with only a few white puffed-up clouds in the sky that were eagerly glowing in the morning-angled sunlight. It was about 10 degrees cooler that morning than it had been the previous evening, and Autumn had worn her favorite oversized blue and red hoodie for the walk to work. She didn't necessarily need it, but she also wore her yellow knit cap just because she loved wearing it whenever she could.

She recognized the young man standing confidently in front of her was Maxwell, the Executive Assistant to the President & CEO who seemed to be a genuinely nice guy but also struck her as naive and misguided. She was convinced he was only promoted to his position because he had a level of physical attractiveness that also had her convinced that he could be a model if he wasn't already employed in his current line of work. Maxwell's jet-black hair was pulled back in a ponytail, and he wore a mocha and navy-blue argyle sweater vest over his shirt and tie that complimented his unbuttoned navy wool overcoat. Maxwell had told her that he had been born and raised in England before moving to the United States to attend college. His ethnicity was South Asian on both sides of his family, but they had lived in England for generations and he said his parents were disappointed that he had chosen to remain in the United States. This was the extent of the details that

Autumn had known about Maxwell since this was only their third interaction since Maxwell had started with the company a year earlier.

Autumn looked at the time on her phone and then looked at Maxwell with a pained expression.

"I'm okay, Maxwell," Autumn finally answered, "just don't tell her I'm late."

Maxwell laughed inauthentically. "You're the only one who can get away with it."

He then turned and walked away toward the coffee shop that was located across the plaza. Autumn estimated there was a 99% chance he was getting beverages and/or sweets for others rather than for himself.

7

Autumn sighed as she stood up from the bench.

She looked through the large window wall behind the bench and saw a vaguely familiar woman in the building's lobby that she knew had worked with her for years, but she couldn't remember the woman's name or her title.

The woman waved to her.

She lifted her hand up to wave back but didn't complete the wave. She didn't feel motivated enough to fully wave back.

She sighed again.

She resigned herself to going inside the building, though she was tempted to either walk back home or follow Maxwell to the coffee shop and hang out there instead.

She stayed silent and made no eye contact with anyone as she walked through the lobby, used the elevator, and then walked down the hallway on the floor her office was on.

It was fairly well-known throughout the building that she didn't like greeting people or engaging in any small talk. Nevertheless, a couple of co-workers she didn't know so well did greet her with "good morning" to which she only responded with a hurried, half-hearted nod.

As she approached the door to her office, she could overhear one of her coworkers on the phone in the office that was across the hallway from hers: "I wish there were more non-profit organizations that helped everybody instead of just separate specific groups of people. It's great that we have any organizations at all that help people, but it's like we don't have organizations that help everyone. Each organization only seems to help a specific group of people who meet their criteria. No one seems to realize how even well-meaning organizations divide people in the world. It's like we are destined to have separate, competing principles and that will always make it easier to forget that we all need help sometimes," her co-worker asserted.

As usual, it was one of those calls where she couldn't tell if it was a work call or a personal call. The co-worker had started there three weeks ago, and Autumn still wasn't sure of her name either. When she reached her office door, she overheard her coworker say "oh, hang on a second" to whoever she was speaking to.

"Oh Autumn, Casey wants to see you in her office immediately!" her co-worker called out into the hallway in an annoying way that anyone else with an opened door in the hallway could hear.

Autumn stopped dead right in front of her office door and felt her heart skip a beat. Casey was the President & CEO of the company.

She briefly thought of peering around the side of her co-worker's door for further interaction with her but didn't want her co-worker to see her looking either worried or discombobulated. She could sense herself alternating between both expressions.

She opted to stand in the hallway so they couldn't see each other.

"She does? She didn't text me or anything, or at least I don't think she did," Autumn muttered as she pulled out her phone from her hoodie pocket to double-check it.

"She came by here like 5 minutes ago, looking for you," her co-worker added before saying "sorry about that, I'm back" to the person she was talking to on the phone.

Autumn looked at her phone and saw two missed calls from Casey as well as a text message from her that asked "where are you?!", in addition to observing that she was 11 minutes late to work and that her phone was still apparently on 'do not disturb' status (she usually kept it that way unless she was expecting a phone call). Casey had an over-the-top way of signing the end of her text messages with only her first initial ("C.") in the same way that she signed every email and document. To Autumn, it was an obnoxious habit that looked more like a signature of Casey's narcissism than an actual signature.

She had already experienced one of those rough nights in which she didn't get enough sleep and only came close to a deep sleep just when it was time to wake up. As if that wasn't enough, it had also been one of those mornings in which she woke from a dream and discovered the better life she had in the dream was not the one she was having in real life. It all had prompted her visit to "the other world" while sitting on the bench outside after she had arrived at her work building slightly earlier than usual that morning. Now that she knew Casey was wanting to see her, she felt an odd satisfaction that she had ended up being late instead of being early.

She sighed.

She tried to think of reasons not to visit Casey.

When she couldn't think of any, she went back down the hallway. She re-entered the elevator she had exited a few minutes earlier, and once inside, she entered the private code that was required to access the 50th floor. Casey had included the code in her text message.

She figured she might as well get it over with.

Autumn had known Casey since they were in the same fifth grade class together. They were subsequently in classes together on and off through middle school and high school. They never said a word to each other unless they were assigned to work as partners or on a group project together in their classes. Whenever they did work together, it was strictly business, and they found they worked well together despite having almost nothing in common beyond a high intellect that was observed in each of them from an early age. Autumn was a very shy child. She was a loner who was awkward, nerdy, and considered an outcast, even in kindergarten (when most kids are still relatively open and considerate to each other). Casey on the other hand, was privileged, extroverted, narcissistic, and popular. Around the seventh grade, Casey began relentlessly bullying other girls with her entourage of friends but always spared Autumn. When other girls would try to bully Autumn, Casey would rein them in and justify her behavior with lines such as "she isn't worth your time" and "she's not even worth you acknowledging her existence." It was Casey's twisted back-handed way of maintaining her reputation while respecting Autumn. Autumn was simply relieved she didn't have to go through what she would see the other girls go through, so she reciprocated the unspoken agreement they seemed to have not to interact at all unless a teacher assigned them to interact.

This arrangement regarding their communication lasted until they were 22 and Autumn was struggling to find work after she graduated from college. Autumn had started college majoring in computer engineering but changed her major to communications after her first year. She also dropped out of the honors college. Autumn switched majors and left the honors college because she wanted a less rigorous courseload despite being a straight-A student throughout her freshman year. Although she had an impeccable academic record, Autumn interviewed poorly with every company she initially applied to. She eventually settled for applying to an Administrative Assistant position at Dark Forest Solutions, which was then a rapidly expanding digital technology startup company that Casey had founded two years earlier with the financial support of her parents. To Autumn's surprise, Casey not only messaged her personally without being present at the interview to tell her she was hired but also designated her as the company's first Digital Marketing Manager, rather than hiring her as an Administrative Assistant. Despite having no experience, Autumn was expected to learn the job on the fly with Casey's assurance that the company would finance any additional education that was needed (Autumn would eventually obtain a master's degree in marketing).

Together, Casey and Autumn elevated Dark Forest Solutions into an international conglomerate with subsidiaries in technology, defense, health care, retail, and real estate and with locations in at least eleven other countries around the globe. Outside of financial gain, these diverse investments were seemingly unrelated to market observers and nearly everyone who worked for the company, but they were all interrelated in the mind of Casey, who had become a billionaire by the age of 28. Throughout the period they had worked together, Autumn was the ideal employee for Casey. Autumn never worked beyond 40 hours a week and frequently showed up to work late and left early, but Casey quickly discovered that Autumn could accomplish the same work in an hour that would take other employees trying to do the same task a few days. Autumn never complained, did everything she was asked to do within her regular working hours, and never asked for more money. Autumn also accepted a much more modest paycheck than the other employees at her level, as she was making $150,000 per year at 40 (which was the same salary she had been making when she was 30).

Other employees would complain that Autumn was detached, and aloof outside of the immediate tasks assigned to her. They also complained that she was sarcastic, moody, occasionally mean, and almost never socialized with them outside of special occasions or required meetings (which Autumn would often skip anyway if she felt it wasn't pertinent to a project she was working on). But Casey didn't see any of these complaints as an issue for her as she felt that she was in full control of Autumn's rare level of intellect and creativity. Casey was known to swiftly fire or demote anyone who she perceived as insubordinate or a threat to her power and rarely showed any preference for any employee. Autumn, however, was one of the few exceptions. Because Casey either defended Autumn whenever there was a complaint about her or outright rejected it without hearing the full complaint, Autumn was perceived as a "favorite" of Casey's despite having the lowest salary of anyone in her pay grade. Autumn was still seen as a "favorite" of Casey's in the eyes of her coworkers even after they would learn that Casey and Autumn hardly ever interacted after Autumn's first five years in the company. In fact, Casey had promoted several people above Autumn, gave substantial raises to people with less time in the company than her, and had created several positions above her in the years that followed their initial five-year period of working closely together.

Autumn's office was located on the 36th floor in the main building of the headquarters of Dark Forest Solutions. The main building had 50 floors total and was located at the center of a massive office complex downtown that included five skyscrapers (the other four buildings that circled the main building were 35 floors each). Casey's office was on the top floor of the main building. In fact, the entire 50th floor was dedicated to space just for Casey. To access it, Casey would text her employees the code (which automatically changed every half-hour or manually at Casey's discretion) that needed to be entered on the panel of the elevator to reach it. The 50th floor was much larger in volume that the other floors because it measured 50 feet in height. Half of the floor was dedicated to a large open garden area with trees, fountains, a large outdoor meeting area, and a pond (this was accomplished by adding an additional 12 feet in the space between the 49th floor and the 50th floor).

The "garden-half" of the 50th floor was completely encased by glass windows (including the ceiling) to maximize sunlight for the plant life and to give Casey the impression she was outdoors without exposure to bugs. Casey had married her husband, Gray, in that garden when they were 32. Casey and Gray had been high school sweethearts, but she had pushed back their wedding by over decade specifically to get married in her own rooftop garden and then hold the reception on a large, elevated mahogany deck within a forest on land she owned on the outskirts of the city. She designed the deck for a prolonged wedding reception and got married at 9am so that she could have her wedding party make the half-hour drive to the deck in time for brunch because she wanted her wedding day to be an all-day event that also included dinner and then dancing until midnight. Autumn was well aware of every detail of the itinerary as she had stayed for the entire wedding despite not wanting to go at all. She saw it as a work assignment and knew that Casey would notice if she wasn't there at any moment despite the presence of 299 other guests at her wedding.

The other half of the 50th floor included Casey's office, a large indoor conference room, and a penthouse apartment that Casey occasionally stayed the night in if she worked late. Casey didn't stay the night in it often but frequently worked in it instead of her actual office to give herself the illusion she was working from home. She kept the office primarily for virtual meetings and to meet in-person with staff or visitors. She would receive an alert from the computerized smart home system she had installed throughout the 50th floor that would inform her when someone was approaching her floor in the elevator. The smart home system included voice activation of appliances, lighting, the thermostat, security cameras, a watering system for the garden, and a dozen smart TVs that were installed within an entire wall of Casey's office. Casey's desk in her office faced this wall of TV screens with her back to the floor-to-ceiling windows that lined the wall behind it. The TV screens included one large primary screen (that measured 8 ft. x 4.5 ft) directly in front of Casey's desk that was used for virtual meetings. The series of secondary screens on either side of the primary seen were often tuned into a live feed with various stock market updates, international news stations, and calming aesthetic scenes like South American waterfalls, scenes at European coffee shops, rainy days in Bali, beaches from around the world, and winter bonfires.

When Autumn exited the elevator, she entered a narrow hallway that led directly to Casey's office. Casey only allowed access to the 50th floor from another set of elevators that were on the garden side of the floor if she was hosting a special event or a visit from dignitaries representing foreign governments or other corporations. For her employees and undistinguished visitors, she used only the elevator that Autumn was in for access to the 50th floor. The hallway was installed to minimize employee contact with the rest of the 50th floor. Both sides of the wall in this hallway were covered with photographs of Casey and her family over the years. There were also speakers that played middle-of-the-road and overplayed acoustic pop music that was positive and upbeat. These speakers were scattered along the length of the hallway. To Autumn, this hallway felt like a bizarre recreation of any millennial's social media page that included pictures of every insignificant moment in their lives that didn't necessarily warrant a photograph. There were unintentionally embarrassing framed photos of one of her daughters sitting on the toilet during her first use of it after potty training, a photo of what Gray's knee looked like after a knee surgery, and a photo of what their new refrigerator in one of their houses looked like next to the old one, among others. Of course, every picture of Casey appeared as though it had been carefully evaluated and photoshopped to present her in the best possible way before being added to the hallway. Lastly, the hallway included ceiling cameras with accompanying ceiling speakers which enabled Casey to view the visitor and speak to them as they approached her office. If someone spent too much time looking at the photos, Casey would thank them for their appreciation of her family before prompting them over the nearest ceiling speaker to expedite their movement through the hallway (this happened to Autumn the first time she ever used the hallway).

By this point, Autumn had adopted a policy of briskly walking through the hallway as though she was in a hurry to meet with Casey. This way, she could minimize what had increasingly become an irritating gauntlet to navigate.

She was relieved to see Casey's door was already open at the end of the hallway.

"Well, there you are, I see we are still ignoring my texts and showing up to work late," Casey said as she stood up from behind her desk.

~ 8 ~

Autumn smirked as she stood at the doorway and then gazed around the office as she slowly approached Casey's desk.

Casey's office had a mix of an old money aesthetic that was augmented with modern architectural and technological features. The side walls between the wall of screens and wall of windows were covered with bookshelves that were filled with books from floor to ceiling. The walls of bookshelves each contained a wooden ladder on wheels that were attached to their respective rows. There were pairs of brown leather reading chairs with end tables in front of both walls of bookshelves. The end tables each had a small, green-shaded banker's lamp on them. Essentially, Casey's office looked like a late-19th century university library with modern technology. Casey's desk had two brown leather guest chairs immediately in front of it, and this set of chairs also included a small end table between them with a banker's lamp. Casey had nothing on her desk except for a larger banker's lamp and two control panels at either side of the desk that operated the smart technology around the 50th floor. As Autumn recalled, Casey's other desk inside of the penthouse side of the 50th floor was much more crowded and elaborate, with multiple computer monitors, documents, and books scattered around her desk (Autumn only saw Casey's desk in the penthouse twice in all the time she worked there).

The fact that the sun was sun shining outside through the tall windows (with the shades pulled up) belied what otherwise would have been a dim, musty appearing ambiance.

Autumn stopped short of sitting down in one of the guest chairs in front of Casey's desk and remained standing with an aura of attentive impatience that fully indicated a preference to exit the room as soon as possible.

Casey was wearing a formal navy-blue skirt suit with no discernible shirt accompanying the jacket as if to augment the appearance of her breast implants underneath the V-neck of the jacket. Autumn had noticed over the past five years that Casey had become increasingly sexualized in her formal wardrobe and had hypothesized this was to compensate for a losing battle against aging that had heightened her pre-existing insecurities about her physical appearance. In all her years of working for Casey, Autumn had never seen Casey wear the exact same thing twice. Casey had kept her long dirty-blonde hair with natural highlights at shoulder length since high school. Casey's deep green eyes were so penetrating, that Autumn had always found it difficult to make eye contact with her. It was like Casey's eyes hinted that she was making a thousand silent judgments per second of whatever she was observing. Casey seemed to be aware of this and didn't hesitate to use this "ability" to her advantage in terms of intimidating rival CEOs and her own employees. Casey's skin was naturally tan and the appearances of both her and her father (from what Autumn remembered of the one time she saw Casey's father in childhood) suggested possibly either Latin American or Asian ancestry from one of Casey's grandparents or great grandparents, but Casey denied having anything but European ancestry.

Casey spent hours each morning and at night dedicated to improving and/or maintaining her physical appearance. Growing up, Casey was not seen as a natural beauty and always felt she had to compensate for it with her intelligence and with a strong personality. Once she found success as business owner, she began the process of undergoing various cosmetic procedures in an effort to improve how she perceived herself and how she thought others should perceive her. However, despite positive feedback from her inner circle, she was never completely satisfied and eventually became convinced that cosmetic technology had not yet caught up to what she needed. As a result, she started a new cosmetic science research department at Dark Forest Solutions. She remained convinced that she could find procedures to perfect her own appearance, even if she had to sponsor the invention or innovation of these procedures herself.

Casey looked at Autumn with a feigned sheepish grin that suggested she had been looking forward to this meeting for quite some time.

"Autumn, I'm placing you on paid administrative leave for the next three months effective right now. You can go home. I'll reach out near the end of your leave period and give you instructions from there," Casey casually dictated without any show of emotion.

"Sounds good," Autumn replied without hesitation. She started walking back toward the door and added: "I'm just going to get a couple of things out of the mini-fridge in my office and I will be out of here."

"That..." Casey began with an amplified volume, "won't be necessary."

"Wait...what?" Autumn asked, turning around.

"You mean the yogurt and the bottles of that nasty carbonated water you drink, right?"

"Well...yeah."

"I think AI Autumn thought they were hers," Casey wondered as though thinking aloud. "I think she assumed I put them in there for her first day in your office. She started work four hours ago and when I went down there to look for you a few minutes ago, she was eating the yogurt at your desk. I tell you what, I'll have Maxwell personally deliver a case of your ridiculous carbonated water and a pack of your cheap yogurt later this afternoon."

"Wait, what?!" Autumn asked. "I should have known..."

Casey didn't immediately respond and looked at her with no perceptible expression.

This was by design.

She wanted to see more of how Autumn would handle this revelation before providing any sort of explanation.

"Well?!"

"Well, what?" Casey asked with a smirk.

"Let's start with 'Why?'!" Autumn demanded as she approached Casey again but ultimately remained in a standing position (she couldn't remember the last time she had sat down in the guest chairs that Casey had in front of her desk).

"Since the onset of the COVID-19 pandemic, nobody knows what they are doing anymore in the workplace. You don't have people around who really know their professions. They just wing it and fly by the seat of their pants. With so much mediocrity, insecurity, misguided selfishness, and general laziness in our generation and now in the younger generations, it's easier than ever for the cream of the crop to rise the top," Casey explained. "Do you think most people know what they're doing? They don't pay attention in their mostly underfunded schools when they are kids. Then later in life, they are overpaid doing work they barely know how to do. Meanwhile, they pay minimal attention to their children in a vicious generational cycle they learned from their parents who also had no clue about what they were doing. All the while, they complain that life isn't giving them enough of what they think they deserve. They look at rich trust fund kids and well-connected wealthy geniuses like me and think they can replicate what we have but they can't. They don't have our connections, they don't know our secrets, and they falsely believe that either just being themselves or actual merit will help them succeed. The irony is that they can't put in the effort to earn what merit would offer them, even if it was all about merit, which it isn't. It's all about who you know and the connections you have.

Maybe you can sprinkle some dumb luck in there too, especially in your case since you are lucky enough to work for me and lucky to have grown up with me. I don't like you, Autumn, I never have. But I'll admit that since I grew up with you, I have that weird unwanted soft spot for you and that's why you are here in the first place. Thankfully, you do a good job, and you are one of those few people who actually knows what they are doing."

"If I do such a good job, then why create AI version of me?" Autumn asked flatly.

"You ever notice how our generation is dumber than previous generations and lacks the work ethic of previous generations, but has higher ambitions in terms of the money they want to make and the type of lifestyle they think they deserve?" Casey continued (leaving Autumn unclear if she had noticed her question). "No wonder our generation has so many issues with anxiety, depression, and drug use. It isn't just social media; it's their continuous state of cognitive dissonance from always wanting what they haven't earned but believe they still deserve. The media they consume totally mirrors those shortcomings with anxiety-provoking headlines promoting articles that are much more fear-based than informative. They consume addictive gossip stories about the celebrities they want to be instead of engaging in educational pursuits. The podcasts they embrace are pseudo-educational opinions and aren't science-based. The media knows they are dumb, so they cater to them with dumb shit which reinforces their failure to learn more about the world and themselves. The difference between people like you, Autumn, and people like me, is that I never get tired, I keep going. I never get lazy. You get tired and you get lazy. You lose sight of your goals and go into your own little world. You lose focus. That's what makes me better than people like you. I'm constantly working. You come and go as the spirit moves you and you'll never catch up to me. Lazy, smug, non-doers like you sit back and judge and criticize what doers like me do but offer no realistic alternatives. You are just like the media."

Autumn simply squinted quietly at Casey. Autumn had learned to do this as a cue for Casey to directly answer her questions whenever she continued with her long-winded explanations in lieu of directly answering her. Autumn also knew that if she offered a response to everything that Casey had shared, it would further delay a response to her initial question.

"AI Autumn is simpler and not all complex and weird like you are. That's another problem with our generation: people are too individualistic and complex when they don't know how to be and aren't mature enough to learn how to be. That's why so many people our age don't have jobs and still live with their parents or depend on them for financial support. If we can create AI versions of them, we can tap into their potential and get the best out of them. We can leave the undesirable traits out. It's the only way I can maintain an effective, stable workforce that will be as consistent and as loyal as our grandparents were with their jobs. I need people who will stay with me and have the kind of lives outside of work that will keep them efficient here. You only work four days a week, and you only have to come into the office two days a week. I don't have to give any of those perks to AI Autumn. She doesn't want to work from home. She'll work overtime without pay. I actually pay her less than what I pay you. AI Autumn is just happy to have a job and happy to be here in the office. It's the way I eventually want all my employees to be and the way they will be. Immigration used to fill those roles in the workforce but now we have AI. A lot of people in my position are considered 'smart' because they know how to game the system, manipulate consumers, and maximize profit even when it goes against their values, but they aren't as intelligent as I am. I have a morality they don't have and a humanity they lack because I'm working around abusing people like immigrants by creating my own AI version of people. I understand that you can't get away with burning people out like the other corporations do. By instituting this AI program, I'm not burning people out or exploiting immigrants like they are."

Autumn stayed silent as she processed everything Casey was sharing with her. Everything that had transpired within the last 16 hours felt overwhelming. It was all too much. She looked blanky at a large white fluffy cloud that was passing in the sky through the window behind Casey.

She loved when they sky moved so visibly like that.

"Our society doesn't value smart people, at least I know our generation and younger generations don't. Most people are threatened by smart people. Unless you are smart person who also has a lot of money to show for it, you aren't going far. Look at the way teachers and college professors are barely paid and undervalued. They don't get much for what they do. A lot of kids now don't want to go to college or feel like they need it. Haven't you noticed how expensive college is? It's like our society indirectly doesn't want more smart people around. The crazy part is that smart people haven't figured that out because they value being smart so much within themselves personally that they don't see how it isn't valued outside of their own subjective experience. The smart people with money seem to assume all other smart people have money and can look out for themselves. The smart people without money are some of the most depressed people you'll ever meet because we measure success with money, and they regard themselves as failures rather than seeing how society has failed them. I don't want you to be one of those people, Autumn, but let's be honest, you already are one."

Casey's insult seemed to give Autumn the ability that she needed to refocus and shake herself out of the daze she had briefly entered while looking out the window. She chose to ignore the insult to try to avoid going down another rabbit hole of endless philosophical dialogue from Casey.

"How were you able to create an AI version of me?" Autumn asked in her most professional sounding voice (that she rarely used) as she hesitantly looked back at Casey.

"You should be proud," Casey declared, "AI Autumn is a magnificent work of art in my opinion. She turned out better than I ever could have imagined."

"She is an 'it' and it's a robot," Autumn grumbled.

"You were a failure as Autumn, but 'you' will achieve everything you should have ever wanted to have achieved as AI Autumn. People already believe every lie they see in the news or in social media, they'll easily believe AI Autumn is you."

"How were you able to create an AI version of me?" Autumn repeated, sounding almost exactly like she did the first time she asked this question as a continued conscious effort to demonstrate to Casey that she wouldn't be phased by her insults.

~ 9 ~

"Years of research and study. We used your employee health records including the psychological testing we did with you about five years ago when you completed that leadership training that I made you go through. IT records your usage everyday of how you work on your computer: when you are working, when you aren't working, and the work-related and non-work-related websites and applications you use. We bundled that data and parsed out the productive elements to use when we created AI Autumn," Casey finally revealed. "We also used data collected from video footage recorded of you by security cameras over the last decade that captured your habits, mannerisms, tendencies, and important decisions, even when you thought no one was watching. Again, we took out most of what we didn't like while leaving enough of your core characteristics in to retain a realistic, but improved copy of you. Everyone around here who meets AI Autumn without knowing the AI project believes it is you because they never truly got to know you. Contrary to popular belief, we all do use our entire brains, but studies have shown that more intelligent people use their brains more efficiently than others do. When you are focused, you use your brain much more efficiently than others do. AI Autumn uses her brain more efficiently than you do. Since AI Autumn is higher functioning and infinitely more likable than you are, the people who would meet both of you will think you are her dysfunctional twin. But we are thinking and hoping that you will disappear."

"How do you know how efficiently my brain operates?" Autumn asked incredulously. "You can't verifiably make that assessment just based on the work I do here."

"You're right." Casey smirked.

Upon Casey's response, Autumn finally remembered a "three-day employee health checkup event" as part of that leadership training five years ago in which employees who signed a disclosure agreement underwent a full physical, a psychiatric evaluation, brain scans, full body scans, lab work, and a battery of testing to determine physical, cognitive, and mental faculties. Casey had hand-selected the employees who were invited to the leadership training. At the time, Autumn had been focused on the fact that you were exempt from work for those three days and supposedly got to see the results of the testing (which she never saw), but now it all made sense. The leadership training, the employee health event, and the security cameras were all ways of Casey spying on her under the clever guise of being offered or utilized either for her career growth or for her safety and well-being. The IT tracking of her computer activity had seemed like another move on Casey's part to micro-manage her employees, but even that had turned out to be part of an industrial-organizational psychological study on the relationships between her behavioral patterns in terms of her procrastination vs. her productivity throughout the day.

Everything now seemed to align except for the access to AI technology.

"But there isn't an AI department here," Autumn stated.

"There is at another undisclosed location," Casey revealed. "I started it pre-pandemic but accelerated the AI Autumn project after the pandemic hit. We had a lot of downtime there for a while during lockdown to concentrate our resources on it."

"Is this even legal?!" Autumn asked. "I should hire a lawyer."

"Good luck with that," Casey countered scornfully. "You wouldn't be able to sustain the legal fees for a good lawyer with your salary and if you could, you wouldn't win because you signed all kinds of approval and disclosure forms for the project without even knowing it throughout the duration of your employment here. You didn't read them. Not that I can blame you, most people don't. As intelligent as you may be, I correctly took a chance on assuming you were one of those people who accepts the terms and conditions of agreements without reading what you are signing. Do you ever notice how most people are too stupid to realize we are invading their privacy? Most of them don't read the fine print associated with shopping websites, social media platforms, or doctor visits. They don't notice the little details of how we dig deeper into learning so much more about who they are by giving them a little bit of what they think they want or need. We know everything about everyone who signs anything that is associated with this company. 95% of people have no idea how much we know about them, and we just call the other 5% crazy and marginalize them. The era of misinformation and conspiracy theories has never worked more in the favor of big business like me."

"It's still worth exploring my options," Autumn mused, but unconvincingly.

"Why don't you go back into your little world and let it go. I am giving you what you always wanted. Maybe you and I aren't all that different, since I have dreams of my own too, but I keep mine based in the real world. I don't think I ever told you this, but one of the houses I own is so close to the ocean that the waves hit the glass wall of windows facing it in my living room. You can see some of the sea life underneath the waves."

"Is that up to code for building inspectors?" Autumn asked dryly.

"When you are as rich and influential as I am, does it matter?"

"Touché."

"See this is another difference between you and AI Autumn, the little comments like that," Casey noted. "No wonder nobody talked to you in high school, you have these random sarcastic observations that no one wants to hear when you do talk. Maybe it sounds fake or inauthentic or whatever to you, but people want you to be nice to them. It's common, basic, simple etiquette that people like you never learn. If you had learned that, you'd have real friends and would have started a family of your own like the rest of us normal people have. But instead, you are alone. You're always alone. Like you were in high school. Like you were in middle school. Doesn't it bother you that you're 40 now and still never learned how to talk to people and have relationships with them? Doesn't it bother you that you could have been more successful here, but I keep promoting less experienced people above you because they know how to talk to people better than you do? People want you to listen to them, and they want you to at least pretend to take an interest in their lives, even if only over a brief interaction. People want kindness. You may think you're funny with your caustic observations about the little details of life, but most people aren't laughing with you and if they are laughing at all, they are still laughing at you."

Autumn initially looked at Casey as though she was about present a sharp, anger-laced rebuttal, but then looked down at the floor instead. Finally, after several seconds of deep but expedited contemplation, she looked up and made eye contact with Casey again.

"I seriously don't understand what I am doing wrong, I'm 40 and I'm living the life I thought I wanted. I have a job that pays more and is easier than anything I thought I would ever get coming out of college. I get to spend as much of my free time in the other world as—" Autumn abruptly paused after reflecting in a way that sounded more like she was thinking aloud to herself rather than talking to Casey. It was an unusual moment of vulnerability that she rarely showed to anyone, much less Casey. But she had felt different in the last 16 hours since meeting AI Autumn and seeing Grandpa in hospice. She had suddenly stopped herself from continuing to speak out of habit when she had mentioned "the other world." She had never made that mistake with anyone in the real world who didn't know about the other world. But Casey had been hinting that she somehow knew about it, and sure enough, once Autumn had stopped herself, Casey smirked in a way that suggested she knew exactly what the other world was.

"...you know you could have at least told me about the AI project," Autumn continued, "and you know, let me know that I was your guinea pig. I did a lot for you and this company. Especially in the early days."

"You're kidding me! I gave you several opportunities to move up in my company and to be in positions where you would know more about what is going on around here!" Casey exclaimed. "This is what kills me about you, I was trying to help you, and you didn't acknowledge it. Now in a roundabout way, I'm still helping you by giving you the freedom you wanted, and suddenly you don't want it?! I don't know how you can still complain about anything. I mean you were a total loser in high school, and I still basically made you my social media person. Did you know that people we went to school with still laugh when I tell them that?"

"You actually still talk to other people we went to high school with?!"

"See, there you go again..."

"Well, you're always bringing up when we were kids in school. What does that matter, Casey? We are 40. That was like over 20, 30 years ago."

"You ever notice how people in their 70s and 80s talk about when they were kids or when they were in their 20s? You don't usually hear them reflect on their 40s or 50s. Why would they? The prime of their lives occurs when they are in their teens or 20s. You hear people in their 30s reflecting fondly on their teens and 20s as if they are already in their 70s and 80s. You establish what your life is going to be like when you are in your teens and when you are in your 20s. In their teens and 20s, people generally make decisions that will stay with them for the rest of their lives: the type of people they prefer to spend their time with, the hobbies they are most interested in, what they will do as a career, whether or not they want to go to college, whether or not they join the military, whether or not they want to jump into trying to get married and having kids— all of those things. Trust me, it matters. You should know that better now than you ever have. You literally wasted your potential. You wasted your life up to this point by living like a kid as an adult and doing the bare minimum at work to maintain your kid-lifestyle."

"A lot of people grow up more slowly these days, 40 is the new 30, or maybe even the new 20. It's common in our generation. There's nothing wrong with that," Autumn asserted. "You're acting like the dream is over, just because we're 40. We obviously both know some people who might feel that way, but there are other people who say their life didn't really come together for them to do the things they really wanted to do until they were 40."

"There's nothing wrong with living with your parents until you were 35? There's nothing wrong with ignoring taking responsibility for yourself? There's nothing wrong with not living to your full potential to contribute productively to this world we live in? There's nothing wrong with contributing far less to this world relative to how much you are taking away from it? I guarantee that the people who live like you do feel unfulfilled deep down and aren't happy with themselves living in basements, dorm-like apartments, or old childhood bedrooms playing video games all day and creating videos of themselves sharing their non-sense opinions to get a bunch of likes on social media and temporarily feel better about themselves."

"Some people make great money doing that," Autumn reminded her, "and I've helped this company make money doing that."

"You've honestly done an okay... ah, a decent job," Casey reluctantly acknowledged, "but you could've done so much more here. Instead, you'd rather daydream about traveling the world and making passive income with your own social media when you could be making a lot more money with me to travel more of the real world, like I do. You live in a fantasy world, Autumn, like you did as a kid. Don't pretend that how you lived your life and made choices as a kid doesn't impact your life when you are 40, you are literally the poster child for it. You're still a kid. Do you know who you are yet? Be honest with me, are you gay? Everyone who knows you always asks me, and I don't know what to tell them. I can't even tell myself. We weren't sure, so we programmed AI Autumn to be heterosexual. Have you had sex yet?! Are you still a virgin? Again, we weren't sure, so we programmed AI Autumn to have a healthy sex drive. Did you ever want kids? Do you know how to talk to kids? We didn't know, so we programmed AI Autumn not to want kids so I could maximize her work effort. Are you just mentally incapable of being in meaningful long-term relationships? You know what your testing indicated in all these categories? 'Null.' That's all you apparently are in your personal profile, Autumn, you're null."

~ 10 ~

Autumn didn't initially know how to reply, so she looked outside the window behind Casey instead and saw that the cloud had gone. She then looked around the office again and for the first time in her life, briefly wished she had a life that was more like Casey's life. She quickly dismissed that thought but still found herself without a response that she would've wanted to give for all of Casey's questions.

"You look like you are trying to come up with another one of your excuses or trying to think of a way to change the subject," Casey observed. "Look, you don't have to answer those questions. At this point, I was asking as your friend anyway. I already made up who you are for my purposes here at work. Like I said, you're getting paid during your leave, but if I were you, I'd use that time to find another job."

Autumn felt both a sense of relief and a sense of sadness upon hearing Casey say that. It was a feeling similar to what one might experience when they wanted to break up with someone they were dating for years, but their partner broke up with them first. On the one hand, Autumn was relieved that she wasn't getting fired or immediately laid off, but on the other hand, she had invested so much into the job that there was a sadness that came along with the idea of leaving. She didn't like her job and didn't like the people, but it was still oddly comfortable in a way that she didn't want it to be.

"Don't take it personally, Autumn. In this era of social media and in a time when people are more transparent about their personal lives than ever before, people see the increasing disparity between the ultra-rich and everyone else. As recently as five years ago, it was still a worthwhile endeavor for big corporations like me to invest more in my employees. It used to be that by improving work conditions, adjusting to flexible hours, and raising salaries, I could maximize the effectiveness of the workforce and increase retention. But even that strategy is no longer good enough to try to reconcile the increasing demands of employees for pay raises and more paid vacation days with meeting the ever-expanding goals I want us to reach. I'm smart enough to realize that and as a business owner, I always want to maximize productivity and minimize the expense of maintaining a workforce. But this is no longer just about productivity; it's about maintaining the integrity of the organization. Therefore, I found a way around that by creating my own workforce that won't be so demanding and won't complain about the difference between a 32-hour workweek and a 60-hour workweek. I want and deserve a workforce that is unconditionally devoted to the organization. I've earned that. I won't find that in millennials approaching middle age who still wish they were children, and I certainly won't find that in the self-aggrandizing trends we are already seeing in Gen Z."

"You don't understand that by the time you get to our age, there are a lot of people who aren't really alive. They are in pain, they are worried, they are suppressed, they feel trapped, and they are numb. They are living ghosts," Autumn replied. "They live only for self-preservation and to preserve their families, but they aren't truly alive. Little victories that involve climbing up to the next rung of the corporate ladder are mostly what they think about when they try to think of ways of how to motivate themselves at work. They think about that next pay raise or that next vacation. It's the only way they feel like they have any semblance of control over their lives—"

"That's not what you think about," Casey interjected before Autumn could go on any further. "You have over three hundred hours of accrued vacation time that you still haven't used. You haven't had a pay raise in years, nor asked for one. I'll be real with you; I've wondered about it for years. I wondered about it back in high school. I would wonder to myself: 'How does Autumn get by?!' Then finally, three and a half years ago during the pandemic lockdown I figured it out while I was working on the AI Autumn project. I'll be real with you, Autumn. I finally know everything there is to know about your other world. In fact, I now know more than you do about it."

"What other world?" Autumn asked, trying to look as genuinely confused as she could by pretending that Casey could have been referencing some other random world that she legitimately wasn't familiar with.

Casey laughed.

It was that odd brand of laughter she occasionally had where it sounded half-genuine and half-insincere.

"I also made AI Autumn more normal with guys than you've been," Casey added, "even outside of the context of a romantic relationship."

"What is that supposed to mean?! I'm fine with guys." Autumn folded her arms in defiance.

"No, you're not," Casey laughed, leaning forward further over her desk, "you barely acknowledge them."

"Sure I do."

"Did you download that dating app I told you to use and offered to pay for?"

"I did not."

"Ahh, you're impossible! I still don't know how you live even after knowing everything about you. I don't know how a creature like you breathes the same air as me."

"I don't need a man," Autumn retorted, "nor do I need you."

"Oh, you need me," Casey contended, "you can't make a living by spending your time in your little fantasy world. Like I said, I didn't know what it was about you in high school, but I knew something was off. I knew something was wrong with you mentally, but it was more than that. Something else about you was off. I thought you were either high on something all the time or you were one of those people that naturally looks like they are perpetually half-asleep. But now I know that even back then, you were spending every waking moment you could in this other world. The difference between you and I is that I live a fairy tale life here in reality, you on the other hand, just live in a fairy tale."

By this point, Autumn looked exhausted from the interaction itself. She looked down at the dark mahogany wood flooring. She felt that extra fatigue she would get in her legs that only seemed to come along when standing somewhere too long in a place that she didn't want to be in. She tried to slightly exaggerate this appearance that she sensed herself having, with the hope that Casey would take note of this struggle and allow her to go. She figured she probably had that same look of being half-asleep that Casey had observed about her in high school.

"I'll tell you something that even I recently had to learn to accept. You know how people do this whole anti-aging routine of various creams and oils to pretend they are 10 or 20 years younger than they really are? They also may become vegans, or born-again in any religion, start doing body cleansing herbal remedies, listen to new age sound waves to stimulate their brains, cosmetically whiten their teeth, attend a spiritual retreat, or try new and different forms of exercise. People try all kinds of things to start over and be younger and healthier again. They keep up with all the healthy trends that are supposed to be the fountain of youth for them. They think they can 'transform' themselves, but they are never clean. By our age, you've been down these rough roads, you have scars, baggage, or mileage or whatever you want to call it.

You still carry all the things you did wrong or failed to do right. Every experience you've had stays with you no matter what you do, and when you present yourself to someone new you might as well wear them like merit badges because no matter what, they are going to be there. You can't get rid of your regrets, flaws, or mistakes. But I've learned you can do an incredible job of hiding them, and not in the way you are thinking. The most successful people I know are the best people at masking their mistakes, their flaws, their regrets— as if they never happened while still acknowledging that the events that precipitated those mistakes or exposed those flaws occurred. When others inevitably find out about their flaws or mistakes, the most successful people I know have ways of distracting them or redirecting them from their mistakes and flaws with their achievements, their promises, and their confidence. Successful people like me know how to get people to accept who we are when they wouldn't normally accept us. We don't avoid, but we deny, we distract, and we redirect. That's how you win, Autumn, because all that is wrong with you is still there regardless of whether or not it's said out loud."

"What do you mean by clean? What's that supposed to mean? Do you mean perfect?!" Autumn asked. As she asked these questions, she looked up and noticed how the sky through the window behind Casey had suddenly become filled with many clouds, but they were not a pure white color like the previous cloud. All the new clouds were partially imbued with varying shades of gray.

"Maybe that's part of the reason why I have a soft spot for you," Casey continued as though she hadn't heard Autumn's response. "You are a mystery. You don't reveal much of anything. And why do we have to know everything? It's amazing, really— the very personal things that people will post online in their blogs, videos, in the comment section of other people's posts, and all that shit. Sometimes I wish I lived back in a time when the only people who you were exposed to in terms of expressing themselves were those who were worthwhile and had something to contribute to society. Now we need to know and hear about everyone on TV, on the Internet, and on 24-hour news cycles. We hear about all the shit, all the trash, and it's mostly about ordinary, mediocre people who aren't worth our time. All it does is take up the space of the true art, actual creativity, and real contributions toward the betterment of society. I literally think to myself sometimes when I'm scrolling on social media or listening to a podcast: 'Why do I need to know everything about you? What good will it do me? Where is the mystique? Where is the challenge? Where is the excitement? What do you know that I don't already know?' I'll give you this much, you are at least interesting enough that I would ask to know more about you. If you're really as smart as I want to think you are, you'll keep up the mystery and you'll keep your little secrets to yourself."

"I don't know," Autumn pondered, thinking about Grandpa in that moment despite the tension in the room, "maybe I'm changing as I'm getting older. Sometimes I wonder if it's good to share and communicate as openly as possible. Maybe there are a lot of exciting or educational stories that people still never know about each other because they are too embarrassed, too afraid, or too egotistical. People might be able to appreciate other people more if they knew everything about one another. I mean, I guess you're right; nobody is clean— whatever that really means. But sometimes I wonder if we were all completely open, then maybe there would be less judgment, and maybe there wouldn't be so much of a tendency for people to think they are so much better than other people without understanding them. It seems like society is going downhill because we are all more inclined to air out everything about who we are, including our dirty laundry. But maybe it's also good for people individually to feel free to be themselves and to be as open as they want to be, even if a lot of people may not want to understand them right away. Most importantly of all, maybe if people felt more comfortable to be open to share who they are, we wouldn't have the cancel culture or people shaming people so much for making mistakes because they would be open and acknowledging about their own mistakes too. Forgiveness could be seen more as a virtue rather than a weakness. It's hard to say right now because I think people are still learning how to be responsible with sharing themselves with the world in a way that is good for their own well-being."

"Don't be mistaken. Society is going downhill, and we have no social restraint. It's like everyone is drunk on hearing themselves talk, seeing themselves on video, and reading their names on other people's social media posts. It's like they forget that the more you learn about someone, the more you find out not to like about them, the more freaked out you get, and the less you want to be around them. A person you know everything about is no longer useful to you most of the time because you already know everything they know and could potentially teach you. 99 percent of people are ordinary and if they recognized that they were ordinary, we wouldn't have all the problems we have these days. Most ordinary people are delusional right now and think they are extraordinary when they never will be. I believe a few people only ever have the potential to be extraordinary. I never admitted this before today, Autumn, but you could have been one of those extraordinary people. I'll be totally honest with you though when I say it's too late for you to be anything more now than ordinary. I tried so hard to bring out the best in you for so many years, and in a way, we can say that I finally have accomplished that with AI Autumn. All my work to try to help you wasn't in vain and now you can also say all your potential wasn't in vain. Again, isn't this what you wanted? You don't have to live in this world anymore. You've been replaced by a better version of yourself, so you can live full-time in your own little world."

"But... this..." Autumn started.

"What?! What now? I'm realizing from this conversation that you'll never figure life out and will never be happy," Casey interrupted.

"But, this... thing... you created of me, doesn't live like I do. I don't trust it to make my decisions, to share my values, and to continue to be who I am."

"Of course not," Casey scoffed with increasing agitation, "that's why she is a better version of you. You should be grateful for that. I expected you to have the opposite reaction to her. She is living the normal life you secretly wanted, and you can't say you haven't wanted that because I know you have. As far as I know, people have ignored you since like middle school. I know I did. In high school, college, and through adulthood, it's been like you haven't existed socially. You've lived like you were a ghost, or you were invisible. Nobody wants to live that way, including people like you who say they do. If you like living that way so much, why have a whole other world that you spend all your free time in? Why be so desperate for social interaction the way you used to be in high school until you finally learned to give up? You were never happy, and it is one of the many reasons why no one wanted to be around you in school and why people politely minimize their interactions with you now as an adult once you start talking to them. People like you need to acknowledge and admit to yourselves that people like you really do exist in our world, and you live your lives alone forever while feeling sad all the time and unfulfilled. It's sad, but it's real. You're 40 now. Every day for rest of your life will only be spent wondering what you are going to eat for lunch, then what you are going to eat for dinner and then needing a coffee the next morning just to get you out of bed. Wake up and accept that you grew up to be one of those weird people you'd see alone on the street that you felt sorry for as a little kid when you observed how all the other adults ignored them like they didn't exist. AI Autumn is accepted; people pay attention to her and even want to be like her around here. You can still live your life in your other world; she will still let you stay with her in this world."

"Stay with it?"

"Sure, she's leaving a couple hours early this afternoon to move into your place. I'm letting her off early to go shopping and pick up a few extra things. Not all of us want to spend the rest of our lives living like a college student like you do."

Autumn looked more enraged than outraged.

"Autumn, I am helping you," Casey reiterated with a more diplomatic tone. "Don't you see that? I am being the friend you always wanted by giving you the one solution to every problem you've ever had in your life. You are one the first people I'm creating an AI replacement for. I plan to do this for a lot of people who work here. It will help this company operate with a level of efficiency you can't imagine, and I know you have quite an imagination."

"Everything isn't as simple— it isn't as black and white as you think it is," Autumn argued. "Maybe my life wasn't as great as it could've been up to this point, but it was still mine and I wasn't as sad as you think I was. I was more confused and yes, with confusion there is often some sadness. But I am finally starting to accept who I am. Not everyone has everything figured out from birth like you."

"First of all, you aren't starting to accept who you are; you're still confused. Second of all, in business, it is that simple. It is black and white. I can be more productive and efficient with employees that don't have all the drama and baggage that people like you have. People don't like to work nowadays anyway. I am doing you a favor. You don't have to work, you can stay at home, you can travel if you want, you can live full-time in your other world, you can go on social media, and you can play games on your phone all day— you can do whatever. That's what most people our age and younger want anyway, right? They want to be able to do whatever whenever they feel like it. Even a lot of people who chose to get married and have kids still secretly want that. Now you get to do that with the freedom of being an eternally single person. AI Autumn has your job and will pay your rent. You are free."

Autumn stood there like a statue that was unfazed by a windstorm howling all around it as she thought about that: *I am free.*

"Think about it some more... I know you already are," Casey recommended with her trademark smirk.

Autumn instead turned now to a different thought: *Why am I even here?*

She was thinking well beyond why she was there in Casey's office. She was wondering why she was there in the real world. She was wondering why she was there with her particular genetic makeup, her particular brain, and her particular appearance. She wondered why she was there breathing, at that specific point of time, out of all the possible times she could have been alive throughout human history.

She was wondering why she was alive.

She had experienced those existential thoughts on and off throughout in her life, but now at that moment it felt like she was experiencing those type of thoughts multiplied a million times in a way she had never experienced them before.

"I only know how to be alone," Autumn heard herself say out from underneath those frightening and burdensome existential thoughts.

"Do you ever wonder why everyone else we went to school with figured their lives out in their teens and 20s while you are still living your life as an older version of yourself from when we were in high school?" Casey walked out from behind her desk but maintained a distance from Autumn. She exuded a posture of increased confidence that was buoyed by the uncharacteristic vulnerability that Autumn was exposing to her. "You still blame the rest of the world," Casey whispered, "but it's not the rest of the world, it's you."

Autumn awkwardly took a step backward away from Casey and then involuntarily scratched the tip of her nose.

"You can blame your parents for not making enough money," Casey continued with her usual volume, "you can blame gender inequality or racism, you can blame it on having bad luck, or you can blame me, but the reality is that you are where you are because you never grew up and never learned how to play the game."

"That's all life is here, it's a game," Autumn muttered. "A game that's not worth playing and I was smart enough to realize that from an early age. If you don't want to sell your soul to be something you're not, then it's pointless to play a game that will forever undermine your character and values. Everyone eventually regrets living a life of being something they are not."

Casey laughed. "That's where you couldn't be more wrong. The secret to life is having the knowledge that you are rarely true to who you really are. You are never really your true personality around other people. People around you never really know the real person they think they know. You could talk to them for twenty or forty or eighty years and they still won't know the real person you are. You adjust your personality depending on the person you are taking to. You only have the opportunity to really be yourself when you are alone. Even then, you aren't always being true to yourself because most of the time when you are alone, you are tainted by the voices of hundreds of people who have walked through your life telling you or modeling for you who they think you should be. Since you rarely get the opportunity to be yourself, you might as well be the best composite of what you and other people think you should be in order to succeed in this world."

"You only say that because your parents already laid out your whole life for you in advance. You'll never have to do any deep exploration to find out who you really are because your parents played the game for you, and you've benefited from it your whole life. You never played the game, you inherited the rewards from other people who played it for you, and all you had to do was smile and look pretty as you accepted those rewards. Sure, you know how to act in the role of being successful, but you were taught that from an early age when success was already handed to you without any effort on your part. The only success you know of is how to make money and how to take advantage of other people. Your version of success isn't happiness, your version of success isn't peace of mind, your version of success doesn't involve any morals or values, and your version of success isn't accepting who you are deep down inside." Autumn took a step forward and they made silent eye contact that momentarily allowed the tension to speak for them. Once it became clear that Casey didn't have an immediate verbal response, Autumn turned to walk away.

"Something changed in you, Autumn. You are starting to act the same way Joy used to," Casey grumbled, as Autumn started to head toward the door.

"Who is Joy?!" Autumn asked sarcastically as she stopped without turning to look back at Casey. "You mean the girl we went to high school with over 20 years ago? I didn't like her either, remember? I haven't spoken to her since we graduated, have you?! I don't think you have either. Why do you still bring her up? It's like you're obsessed with her."

"I am not!" Casey shouted at her with a seemingly younger tone in her voice that oddly sounded like the one she had in high school.

"Didn't you get suspended in high school for jumping Joy in the gym locker room with your friends?"

"I didn't," Casey replied. "Natalie did. Kaela did. Madison did. Lizzie did. My friends did, but I did not. You need to keep your facts straight. They almost suspended me too, but I'm like a cat. I land on my feet. You know people like me always do. It's why we can get away with anything. It's also why I love cats."

"I thought you were a dog person," Autumn wondered aloud as if she had temporarily forgotten she was angry at Casey.

"I'm really neither, animals are a waste of time and too much of what I call 'rabbit hole work.' I love dogs and cats as long as I don't have to do anything for them," Casey clarified. "But I do love to reference how cats land on their feet, because I do too. See, my 'righting reflex' is the people I surround myself with. Sure, it started with my parents, and I was lucky there, but beyond that, it's been me networking and making the system work for me rather than pretending to be a victim of it, which is what you've spent your life doing. It's why I am here in this beautiful top floor office that's probably bigger than your apartment and you're 14 floors below me with the most annoying employee in the building with an office across the hall from yours."

"You didn't really beat Joy up in high school, did you?" Autumn asked as she finally turned to Casey with a smirk that she couldn't hold in. "Maybe all the rumors are true. Joy got the best of you and obviously you can't let it go because you were never quite the same after that day you supposedly beat her up. You literally run a billion-dollar company, have traveled the world, and have everything in it, but all you think about is some random girl in high school that you unfairly bullied enough that one day she probably fought back and won. Maybe that's why you can't let it go. Listen, I appreciate all you have given me with this job, Casey, but you really need to seek help."

"Shut up and get out before I change my mind and fire you," Casey cried.

"I'm just trying to help," Autumn mumbled as she closed the door behind her.

11

Joy couldn't ignore how Autumn had been almost continuously looking at her since she had arrived at the coffee shop.

Autumn had already been there for a while and was at the front of the line to the barista at the register when Joy arrived. They had only nodded to each other from a distance up to this point and then separately purchased a coffee for themselves.

Autumn wasn't sure if she was supposed to let Joy cut in front of her in line, or if she was supposed to go to the back of the line to join Joy. She then decided her relationship with Joy wasn't close enough to make a move and her desire for a coffee outweighed any sense of responsibility she felt to observe some kind of etiquette in this situation.

Autumn looked Joy up and down as she about to join her at the table she had selected for them. At least in terms of sharing classes together on and off throughout their childhood, they had pretty much grown up together, and throughout that time, she had never seen Joy appear as glowing as she was there at the coffee shop. Both Joy and Autumn had been teased throughout grade school about their weight (Joy much more so), even though they weren't necessarily overweight at that time, either.

They just weren't naturally thin.

Autumn had spent most of high school and all of adulthood trying to be thin or stay thin, and now appeared thinner than Joy, but didn't appear healthy. Unlike high school, Joy now looked comfortable and content with her healthy weight. Like high school, Joy still had long dark hair that stretched over and well beyond her shoulders. However, in high school, her hair had been wild and frizzy, while now it appeared styled, controlled, voluminous, layered, and highlighted.

Joy's hair had so much life to it that Autumn imagined it could be its own person.

It was the type of hair that Casey spent hundreds of dollars per hairstylist visit striving for, but never quite pulled off.

Joy was wearing a sandalwood-colored cashmere cardigan coat over a white silk blouse that seemed perfect for the season and more expensive than the entire combined wardrobe that Autumn had seen Joy wear in high school. Starting around middle school, she had always felt that Joy could have been one of the most beautiful girls in school if she had put a little more effort into her appearance, and here, she finally had. Autumn wanted to give her positive feedback for this but opted not to out of envy. Despite these remarkable changes, the biggest change that Autumn observed was that Joy was primarily smiling and didn't have the resting frown she frequently had in high school. She was wanted to ask Joy: "how do you get rid of that?". She reasoned that it must have involved years of work, as a resting frown like that doesn't go away overnight.

There was a unique tinge of loneliness that Autumn felt from seeing someone from her childhood that she hadn't seen in 20 years. It was like a hybrid of the loneliness she recalled feeling as a child and the loneliness she currently felt from getting older.

Joy was still wondering why she had agreed to meet Autumn in the first place. They hadn't seen each other in 22 years since they graduated high school and hadn't spoken at all during that period. Joy noted how Autumn simply looked like an older version of exactly who she was in high school. To Joy's eyes, Autumn had that dichotomous appearance of someone who lived a life of being hard on themselves and therefore looked tired and defeated, but at the same time still also appeared child-like due to a lack of maturity and avoidance of adult responsibilities. Although Autumn's body language was still anxious and tense like it was when they were kids, she also seemed to have mellowed slightly with age and life experience. Joy wondered if this was from maturity or if Autumn was just worn out from reluctantly adulting.

Back when they were kids, Joy would notice how Autumn often weirdly smelled like graham crackers, but on this occasion, she instead smelled like a cinnamon scented candle.

The coffee shop itself smelled like a mix of coffee beans and a rainy day, since it had started drizzling about 10 minutes before Autumn had arrived there.

It was one of those coffee shops that had a large industrial roaster displayed in the corner of it to add to the modern warehouse aesthetic it had. The roaster was around 7 feet high and 9 feet wide. It looked like it weighed at least 1,000 lbs. This coffee shop was one of those shops that had an exposed, unfinished ceiling to add more volume to the room and give it an urban warehouse loft feel. Autumn hated this type of ambiance, and this was one of those coffee shops she had already visited once and then vowed to herself she would never visit again.

She reminded herself she was only there because of the unusual circumstances she found herself in.

The closest coffee shop to her apartment was the coffee shop at the plaza of the Dark Forest Solutions headquarters, but she had wanted to get as far away from there as possible after her meeting with Casey. She instead opted for a coffee shop that was closer to where Joy said she was at. When Autumn had called Joy, she was not only surprised that Joy had answered, but that Joy was also willing to meet so soon. For Autumn, the coffee shop they were at was about a 30-minute walk from her work. Autumn had opted to walk to there to "walk off" the array of emotions she had experienced after leaving Casey's office and to match the timeline that Joy had identified as to when she could meet her. She had arrived there in only 20 minutes as her angry-pace and the desire to get out of the rain had helped shave off some of the usual walking time.

Autumn was still wet from the walk. Not soaked, but wet.

Joy was completely dry. Not only had she driven there, but she also had an umbrella with her for the short one-minute walk from where she was able to park her car to the coffee shop. She had arrived right at the meeting time.

Once they sat down, the coffee shop had quieted down. They had run into one of those odd situations where there was a line when they each walked in, but all the other customers had picked up their beverages to-go and now suddenly there was no line at all after they had just waited in one. It made Autumn wish she had set the time to meet 10 minutes later than she did (even with the rain).

They were now the only customers there.

They were seated across from each other at a two-seated table right beside the front window wall of the coffee shop that gave them a view of the busy, rainy sidewalk filled with passersby. The coffee shop was on a busy city street encased with skyscrapers that were filled with shops on lower floors and office space or residences on higher floors. The sidewalks along the street were lined with trees that were decorated with lit string lights. The string lights provided additional light to what had quickly transformed into a dreary, dark, night-like morning.

The rain outside picked up to a steady pour.

It was difficult for Autumn to think of something to say to Joy as she was so awestruck by her appearance. A part of her instantly regretted asking Joy to meet her there as she didn't anticipate Joy's appearance would make her feel this much more insecure and self-conscious. If anything, she had thought she would be getting the added bonus of seeing Joy again and encountering some kind of older version of Joy's appearance in high school that would enable her to feel better about her own appearance.

She continued to gaze quietly at Joy as she took her first sip of coffee. The coffee tasted too strong again like it did the first time she was there— even with the vanilla oat milk added. If she was alone, she would have asked for a new one. But since this was a rare occasion where she was hanging out with somebody this time, she decided to bear it. She decided to take tiny sips. She was mainly drinking coffee because she remembered Joy loved coffee back in high school. She otherwise would have opted for tea since she didn't like the coffee at that shop the first time.

Joy looked down at her own coffee but before she could have some, she felt awkwardly obligated to break the ice. She opted to go directly with the question that had been foremost on her mind ever since Autumn had contacted her.

"So, I am dying to know, how did you get my number?" Joy asked with a tone of forced diplomacy.

"I still had the number to your parents' house from an old elementary school directory, so I called it and spoke to your dad. I told him I'm old friend from when we were kids. He recognized my name and gave me your number." Autumn had figured this question was coming and felt the need to tell Joy before she asked it but had also been hoping they wouldn't have to discuss it because just the thought that she had resorted to that move made her feel more embarrassed and desperate.

"Ooh yeah, I can see him doing that. He still encourages me to make more friends."

"I kept everything from when we were in school. Yearbooks, notebooks, folders, I think I have a couple unreturned library books," Autumn laughed uncomfortably.

"I kept nothing," Joy reflected. "Maybe I should have, but high school was miserable. Weren't you miserable?! I thought you were."

"Apparently not as much as I thought I was."

There was a renewed awkward silence as Joy took a sip of her coffee.

Joy already looked like she wanted to leave. She was suspicious as to why Autumn had contacted her and wanted to meet with her. This strange delay in conversation only fed her suspicion.

"I really appreciate you making it here on such short notice," Autumn said with an uncharacteristic tone of sincerity.

"You mean desperate, last-minute notice?" Joy laughed.

"Something like that," Autumn acknowledged while including in a bit of her own fake laugh.

"Well, you picked the perfect day. I'm off work on Fridays, my partner is at work, and my kids are in school. I don't have anything planned for another hour until I go in for a hair appointment, and that's right down the street."

Autumn couldn't think of an immediate response she felt comfortable saying aloud and instead silently avoided eye contact. By now, she was about to burst with everything she wanted to tell and ask Joy but couldn't help but maintain a defensive posture around her like she always did with almost everyone. She instead looked outside at the pedestrians breezing by them on the sidewalk through the rain. A few of them looked at her and briefly made eye contact with her in passing, quietly sharing their dreary and perturbed expressions with her.

As she was about to look away, she saw AI Autumn walking by in a black hooded rain jacket with a smirk on its face as it looked directly at her while maintaining the same pace of walking with others around it that were going in the same direction.

Autumn immediately looked at Joy to see if she had noticed AI Autumn, but Joy had been looking into the coffee shop as opposed to looking outside. Joy's back had also been to AI Autumn as AI Autumn had been walking from the direction that Autumn was facing. She quickly sighed to cover up any unusual facial expression or reaction she may have been exuding in response to seeing AI Autumn. It was peculiar to her that AI Autumn was wearing a black hooded rain jacket. She owned a rain jacket, but it wasn't black.

Joy turned back to Autumn. It had become clear to her that she would have to lead the conversation even though Autumn had been the one who asked her to be there. Autumn's odd mannerisms only made her want to expedite the visit.

"Sooo...what are you up to nowadays?" Joy asked.

"I'm a digital marketing manager at Dark Forest Solutions," Autumn stated, looking away from Joy indiscriminately at the wall over Joy's shoulder as she revealed her job position.

Joy's eyes first widened and then her lips slightly parted. "You..." she hesitated. "You actually work for Casey?!"

"I guarantee you it won't be for the duration of my whole career, she—" Autumn thought for a moment about whether she should continue and then rolled her eyes to herself before proceeding: "...well, the pay is decent, and I know she is more flexible with me than anywhere else I would potentially go to. Trust me, I've looked around. I'm still looking around. Why?! What do you do?"

"I'm an AI engineer at Red Mosaic Technologies," Joy answered. "Have you ever applied there? I could introduce you to some of the digital marketing staff there if you are interested."

"AI?" Autumn asked, visibly cringing as she ignored everything Joy had said after identifying herself as an AI engineer. Joy's identification of her career path had seemed to release the pent-up anxiety that Autumn had kept corked since the appearance of AI Autumn through the window. She became aware that she was no longer breathing normally.

"Yeah, you don't like that?" Joy asked as she still appeared distracted by the shocking concept of Autumn working for Casey. She didn't seem to notice the level of Autumn's discomfort.

"Oh no," Autumn gasped, catching her breath to reset herself to a normal breathing pace, "that sounds great. I would love to talk to you more about that particular subject, actually—"

"I can't believe you work for Casey," Joy interrupted her, "and that you work in digital marketing. I don't know why. I mean I am sure you are awesome at it. I didn't imagine you doing any of that."

"Oh really?! What did you imagine me doing?" Autumn asked with a hint of annoyance as she sensed herself gradually returning to normal breathing.

"Well...um, I don't know," Joy stumbled, "something creative for sure, like maybe a graphic designer?"

Autumn looked down at the table. "That was what I wanted my major to be in college, but I ended up starting with computer engineering instead at the insistence of my parents. I ended up with a degree in communications."

There was an uncomfortable silence after that, and Joy decided to compensate for the new pause in conversation with another drink of her coffee.

"I must say I'm surprised," Joy said after she finished a long thoughtful, reflective sip, "that you asked me to meet you here."

"Surprised?" Autumn asked. "Really?"

"Yeah, I mean you hated me in high school."

"I still do," Autumn responded without hesitation or a hint of sarcasm.

Joy looked around the coffee shop uneasily like she would rather be anywhere else than where she was— sitting across from Autumn.

Autumn looked outside again.

Numerous pedestrians on the sidewalk and cars on the street continued to zoom by them but with increasing density each time she looked outside. While the street outside had become more crowded since their arrival, the coffee shop itself remained relatively empty. The two baristas working there had disappeared somewhere in the back room of the shop.

"Does anybody work anymore?" Autumn asked as she was still looking outside. "Rush hour should be over, and I see more people walking around now than I did earlier."

"Doesn't it seem like people don't really talk to each other anymore?" Joy asked with a tone that didn't seem to intend to ignore Autumn's question. Her tone instead indicated that she had so deeply contemplated the string of thoughts that led to that question that she had missed Autumn's similar-sounding question.

"We know too much about each other anyway." Autumn turned back to Joy. "I mean, we know everything now with everyone posting every single insignificant event of their lives on the internet, and with people pouring out every little emotion they are experiencing to each other on the rare occasion they do talk because they realize they don't talk to each other enough but then do nothing to make it happen more frequently since..."

"...it seems like too much already," Joy finished.

"I miss high school," Autumn heard herself say to her own surprise, "but I especially miss college."

Joy first looked at her for a moment, before her eyes wandered around the coffee shop, clearly searching for something to say as though the coffee shop had a sign on the wall that would tell her what to say. But instead, she only found herself reobserving the odd morning emptiness in the coffee shop with mild gray-light streaming into every exposed corner through the front window walls. She wondered if Autumn was conscious of the irony that she was already spilling out random repressed emotions herself despite previously highlighting this as a tendency that socially sheltered people in their generation had.

"I miss the nostalgia of the life I should've lived in my teens and my early 20s, not the life I actually lived in my teens and my early 20s," Autumn clarified. "It's like I'm lost in a state of convenient revisionist hindsight while searching for greater truths and insight. My mind keeps going to either the past I lived through or the past I wanted to live through rather than living here in the present moment. It's exhausting in a way that leaves me feeling numb and kind of sedated. But I'm trapped in this cycle of thought and wonder if I'll ever be free to wander and then identify where my life will go."

"It's like living in a time loop of the same day over and over again?" Joy asked with searching eyes.

"Kinda, but it's worse," Autumn indicated. "Time keeps passing by and I keep re-running my life through different alternate histories of how my past life could have been. Intellectually, I am aware of the passage of time, but emotionally, I am stuck in a time loop."

"Are you sure it's not an actual time loop?" Joy asked.

Autumn suddenly smiled ever so slightly as one might upon encountering a hidden memory that they hadn't thought about in decades.

"Wow, you remember when I told you in high school about how I experienced a real time loop as a kid with the day repeating over and over again?" Autumn asked rhetorically. "I wish it was. You know I had forgotten I ever told anyone that story. You are the only other person who ever knew about that. I only told you because you are the only one who would ever believe me, you know, since you have had similar experiences."

Joy looked around the coffee shop self-consciously again.

Autumn was now visibly getting annoyed by this ongoing pattern of strange behavior from Joy.

"What?" Autumn asked, looking around the coffee shop with Joy sarcastically with her eyes. "You think you're above it all now that you're living what is left of the American Dream with having a family and a great job and all?"

Joy raised her brow as though still unsure she wanted to revisit the topic she had known would inevitably come up when Autumn had asked her to meet.

"I take it you still spend a lot of there?" Joy eventually asked. "The other world?"

"Every chance I get," Autumn confirmed, "but it's not the same."

"Not the same?"

"Well, there's more to do. There are more places to go to when I'm there. It's more elaborate, more sophisticated, it's more beautiful..."

"But...?" Joy asked after Autumn had trailed off.

"But..." Autumn resumed, "it feels like I've plateaued there. It's like a job or a friend you feel like you've outgrown. It's become kind of boring."

"Boring? Wow. I can't imagine it ever being like that."

"I know, but you probably haven't been there lately," Autumn assumed. "I imagine you remember it with all those good nostalgic feelings like some people do with high school or college...like I am even doing with high school and college."

"I do have some nostalgia for it," Joy said, smiling.

"It's like anything else that you moved forward from in your life that you can't go back to without feeling different and without you knowing it doesn't feel the same," Autumn lamented. "But I keep going back, hoping it will be the same. It didn't really start feeling different until I was like 30."

Joy didn't reply and instead took another long swig of coffee but then slowed down as she realized it was already running lower than she expected. She had ordered a smaller sized coffee than what she usually got in case she didn't like the experience of seeing Autumn again and wanted to leave early (she had surmised on the way to the coffee shop that the probability of that happening was about 50/50).

"The other world is still the best thing that ever happened to me. I meant everything good I ever said to you about it when we were kids..." Autumn paused again and took a deep breath that looked unusual and interrupted. "I don't know about you, but I think we should feel proud of ourselves. I don't think I would've survived my childhood if it wasn't for the other world, and I don't think you would have either."

Joy involuntarily took another sip of her coffee, this time without paying attention to the fact she was running low. She briefly continued to sip a bit of air after the coffee had gone.

Autumn watched Joy finish her coffee with the slight smirk she would often get that she couldn't hide when she occasionally tried to. "You know, Casey still claims she beat you up in high school. I wasn't there in the locker room, but I know that's not true, because I saw you that day and saw how that experience transformed you."

Joy was expressionless as she lowered her empty cup toward the table. The empty to-go-coffee cup made a louder sound than she intended when it hit the tabletop. It seemed to echo through the emptiness of the coffee shop in such a way that Joy couldn't tell how much of the sound was echoing through the shop and how much of it was echoing through her mind.

"What really happened in that fight you had with Casey and her friends?" Autumn asked.

12

Joy looked down at her empty coffee cup on the table. Right before she was going to excuse herself from the table to avoid answering the question and head to the cash register to order a refill, a large white coffee mug was placed beside her empty to-go cup. The new coffee was a latte with a microform design on its surface that resembled an orchid.

Joy looked up at Autumn, and upon seeing that Autumn looked a little surprised, she looked over and saw the suntanned barista with blonde highlights who smiled at her every time she saw her standing beside her with a smile. Despite going to that coffee shop often, Joy had trouble remembering her name.

"This one is on us, Joy," the suntanned barista with blonde highlights offered.

"Aww, thanks," Joy expressed meekly as she placed both hands around the mug to allow the warmth of the mug to travel through her hands. Joy knew from previous visits to this coffee shop that the large in-house coffee mugs that were there were so insulating of the hot beverage inside of them that the coffee was never too hot to put her hands around the mug. She loved that.

It was a cozy sensation that made her feel like she was in a hug.

As the barista walked away, Joy looked at the orchid thoughtfully and then looked back up at Autumn.

"It's so hard to describe those moments of freedom you feel when you finally get out of something that was hurting you," Joy replied to Autumn's earlier question. "It's like being born, but as an adult who knows what's going on and recognizes the gift of new life you're receiving. Some people might say 'well yeah, you're being reborn' but I don't say 'reborn' because it was like I was being born for the first time when I finally stood up to Casey and her friends that day in the locker room. Before that, I was only experiencing a living death. It was like I was breathing and walking around, but it was as if I hadn't been born at all. When you are happy, you don't ever want that feeling of being alive to go away, but if you lose that feeling or feel like you never had it to begin with, then it can feel like it's impossible to feel alive and you may eventually accept that's how 'life' is. I think that feeling of being born to reset ourselves or renew ourselves is what we all strive for deep down at some point in our lives, whether we try to find it in earning awards and accolades in our careers, or experiencing a spiritual epiphany, or trying to find it in a new relationship, or trying to find it by having our own children. It's a feeling that is kind of like how my partner and I recently renewed our wedding vows, but in this case, you renew a vow with yourself to live your best life."

Autumn took a sip of her own coffee and discovered it was already cooling down (while being reminded it was still almost full).

"I envied you when we were little kids. I envied you when we were in high school too," Autumn admitted as she pushed her coffee cup a little further away from herself after putting it down on the table. "You had that castle in the other world, and didn't you also have a space station or something like that?"

"You had more going on in the other world than I did," Joy recalled, prompting a broad smile from Autumn. To Joy, it still and had always looked unusual to see Autumn smile. Joy wasn't sure why beyond observing that Autumn was simply one of those people who wasn't naturally constituted to smile.

"I didn't quite have all the things you had there," Autumn conceded. "Do you have anything new going on there?"

Rather than directly answer Autumn's question, Joy opted to share a thought she had always wanted to share with Autumn that had come back to her mind on the drive over to the coffee shop: "I regret not spending more time with you there as well as here," Joy disclosed. "You asked for that, and I realize now that you really wanted that and weren't just trying to mess with me. I realize now you were as lonely as I was. But on the other hand, you acted like you were happy with the way things were even though you didn't have any friends at school either."

"I wasn't ready to have a great friend like I know you would be," Autumn reflected. "I wasn't mature enough. Trust me. I don't say that easily. I resented you for years for being—stronger— than I was. I also resented you for having the same access to the other world that I have. I resented you long after we graduated high school. I resented you but at the same time, I don't know how else to say this because I know it sounds weird, but I respected you too. So maybe I don't hate you." Autumn laughed her fake laugh and did the thing Joy remembered her doing as a kid when Autumn would laugh and then wait a little bit to see if the other person would start delay-laughing with her if they didn't initially laugh with her.

"When we were in school, the other girls and the guys all teased you constantly and humiliated you," Autumn continued after she had established that Joy wouldn't laugh along with her. "Back then, I rationalized that I was better than you because they mostly left me alone. They never tried beat me up like when Casey and her friends jumped you in high school. I thought I was lucky, but now I realize it was like they didn't know I existed. I ask myself 'what is worse: being ignored or being bullied?'"

"Being bullied," Joy responded without hesitation. "I've been through both. Trust me, it's being bullied. Being ignored is brutal too in its own way, but I still feel like Casey is somehow watching me. I haven't seen her in years, but I can sense it. After all these years, it's like she's still waiting for the next opportunity to come after me."

Autumn leaned slightly forward: "Is this a conspiracy theory?"

"It's more like subconscious intelligence," Joy indicated.

"Ahh, subconscious intelligence is what I live on," Autumn said. "It's underrated. Never underestimate the great ideas you come up with and the cool things you accomplish without consciously thinking about it. It also has a way of calling your attention to things you need to know that you otherwise wouldn't know."

"Exactly, like an intellectual form of intuition."

"But I will still say that being bullied and teased implies people see something in you. They have an interest in you, even if it's just to hurt you. They are threatened by you. They indirectly direct you to learn something about yourself," Autumn explained. "But when they ignore you, you are nothing to them. You aren't worth their time. You start to question if your life is one worth living."

"Being bullied makes you feel like life is not worth living," Joy retorted with a tinge of unexpected emotion.

Autumn's eyes widened.

"I mean being bullied can make you question if your life is one worth living," Joy clarified, not wanting to bring up the fact that she had secretly almost committed suicide once while they were in high school. "When you don't know any better at a young age, you don't realize how people are preprogrammed by evolution to fight and eliminate any perceived threat to them and their well-being. Without this intellectual understanding, you are pretty much predisposed to think there is something wrong with you. People are implicitly aware that other people are inherently wired differently than they are, but they still often default to negative narratives within their own minds about the people who are most different from them instead of automatically trying to understand them. This is how they are more threatened by someone born completely different from them than they are by someone who appears to be more like them but might make different life choices than they do. They may loathe the latter more for their choices, but they aren't as threatened by them as they are by the former. Parents often consciously or inadvertently conjure up these inclinations by teaching children their own negativity, insecurities, and hatred. It's a subject I wish they taught you early on in school since children are less inclined to be rational and to control their impulses when they are triggered to demonstrate inclinations learned from parents to judge and hate. Instead, it's easier for adults in our society to tell every kid they are special and wonderful, while it's also just as easy for other kids who may misunderstand them or envy them to tell them that they're not. Kids are more empowered now than they've ever been, and I can tell you as a mom that kids listen to other kids more now than they ever have."

"I get it," Autumn accepted, "being ignored and being bullied are both terrible and it's subjective in terms of how deeply they can hurt any individual person. Were you ever suicidal back then?!"

Joy took a deep breath and looked down at the orchid design that was still somewhat intact on the latte.

"I keep a much lower profile in the other world than I used to," Joy shared, opting to change the subject back to Autumn's earlier question to bypass the current one, "but my kids have inspired me to spend more time there again after several years of being away from it after high school."

"Wow... your kids spend time in the other world?"

"I still spend time in the other world too," Joy explained. "I don't know where you got the idea that I wouldn't. You always knew when I was there when we were kids. I guess I did stay away for about fifteen years though."

"The castle you used to hang out in over there is—"

"Abandoned, right," Joy interjected before looking down at an alert notification that suddenly appeared on her phone. "Yeah, I don't spend any time at the castle anymore. But I still go to the other world when I can, I obviously have a lot more responsibility here."

Autumn was unable to discern what the alert was about on Joy's phone from where she was sitting. She had noticed how Joy had an unusually large smartphone that was face-up on the table near her latte mug. It was larger than nearly all the smartphones she had ever seen.

"Um, do you have to go or something?" Autumn asked.

Joy was now holding her phone and appeared to be responding to a text. Autumn hated when people responded to text messages in front of her during a conversation and was about to say something more, but Joy finished right before she was going to protest.

After she set her phone aside, Joy looked at her latte and saw that there was still slight steam rising from it. She then noticed that Autumn was considering taking another drink of her coffee but appeared reluctant to.

Joy carefully slid her mug over to Autumn's side of the table.

"I still have a little extra time," Joy finally said, "have a sip of my orchid latte."

Autumn took a seemingly reluctant sip that was only out of kindness in return for Joy's insistence she try it. Her eyes immediately brightened upon tasting it and she found it so incredibly delicious that she felt (but didn't follow through on) the unusual urge to fall out of her chair, lay down on the floor, and look up at the ceiling. She couldn't remember if she had ever tried a latte before (maybe once, and it wasn't like this).

"You know, I know I wasn't very kind to you in high school...or middle school..." Autumn began as she slid the latte back to Joy after trying it.

"Or elementary school," Joy added before taking a sip of the orchid latte herself.

"Or elementary school," Autumn acknowledged. "But like you said, deep down I wanted to be your friend. I always felt like we should have been friends. For a long time, you were the only other person I knew who had access to the other world. We were also the only mixed kids in a lot of our classes. We both have Asian moms. We both have Mexican dads. Our birthdays are in the same month."

"Um, my birthday is in September, and my dad isn't Mexican... he's Native American," Joy corrected her, sounding perturbed by the inaccuracies.

"September? Oh...well, I remember our birthdays were kind of close together..."

"You thought my dad was Mexican?"

"Well yeah," Autumn mumbled nervously, "he was never close with my dad, but they lived in the same neighborhood and knew a lot of the same people. And I remember your mom was Asian. My mom is Japanese."

At this point, Autumn had decided just to share her mom's ethnicity rather than share her assumption that Joy's mom was Chinese.

"Yeah, my dad lived in a mostly Mexican-American neighborhood when he was in high school, but he's Native and originally from the rez. My mom is Korean and met my dad when he was stationed in Korea with the army."

"Oh wow, I didn't know," Autumn admitted, but upon seeing at how disappointed Joy appeared to be by her ignorance of Joy's heritage despite growing up in so many of the same classes together, she added: "or I knew, but must've forgotten."

Joy stayed quiet. She was reminded of how Autumn frequently inadvertently offended her growing up and was amazed at how she still wasn't quite sure how to respond to her in adulthood.

"Yeah, I can understand why you wouldn't have been my friend," Autumn laughed uncomfortably (once it became apparent to her that Joy wasn't sure how to respond to her).

"It's amazing how long people go by their assumptions before they ever learn the truth or finally admit to themselves that they don't know the truth," Joy observed as diplomatically as she could (considering her current frustration with Autumn). "I know I can be guilty of that too."

"Uh, huh...this is pretty awkward," Autumn murmured.

Joy took another sip of her orchid latte, before realizing that she couldn't keep taking too many more uncomfortable sips of these delicious beverages to fill the awkward pauses in the conversation because she would then end up consuming too much caffeine (even for her).

"Autumn, what are we doing here?" Joy asked. She felt like she had released a large weight off her shoulders in the process of uttering that question and instantly regretted not asking it sooner.

~ 13 ~

"I suppose maybe I'm going through a similar situation like you did in high school," Autumn suggested with a casual tone that implied she had been anticipating the question for a while.

"Really?" Joy asked with a tone of immediate skepticism. "I don't know about that. I was pretty lost throughout the first half of high school and worked on getting myself together through the rest of it. Whereas you seemed to know exactly what you wanted—"

"Thought! Thought I knew what I wanted," Autumn interrupted. She then repeated it again with a softer tone as if saying it to herself: "Thought I knew what I wanted."

"Maybe it really was what you wanted back then and now you've changed."

"I suppose we all think we know everything when we are sixteen." Autumn laughed.

But Joy wasn't laughing.

"Well, some of us," Autumn added as a reply to Joy's non-response. "You know you should give yourself more credit, you really turned it around in high school and look at you now. This is the happiest I've ever seen you. Not everybody who was treated the way you were at school when we were kids can do what you did. I truly think only a very few of them can."

Joy wasn't quite sure how to take the unexpected complimentary feedback, so she smiled mildly at Autumn and then looked down at her latte without taking another drink of it.

After observing Joy's reaction, Autumn looked down at her coffee too and wished she had ordered either one of the exotic-looking flavored teas she had noticed when she was ordering earlier or a latte instead. She closed her eyes and took a quick, reluctant, "I paid for this so I might as well drink it"-kind-of-sip of her coffee.

"I am starting to think the sadness we experience, even at an early age, never goes away. It's always there. It ages and changes with you," Autumn stated as she put down her coffee and slid it a little further away from herself again.

"You're right," Joy responded with a more energized tone that indicated she had more of an interest in the conversation again, "it doesn't ever totally go away, and it ages and changes with you, but that doesn't mean it has to keep you sad."

As she finished her last sentence, Joy's eyes seemed to light up as though they were windows to an actual light bulb in her head that lit up whenever she had an epiphany or a thought that had suddenly occurred to her that she really wanted to share in the middle of a conversation.

"Life is harder when you don't settle. It's easier when you settle, because you simply adapt to life when you settle, rather than trying to make life adapt to you. You haven't settled. You've lived your life your way, so your career objectives, your personal goals, your relationships— they've all been harder for you to achieve than the people around you in your life because most people chose to settle in most if not all those areas of life. There is nothing wrong with settling. In many ways, I've chosen to settle in my life. I have a decent job that isn't too stressful and gives me more time with my kids. Just like we need followers in life as much as leaders, we need people who choose to settle as much as we need the kind of people like you who choose not to settle. But when you don't settle, sometimes other people who have settled will envy you. They may make things harder for you because they know that a life of not settling was too hard for them. I believe that settling is a choice, and I chose that. But not everyone who settled believes it was their choice. They think life forced them into settling for a lesser life than what they wanted, and they become bitter and resentful about it. It's easy for them to take out that resentment on other people they meet who haven't settled," Joy explained. She sounded like an underpaid, underrated college professor who was passionate about the subject she was discussing and still in the job because of that passion.

"You feel like you settled?!" Autumn asked with a mix of skepticism and astonishment. "I've thought of you as the type of person who had this strength in you that wouldn't settle for anything."

"I settled at a certain level in my career because I wanted a family. I had a great partner who also wanted kids, and we wanted to spend as much time together as possible. At first, I thought I could both maximize my potential in my career and have a family. Some people can do that; I was not one of them. A hard work ethic can be both a virtue and a curse. People have a misconception about working hard. On the surface, it's easy to see how working hard and burning yourself out isn't worth it, but the value of a hard work ethic isn't just effort, it's a skill. The skill component comes into play with how your goals and priorities dictate your effort. Burnout often happens when you don't believe in what you are doing, have changed your priorities, or don't have an end goal but are still working hard. Burnout can obviously still happen if you believe in what you are doing and you are on the right path, as overthinking and lacking balance can happen to anyone, but that kind of burnout is different and not as deep. What I call 'deep burnout' happens when you feel you are no longer in alignment with your goals and priorities. In my case, I had the best possible work/life balance, believed in what I was doing, and had goals associated with my career, but my priorities changed, and I started to burn out. I had to decide what I believed in more: my family or my career. I was at a crossroads. I chose my family first. I did what was best for me and for them."

"Did you settle for your partner? Do you love him as much as you loved Gray back in high school? You know Gray and Casey finally got married, right?!"

Joy gazed vaguely at Autumn as she considered how much of her truth she really wanted to share. Meanwhile, the resting frown that Autumn had remembered Joy having in high school returned to Joy's face, but it remained only briefly. Eventually, Joy raised her eyebrows as if to signal that she had decided to open up completely.

"I settled...but in the right way," Joy concluded, with her voice sounding weighed down by the extra layer of emotion that had made her somewhat hesitant. "I say 'the right way' because when you consciously choose to settle, rather than subconsciously surrendering into settling, you are in a position to consider your options and make healthy choices. And yes, I love him as much as I think I loved Gray in high school, but in a different way."

"As much as Gray?!" Autumn asked in a condemnatory tone. "You still love Gray? He ignored you the entire time we were in school. How can you still love someone who treated you that way? How can you love someone that you really didn't know? How could you love someone who chose to be with someone who hates you?"

"We love what we love," Joy explained softly, "sometimes there is no logic or rational explanation for it. Not only do we love what we love, but we love differently at different phases of our lives as we change. People often ironically want to compartmentalize and then generalize the way we choose to live our lives. They then take that generalization they want to make about us and make that a permanent stamp on us for them to see us that way for the rest of our lives as though we don't or can't change. I've named it the 'paradox of judgmental convenience.' We already know it's easier for people to take complex individuals and then compartmentalize them into certain groups or stereotypes and then make generalizations about them based on how they perceive those groups or stereotypes, but it's also easier to assume that they'll never change. We all go down different paths in life that are ever-changing and even our core values can change along the way. People want to view love through this 'all or nothing' lens where we instantly know and fall in love with our true soulmate. It may work out that way for a few people, but the reality is people can also have multiple soulmates too, who play different roles in our lives. Not all of us end up marrying every soulmate we have. Some of us won't end up marrying anyone. People also want to believe that we will always have the same definition of what "love" means to us throughout our lives. But how we view love and what we know about love changes along with us. I loved Gray in high school based on what I knew love to be at that time in my life. I love my partner now based on everything I've learned about love since then and continue to learn about love now."

"So, you have two soulmates," Autumn wryly summarized, "one who is loyal to you and one who acted like you didn't exist."

"I have two soulmates," Joy verified with a calm tone of diplomacy, "one who was my childhood crush and taught me what love shouldn't be and one who is my life partner who taught me that love is much more complex than I ever thought it was in terms of how much you truly have to adjust, compromise, and sacrifice to both maintain and continue to grow with love."

"Some people end up with no soulmate," Autumn mentioned coldly.

"I believe those people either end up being their own soulmate or connect with God as their soulmate," Joy asserted. "The love you are looking for is first found inside of you, and once you access it, you are free to love the others who will love you the way you deserved to be loved and the way they deserve to be loved. They say, 'love is blind' and I think that can also include how someone experiences love within. You can think you genuinely know and love who you are, but it could be either just your ego, or what you think other people think of you. What many people don't understand is that you never know or authenticate your true identity until you fully set yourself free to hear your inner voice instead of just listening to your parents, your friends, your co-workers, your country, the media, your culture, or anything else in the environment life has formed around you. No other human has a right to tell you what is innate in you, it's an area only you can access."

Autumn rolled her eyes.

"Love has been a series of awakenings to me," Joy reflected, choosing to ignore Autumn's reaction. "I had a love awakening in high school, but I also had a love awakening when I met my partner and later had love awakenings when I had my children. Love is a series of awakenings that seems to go in any order according to how far you want to take it, but it went in this order for me: first with self-love, then romantic love, and then thirdly, parent love. At any point within the order you choose, you may also add spiritual love, which I believe enhances the other three forms of love in addition to being a fourth form of love on its own terms. Each form of love has taken me to a deeper place of understanding love that has led me further away from my ego in the sense that learning the depth of love has opened my eyes more and more to see the world from other perspectives far beyond my own anxieties, negativity, self-doubts and worries. It's also like I become more and more 'as one' with the other people I love, especially my partner and my kids. But if you choose not to get married or have kids, it doesn't make you any less familiar with love. For instance, I think people who choose to remain single open themselves up to potentially deeper experiences with self-love and spiritual love that the rest of us can't have because we also maintain the other forms of love in our lives. Likewise, a couple who chooses not to have kids can open themselves up to deeper possibilities for romantic love that maybe a couple who has kids may not necessarily have. I believe this all balances out and we all have an opportunity to know deeper forms of love."

"Everything you are saying sounds great," Autumn replied with a snarky tone, "but love is overrated and overanalyzed. You either experience love or you don't and you either know it, or you don't. For the small percentage of the population who have experienced these levels of love the way you have, it's great. But most of us don't really understand or feel much of anything if we do fall in love or get married or have kids. I see it everywhere I go."

Joy looked at Autumn with a genuinely concerned and pained expression. She shifted the mug containing the orchid latte slightly toward Autumn as a way of offering Autumn another sip, but Autumn shook her head to decline.

"Are you going to tell me what's really going on or not?" Joy asked firmly as she sat back and folded her arms.

Autumn sighed a long sigh that appeared to need more air than Autumn was able to release.

"There is a humanoid AI version of me running around, trying to take over my life," Autumn disclosed in a reluctant tone with an aura of embarrassment. "In fact, it is specifically designed by Casey to take over my life. It has already taken over my job. It's apparently moving into my place to live with me today. I guess that's okay, I figured maybe it'll pay the bills for me. But I don't know. It doesn't feel right."

Joy initially appeared unable to concoct a verbal reply as her facial expressions and body language displayed a myriad of emotions that appeared both mixed and complex. She ended up taking another sip of the latte herself before looking at Autumn and then looking at the door like she wanted to leave and had wished she had never heard this information. She then looked at Autumn again.

"Autumn, I'm confused. Not that I ever like to agree with Casey on anything, but isn't this what you always wanted? Isn't this what I thought I wanted as kid? This is the opportunity we dreamed about as kids," Joy finally responded.

"Yeah, but you let that dream go in high school and I'm wondering if I should have too," Autumn contemplated with a somber tone. "Even if I get out of working and have an AI version of me taking care of everything, I don't want it to totally live my life for me. I feel like I would be losing something. I am not totally sure what that is, but I don't want to lose it. I have been surprised myself that I feel this way."

"I really believe that to understand the true depth of love in this world, you have to experience every path that life places in front of you to reach it," Joy said, "especially the paths you don't want to take."

"It also knows about the other world, this AI-version of me does," Autumn continued, looking downtrodden at her coffee that was probably now beyond lukewarm. She figured she'd probably end up taking it home and pouring it out in her sink. Since it was in the to-go cup and she was there with Joy, she felt more of an obligation to take it with her rather than leave it there for the baristas she didn't like to clean it up.

Up to this point, Joy had found herself experiencing the layered emotions she would feel whenever she presented a new idea at a work meeting that her team didn't initially understand or whenever she tried to teach her children something new about life that they weren't quite ready for. Autumn didn't seem to either understand or be ready for what she had been sharing about love. She was disappointed, doubtful, and annoyed, but was aware that she couldn't continue to be any of these things if she wanted to continue to demonstrate authentic positive support. She was still hoping that simply providing support and encouragement to Autumn would be enough over this one meeting at the coffee shop and they could then go back to their separate lives. For this to happen, she realized she would need to pivot to giving Autumn encouragement from another angle.

"Autumn, you have 'The Drive' and that's why you are in the situation you're in. It took you a while, but you are finally here," Joy heard herself say as she still sifted through various thoughts on what to say next.

"The what?" Autumn asked, appearing caught off-guard, "I hate driving."

"The Drive," Joy reiterated, "I call it 'The Drive' but I'm referring to the drive you have inside of you to follow your dreams, reach your goals, and achieve your full potential. 'The Drive' is that spark inside of you that aspires to greater things than the nine-to-five job that you aren't happy in, the boring town or suburb you may be living in, and the mundane existence that your family and friends raised you to believe you were supposed to be living in. 'The Drive' is that spiritual sense of purpose that intuitively encourages you to harness the dream you may have had dating back to childhood to do what you love for a living as an adult. 'The Drive' instills discipline in you, wills persistence, maintains consistency, enables you to make sacrifices, and doesn't compromise until you've overcome every barrier that you encounter to achieve your goals."

Autumn remained expressionless in apathetic silence.

The coffee shop remained quiet and sleepy as the rain poured outside.

"You know," Joy added with a tone that didn't quite mask her uneasiness at Autumn's silence, "'The Drive?'"

"Joy, I don't need your help if you are just one of those people who helps people to feel better about yourself," Autumn remarked candidly. "I asked you here because I needed a friend, and I don't really have friends. You are also the only person I know who would get it. But, I mean, you are talking to me right now like you're my mom. Are friends supposed to raise you like parents now?!"

"Absolutely," Joy immediately contended as though Autumn had inadvertently struck upon a recurring thought that she already had been experiencing, "these days I think friends do almost as much as parents do in some ways. Trust me, I have kids. Kids are all about their friends because other kids have parents who aren't all about their kids, so those kids are all about my kids because they aren't getting the attention and love they need from their parents at home. This in turn, pressures my kids to reciprocate and try to be all about their friends who are all about them."

"Are we here together to resolve some of your problems too?" Autumn asked dryly.

Joy initially appeared as though she didn't know how to handle Autumn's response. But then she quietly opened her heart to that understanding she had been so hesitant to experience. The act of opening her heart made her almost want to kick herself for not doing so earlier (in the way that finally opening one's heart to something tends to do when it is delayed). As much as she wanted to simply have coffee with Autumn the one time and give her some encouragement before moving back to living totally different lives again, it was becoming clear that Autumn really wanted that friend again who would spend time with her beyond this one time, just like she had wanted her friendship in high school. This was a second chance at friendship between them and Autumn needed her help beyond a one-time visit there at the coffee shop but had too much pride to be more direct about it.

Joy laughed upon deciding to herself she'd go further with trying to assist Autumn: "I was totally leading to where I think how I've resolved my problem can help you with yours."

"Really..." Autumn muttered with her trademark tone of mildly skeptical sarcasm.

"At one point my kids started becoming consumed by their friends at the expense of family time, so I started showing them the other world on what I would refer to as 'field trips' to give us a new way to bond. My partner doesn't access the other world, but since I started spending more time with them there, they started spending more time with him too doing other things together. Of course, we also do more together as a whole family. It made all the difference we needed to give them more balance between friends and family. Speaking of balance, I call them 'field trips' because we absolutely enjoy those trips when we have them, but I want them to have a much better balance between the other world and this one because..."

"...we didn't?" Autumn offered to finish her sentence after Joy had trailed off in hesitation.

"Exactly," Joy said, "but there's more to it. Since I started spending that time again in the other world, I have made a few discoveries that I think can help you. I think I have access to everything we need to help you stop AI Autumn and Casey."

"Ready!" A robotic female voice suddenly echoed through the empty coffee shop. It was so unexpected that Autumn nearly leapt from her chair.

Joy looked around the coffee shop and found that the baristas had retreated to the back of the shop again and weren't in sight. She then turned to Autumn and blushed.

"It's a software update," Joy explained. "I'm sorry, I thought I had my phone silenced."

Joy picked up her phone and started typing on it as though she was texting again.

Autumn glanced outside at the passersby navigating through the growing fog of misty rain.

"Okay, I'll have another sip of the latte," Autumn sighed as she looked out the window.

Joy slid the cup of latte over to Autumn while scrolling on her phone with her other hand as if she was checking a social media app.

Autumn glanced at her and involuntarily shook her head slightly in disapproval before raising the mug to take another sip of the latte. She took another sip that was much longer than she anticipated as she found that she enjoyed it even more this time than she had the first time. After she was done, she closed her eyes to savor the experience while cradling the mug between both hands on the table like she had observed Joy doing earlier. She started to wonder if it was the best she ever had.

She couldn't remember the last time she had enjoyed a beverage or a food this much (probably not since college).

As she opened her eyes, she suddenly felt a strange electricity through her entire nervous system that prompted her to involuntarily, but quite consciously, blink.

~ 14 ~

As Autumn blinked, her hands suddenly felt empty and the air around her felt different. It felt significantly cooler (but not quite cold) and she had a unique sensation that made her feel like she was sitting in a more open, much wider space than she had been in at the coffee shop.

When she opened her eyes after they had been shut for approximately 0.3 seconds, she found herself at what appeared to be an open-air rooftop bar on a skyscraper in the middle of a small city that was floating in outer space. The rooftop bar was situated on the tallest building among at least a half dozen other skyscrapers surrounding it.

She saw Joy sitting beside her on a barstool. The barstools looked expensive and were made of black leather with cushioned backrests.

At first, she didn't notice how she was still breathing normally and upon witnessing the billions of stars all around them with no discernible barrier between her nostrils and the lack of oxygen in space, she started looking around the bar anxiously as if to find a source of oxygen.

She soon found herself breathing irregularly.

Joy placed her hand on Autumn's shoulder.

"It's all good here, you can breathe normally. We have oxygen misters and gravitational harmonizers installed throughout the rooftop deck so that customers can breathe and walk around like they would on any other open rooftop bar," Joy reassured her. "We used to have a dome installed over the entire space station, but this newer technology made it unnecessary."

"Huh?" Autumn managed to whimper before she was able to take a deep breath to start calming herself down. Even as she was catching her breath, she couldn't help but observe the scenery around her with awe and wonder, like a little kid would upon setting foot in a new theme park or a new toy store.

The overall area of the rooftop bar and restaurant covered at least 5,000 square feet. The restaurant seating section included small garden areas with fountains scattered around what seemed like hundreds of tables and chairs. This restaurant portion surrounded an elevated circular bar that had at least 50 bar stools around it. There was purple neon lighting throughout the restaurant along with eight strategically placed electric "fake" fireplaces that generated actual warmth in addition to being a supplemental light source. The bar, tables, and chairs were black with steel linings and had a futuristic, metallic quality.

Joy and Autumn were the only people seated at the elevated bar, but there were various people, robots, and aliens seated at about 30% of the tables below them. The robots appeared to be of various manufacturers, and the aliens appeared to be of various species as both groups were of all types of diverse shapes and sizes. The aliens had especially striking differences in their appearances: some were more humanoid in appearance, others looked more like animals or plants on earth, and still others had an appearance that was more cell-like or something out of a biology book. The diverse set of aliens suggested they came from all over the universe and maybe beyond. There was no clear separation or disparity in how the people, robots, and aliens were seated as they all seemed to congregate with one another based on personal or work relationships rather than by nationality, gender, race, or status as a life form.

The bar section had no one else around except for one android robot that was cleaning pint glasses at the other end of it. The android robot had clear, translucent "skin" that formed the humanoid shell of what would vaguely appear to be a 25 year-old man. The shell or "skin" partially revealed the inner mechanical body of the bartender and included scattered purple neon lighting (mirroring the exact lighting of restaurant) that lined and illuminated some of its parts, such as its arms, shoulders, brain, breast plate, and fingers. Its eyes were similarly lit with the same purple neon color that lined other areas of its body. It had no hair but did have the outline of ears, lips, and a nose in addition to its eyes. Its hands seemed to have the full agility of human hands in addition to being waterproof.

"This is a perfect time to be here where we can talk," Joy observed. "It opens earlier nowadays because it gets super crowded from lunch until close. It is the most popular restaurant at the space station."

"I can see why," Autumn commented, still sounding out slightly out of breath, "did your space station always have a bar?"

"Well, over the years, I've made it more, um, adult." Joy laughed.

"So... oxygen misters and gravitational harmonizers?"

"Yes! We have oxygen misters installed around the periphery of the rooftop that create a large invisible bubble in which enough oxygen is released for us to breathe. They were developed by the staff employed here at the space station and I named them 'oxygen misters' because they made me think of the misters that restaurants and coffee shops have around their patios on hot days. The gravitational harmonizers were also created here, and they are installed underneath the flooring. They contain body heat sensors that activate a gravitational pull on anyone who enters the area. They have a range that rises up to 12 feet above the floor, so they are activated now even as you are sitting down on your barstool," Joy explained.

"Well, this is certainly different..." Autumn began but then didn't know what more to say about it. Upon observing beer taps within the bar area she eventually asked: "Do you guys have amber on draft here?"

"I'll have the usual," Joy asked the robot bartender as it approached them to take their orders right after Autumn had asked her question, "and she'll try our amber."

Autumn quietly observed as the robot bartender filled a pint of amber for Autumn and then fixed a cocktail-like, coffee-themed beverage for Joy that didn't seem to contain any alcohol. After serving them their drinks, the robot bartender then quietly returned to washing pint glasses at the other end of the bar.

"Your space station bar went to serving non-alcoholic cocktails too?" Autumn asked with a cynical tone. "I see that everywhere now."

"When you have an ambiance like this, you don't really need a drink."

"I still do," Autumn mumbled before she took a sip of her beer right after the robot bartender had handed it to her. She nodded approvingly after she had tasted the beer. "I suppose it's 5 o'clock somewhere," she added with a smile.

Joy laughed. "The environment is like morning at an airport bar here, isn't it? I'm so happy to see you are enjoying the beer. We brew our own beer on site."

"Wow... so, this is where you hang out nowadays whenever you are here?"

"Pretty much... Well, not the bar, but here at the space station in general. It's my old space station I created when I was a kid."

Joy then looked around to reaffirm that nobody was sitting near them as though she wanted to tell Autumn either a secret or something so serious that she wanted no one to interrupt her.

"My entire research team of scientists and engineers are all still here from when I first started this place," Joy continued. "Everything they started working on that I had first dreamed about as a kid are projects that they kept working on even during the years I wasn't around here. One of them was time travel."

"Really..." Autumn whispered with mesmerized sincerity as her eyes widened.

"A few years ago, we finally discovered a way to travel through time but..."

"But?" Autumn was looking at Joy with her full, impatient attention.

"But it's limited... you see, the time travel is based on traveling into the memories of a living person who must be present with you while in a meditative state when you are using what I will refer to as the little 'time machine' we've created here. But there's something else..."

"But?" Autumn repeated.

"But it does have the capacity to bridge the past with the present within the real world through a gateway in this world. We are also able to minimize triggering the butterfly effect that would alter previous events that have occurred in the real world. But that doesn't mean we can't still use the past to pinpoint and alter specific present events in the real world though. In other words, within the context of the real world, we can bring past figures and prior events from memories to life in the present to alter the course of specified events that are occurring at this moment in the real world if we want to, but to achieve that, we are only able to bring the past figures into this world in order for them to have any potential impact on current events in the real world. We can do this in a way where the past figure would have no recollection of coming here or of you visiting them. We haven't figured out how to directly bring people from the past into the present moment within the real world, we can only bring them here. The closest we can come to that is we can bring a person's spirit into the real world, but that's a whole other topic of conversation there." Joy blushed as though to indicate she felt like she was now over-sharing.

"A gateway in this world...how?" Autumn asked. "Like 99% of the population will never access this world the way we do."

"Right, most people don't access this world the way we do, only a small percentage of people do, and they often only do when they are children," Joy explained. "But we discovered nearly everyone has access to this world within the recesses of the minds, even if they have never accessed it before. In order for the present version of themselves to 'meet' the person they were in the past; they must access this world to make that possible. But that meeting doesn't happen face-to-face, it all happens within the body."

Autumn remained still as she deeply considered this concept.

"Because it's like they have to believe that anything is possible when we access the full efficient capacity of the human brain," Autumn observed after a long pause.

"Yes, and just like children forget this world ever existed once they lose access to it as they get older and get wrapped up in the real world, many people who visit here from the past either don't recall they were ever in the future or vaguely remember it like it was only a dream."

"Don't you ever wish we would forget about this world too?" Autumn asked with her trademark smirk.

Joy looked down at her coffee-themed beverage and laughed: "Having lifetime access is both a blessing and a curse."

Autumn started to genuinely laugh along with her before realizing what she was doing and gradually pulled back in the way one would when trying to suppress a coughing fit. Whenever any interaction with another person was going well for her, she still found herself waiting for the seemingly inevitable disappointment or rejection. She was therefore hesitant to enjoy herself too much with Joy.

"So where is it?"

"The time machine? It's right there in front of you..."

Autumn looked at Joy's cell phone which was placed about six inches away from where she had put down her beer.

"The phone?! The time machine is your phone?!" Autumn picked it up and found that it weighed significantly heavier than an average smartphone. It felt like she was lifting a 2.5-pound weight.

"It operates as my personal phone, but I also call it 'The Portal'. It has a different alarm on it than your average phone that enables you to set a full date, including month, day, and year, in addition to the option to select a time. If you have the exact date, then that is all you need to access the memory. You don't need to select the time, because by selecting the date, it will take you to the exact time that the memory occurred. The time is strictly an alarm that you need in the present moment to activate time travel. You only need to set the alarm one minute ahead of the current time while being present in the same room as the person who has the memory you are trying to access. At first, I wanted to call it a 'time-management app' but that makes it sound like a scheduling app for work/life balance, so I went with calling the app 'The Portal.' Since the app required these extra modifications to my phone to make it work, I eventually ended up calling my phone 'The Portal' too."

"Can you access your own memories?" Autumn wondered.

"Yes, but only if you remember the exact date that the memory occurred."

"Wow, that's so weird..."

"The time travel option within The Portal will only know what you know and then it will let you go from there."

Autumn also noticed how warm the phone was, as though it had just been used for a two-hour phone call or had been overburdened by the use of multiple apps all at once.

"I understand what you were doing on your phone now at the coffee shop," Autumn realized as she placed the phone back on the bar in front of Joy. "You must have used an app to take us here."

"Yes, this time I used the same app to get us here. The Portal uses a rapid orange flash that prompts your brain to accept the transfer into this world. More often than not, you can't detect the flash as it happens, it works that quickly. But the time travel option uses a longer, much more pronounced red flash that is easily detectable and impacts your body in a different way to accept the transfer through time. Have you ever wondered how we access places like this?"

"I mean, who cares? I love that we're here."

"It's our own internal biological AI."

"What?!"

"This world is created by our own internal AI program, it's an alternate dimension that you and I are able to fully access anytime we want to. Like AI, we are the initial creators of it, and it wouldn't exist without us, but then it takes a life of its own. If there was ever such a thing as 'natural AI' then this is it."

"Are you sure?" Autumn asked. "Sometimes I kind of either drink a beer, smoke a joint, or eat an edible, and I'm here because those activities seem to also trigger what is left of my imagination. It was easier to access when we were young and had the 'little kid imagination'. I have always seen it as a process where we use our imaginations like anyone else would, but we have this whole extra gear within us that we could shift into within our imaginations that could bring us here to this world. It's like this extra gene or a random bit of additional knowledge we have that is so advanced that it's like the difference between what most people would experience as simple arithmetic, but we somehow experience as advanced calculus."

"It was easier to go to sleep at night when you were a little kid, right?"

"Well, yeah, these days I often use those same things I occasionally need to get here to also help me fall asleep."

"Exactly the same concept, just like you think you need those things to go to sleep instead of choosing healthier alternatives, you also develop a habit of having more trouble accessing your natural AI without them."

"Uh...hmmm...huh?"

"At Red Mosaic, we have a neuroscience department, and I used one of the labs to evaluate my brain responses when I am here. I discovered that the astrocytes in my brain multiply exponentially when I am in the process of transporting here and then the new astrocytes coalesce to form hundreds of star shaped structures around all the neurons throughout my brain. The firing neurons activate the 'stars' so that they brighten just like the stars you see in the night sky or in space. That's what our brains look like while we are here, and the astrocytes maintain those structures until we return to the real world."

Autumn looked up again at the stars above them, imagining them in her brain.

"But just like it's easier to go to sleep when you produce more growth hormone as a kid to improve deep sleep, I discovered that growth hormone production also positively impacts your ability to produce what I'll call 'The Star Effect' of the astrocytes. Of course, it's also easier to go to sleep and access your imagination as a kid because you don't have the distractions of adulting in which you are stressed out about your job, trying to keep up with your kids, or just hoping you can figure out what you are going to have to eat that day with all the complex emotions and problems that we seem to encounter regularly at home and at work. That's all there, in addition to how aging can disrupt our sleep and ability to initiate The Star Effect."

"What? You analyzed the brains of your kids when they are here too?"

"I did," Joy recalled, "and I also looked at my own brain after a couple glasses of wine and noticed drugs like alcohol also independently stimulate The Star Effect as a kind of cheat code around growth hormone production that isn't sustainable without increased use of substances."

"Makes sense," Autumn said dryly.

"I've found other things like yoga, meditation, prayer, fasting, and working out create an environment in your brain that is more conducive to The Star Effect," Joy explained. "I also studied people who don't access the other world, like my partner, and found they are capable of experiencing about 10% of The Star Effect in their waking hours and a little less than a quarter of The Star Effect when they are in deep sleep. Their access to their natural AI is limited primarily to dreams, many of which they don't remember."

Autumn took a contemplative sip of her beer. By this point, she was impressed and intrigued while somewhat overwhelmed by all the information that Joy was providing.

"I appreciate everything you are sharing here. It really is insightful," Autumn eventually shared with a tone of sincerity. "But I am not understanding what this has to do with AI Autumn."

"In this world we are in now, you are AI Autumn and AI Autumn is you."

Autumn had started taking another drink of her beer and nearly spit it out upon hearing that.

"Wait?! What?" She asked, after a forceful, almost choking-like gulp.

"Here we are the AI to them, and they are real. Did you ever think about it? For a long time, I never did. But you can ask them, and they'll tell you."

"We are AI to you?!" Autumn asked the robot bartender, who happened to be walking by at that moment to check on their drinks.

"Completely AI," the robot bartender confirmed, revealing it had a mechanical, gender-neutral voice, "but we understand the role you have in our creation as much as we have a role in yours. You are always welcome here. We think of you as tourists."

"Even Joy?!"

The robot bartender looked at Joy.

"Even Joy," it replied before walking away to welcome a group of four new customers who were sitting down at the other side of the bar.

"I can't believe they think that. I guess I never really thought about it...they think they have a role in our creation?" Autumn asked.

"They do," Joy verified, "look at how much of a role they have had just in our lives. They represent everything we are and want to be and to them we are the avatars through which they can influence events in both this world and the real world."

"Okay, this is getting too weird." Autumn decided, sounding more overwhelmed and fatigued by everything she was learning.

Joy laughed, but Autumn didn't join her.

"It gets better," Joy promised with the kind of beaming smile that seemed to want to leap off her face and be a smile on Autumn's face too. "You know how I used the app to get here? Well, we obviously don't need the app to transport here, but the app has an added benefit you probably have never experienced before. Before I developed this app, my visits here were always at expense of real-time still elapsing in the real world—"

"Yeah, but that's part of what I've enjoyed about it," Autumn interjected. "I want to spend as little time in the real world as possible to be in this one."

"I felt the same way as a kid, but when I started returning here with my kids, I realized I didn't really have as much time to visit here. My life had changed so much during that period of about fifteen years when I didn't access this world at all. From when I was 16 up until I was 31, I thought I had moved forward to other things like you thought I did. While that was true for a while, it's funny how life brings you back through your past even when you are in the process of continuing to move forward with your life. I started visiting again after I encountered the situation that I told you about earlier involving my kids and their friends. I discovered both of my kids had relatively easy access they apparently hadn't been aware of, so it was like rediscovering it all over again through their eyes. But of course, by then, I'd been through college, gotten married, started my career, and had a lot more life experience, so I had this desire I didn't have before to understand this world more, especially with my kids visiting here. Recently, in the process of my research, I found a more advanced portal than the one we had been using. See, we have been using the portal through the astrocytes in our brains, but there is a more advanced portal through glial cells in our heart that are similar to astrocytes. When activated, these cells form a Fibonacci sequence spiral within the heart. The astrocytes in your brain still create The Star Effect during the activation of this portal, but there is an additional Fibonacci sequence spiral formed within the brain as well. It appears on scans as looking like a constellation among the 'stars' formed within your brain. All of it forms this advanced portal we used to get here."

Autumn involuntarily placed her hand in her heart upon hearing this.

"It doesn't just bring you here, it manipulates time as you visit here so that you could be here for hours or days in real time here, but only a split second elapses in the real world. It's incredible, isn't it?"

Joy picked up her phone, swiped around on it and tapped on it a few times to bring up a new screen before placing it directly in front of Autumn.

The screen revealed a live-feed of the coffee shop in the real world in which both Joy and Autumn appeared frozen-in-place while the orchid latte remained cradled in Autumn's hands.

"Oh wow," Autumn said, as she picked up the phone to study them more closely.

"It will be like we haven't lost any time at all when we return," Joy affirmed with a discernible glow in her eyes, "but that's not even the best part of this heart portal. As I indicated earlier, I also discovered that by manipulating the passage of time, this app also gives me the ability communicate directly with another person's soul. I say another person's 'soul' or 'spirit,' depending on how you define each word, but I view them as having the same meaning, so I use the terms interchangeably."

"Okay, now you've lost me...this is getting too insane," Autumn laughed. "Talking to someone's soul?! Do we really have a soul? I guess maybe I was indifferent on the whole 'spirit' versus 'soul' definition thing."

"From what I've learned from using The Portal, we absolutely have a soul. But to communicate with another person's soul, it operates like the time travel option where you must be in the presence of the other person. Ideally, they are either in a meditative or contemplative state when you access their soul to better facilitate the process. You can communicate with their soul directly either within the real world or you can do it here in this one. Either way, just like when you time travel or visit here with the advanced portal, only a split second elapses in the real world when you communicate with another person's soul. It gets a little more complicated though. To activate the soul within the person, the app only activates The Star Effect within their brain, but to communicate with another person's soul and see it, your brain needs to activate

The Star Effect and your heart and brain also need to be in the Fibonacci sequence. The mystery that I'm still trying to understand is that time still freezes for a person when their soul has been generated into human form for us to communicate with it. It's as if the act of manifesting their soul in this way can manipulate time the way the Fibonacci sequence alignment can, but without them needing to experience the Fibonacci sequence themselves."

"Oh, um, whoa...okay," Autumn reacted as she slid Joy's phone back to her. "But I wanted to ask you this when you brought up time travel earlier: What about the time you travel to? Would it really be time travel if you go there and freeze time while you are there too? What is the point of time travel if you are freezing time at both where you are coming from and where you are visiting? I guess it's nice to have the luxury to move around time and simply observe things. I am also guessing that is part of what enables you to only change certain specific things without triggering a full-blown butterfly effect."

"Unless you transport the past version of the person or people you are visiting here to this world, our experience in the past otherwise elapses in real-time within the timeline of the past when you time travel there. We have the work-around of bringing them here if you want to spend any time with a person from your past and impact their lives without affecting everything else going on around them. It's the act of bringing the person or people from the past here that enables you to make any changes in their lives that you want to make without interfering too much with the time they have come from. You can bring them here and allow them to remember their experiences here. I don't know if it's statistically possible that you can totally avoid the butterfly effect in this instance, but you could drastically minimize it to such a degree as though you were basically never there beyond the few people you want to remember you being there."

"Oh really?" Autumn asked with a sarcastic laugh. "You seem to have an answer for everything."

Joy laughed along with her, though somewhat uncomfortably.

Autumn took another drink of her beer as she found herself randomly thinking about how she had never wanted anyone else to know about this other world. She used to hate that Joy knew about it. Now Joy apparently had learned all these details about it that she felt like she should have already known about.

"Why are you telling me this?" Autumn asked.

15

Joy looked away from Autumn and at her own drink as though she was thinking about taking a sip of it but elected not to.

"You love coming here, and I thought hearing these new things about it would be exciting to you and maybe give you something to be happy about, because you seem...well, sad," Joy replied. "When we were kids, we thought of this world as an escape from the real world, but now I am convinced it's a complex gateway to understanding life and understanding ourselves..."

Joy looked like she wanted to say more but needed more time to think about it.

Autumn yawned.

It wasn't one of those intentional yawns she used to hint to someone that she didn't want to engage in conversation any further, but an involuntary, exhausted, burned-out kind-of-yawn that she had become accustomed to experiencing in recent years. She felt slightly embarrassed about this untimely yawn occurring at this point in such a deep discussion with Joy but also didn't feel a need to apologize for it.

She was about to respond to Joy when Autumn noticed a notification illuminate her phone. She picked it up and saw that AI Autumn had commented on one of her posts on social media. Autumn didn't use social media often and her most recent post was from almost a year ago when she was at a work conference in Vancouver, Canada. The photo depicted her on the Capilano Suspension Bridge standing in the middle of the bridge above the Capilano River at dusk. In the photo, she was flanked by giant Douglas fir and red cedar trees on either side while wearing a scarf that looked like it was a size too big for her. The bridge itself was covered in string lights for the holiday season. One of her co-workers in the travel group took the photo despite her reluctance to participate in any of the group pictures they were taking. She had eventually decided she liked the photo enough to post it.

AI Autumn had apparently created a new account using the same profile picture that Autumn was using and commented underneath her post with one word: "delete."

Autumn considered ironically deleting the comment that said "delete" but instead resigned herself to leaving it there. She set her phone back on top of the bar, but this time placed it face-down.

"AI has already changed the world, and if it is used in the right way, it will make the world a million times better for us," Joy reasoned after her moment of reflection that had seemed to keep her oblivious to both Autumn's yawn and her phone usage. "Unfortunately, I'm not surprised to hear anything you've said about Casey. It's like she hasn't grown up at all."

"She hasn't," Autumn groaned. "But I haven't either. In our defense, I don't think the real world is worth growing up in. The more you grow up and mature, the more you understand how deeply horrific the world really is."

"The world is beautiful," Joy contended, "it's the people who refuse to grow up and mature that create horrific events within it and in doing so, try to undermine its beauty. But the world heals, recovers, and goes on being beautiful long after they are gone."

"Yeah, that's cute and everything," Autumn retorted, "but it doesn't help me with my situation. What if AI Autumn interferes with my life more than it already has? I have this weird feeling it isn't satisfied with only taking over my job. It even showed up at the hospice center that my grandfather is in yesterday while I was there visiting him."

"Oh no..." Joy reacted with a genuinely concerned look. "Your grandfather is dying?! Is that the same grandfather you did a project on as your hero in the fourth grade?"

Autumn's lips parted slightly in stunned silence that Joy remembered the research project she did on Grandpa in the fourth grade. She had forgotten about it herself.

"You know, if you bring me along on a visit, we can talk to his spirit before he passes, but only if you want to. We can talk to his soul through The Portal," Joy continued. "We discovered your soul is represented by your ideal self. But in this case, when I say 'ideal self' I don't mean a person you imagine yourself to be or hope to be, but rather the person you were when you were at your best—in the prime of your life. For some people, the prime of your life can be right at this moment, so your soul would be manifested as a person resembling exactly who you are now. But for most people, the prime of your life was at some point in your past, so the physical body of their souls will be revealed as resembling who they were at a specific point in time from their past. Regardless of when their prime was, interacting with someone's soul is still like interacting with them now because their soul has all the knowledge and experience that they have attained up through the present day. You can interact with your grandpa when he was in his prime."

"I don't know..." Autumn began after a moment of contemplation.

"Or we can visit him through one of his memories?" Joy asked.

"I don't know..." Autumn repeated, "I love my grandpa more than anyone else, I wouldn't want to do anything that might mess up his life."

Joy picked up her phone and brought up a screen that she showed to Autumn. It looked like she had opened a music app on it.

"I have embedded an alarm within The Portal that activates a siren song for the duration that I am visiting another time. The song is hidden, and it is not noticeable to either you or the people you are visiting back in time. Nevertheless, it emits a powerful frequency that unhinges astrocytes in the brain of person who is not experiencing the Fibonacci sequence and disrupts their ability to remember any events as they occur while they are exposed to this sound. Once a person is no longer exposed to this sound, they don't think anything of it. It's like when you feel like you forgot something but aren't sure what you forgot about or when you are in a conversation and get so caught up in what the other person is telling you that you forgot what you originally wanted to say to that person before the conversation started. Our brains are not impacted by the siren when we are in the act of using The Portal because we are locked in the Fibonacci sequence to use the advanced portal, but the person from the past is only in The Star Effect to visit this world, so they are impacted by the siren. In other words, the Fibonacci sequence spiral in the brain, but not The Star Effect alone, creates an immunity to the siren."

"When you say siren, do you mean like a police or ambulance siren, or do you mean like a Greek mythology siren?"

"Greek mythology siren. It also places the exposed mind in a mildly euphoric state lasting through the duration of the sound," Joy explained. "Because of the way it impacts people I thought I'd name it a siren because I love the concept that it could be so beautiful and pleasing to the mind, that it enables you to navigate the past relatively unperturbed by the people in it. People will still recognize you are there and otherwise function normally. But as I said, in the end, they won't remember you. While you are there, it's like they will be happy to see you are there without really knowing why."

Autumn took another contemplative sip of her beer. It seemed to taste better with every sip just like the rooftop bar at the space station seemed to look even better the longer she stayed there.

"What if you want someone you visit in the past to remember something?" Autumn asked after she had put her beer back down on the bar top.

Joy placed a seashell down beside Autumn's pint.

"You probably know how seashells can sound like the ocean when you hold them up to your ear because of the way they absorb the ambient sounds of their immediate environment. Well, I was inspired to use a seashell as a design to create a noise cancellation device for the siren sound. You simply give it to the person you want to have a memorable meaningful interaction with before you have that interaction with them. They'll only think you are giving them a beautiful seashell. It was easy to choose a seashell because they've always been around and admired throughout time. It has a range that fully covers the individual who possesses it. You have to be really careful though..."

"...to minimize the butterfly effect, I know," Autumn finished, as she held up the shell. She appreciated how she was unable to detect or suspect that there was an electronic noise cancellation device installed within it.

"That noise cancellation device is specific to that siren sound," Joy added, "it doesn't eliminate or reduce any other sounds but the siren sound. The seashell is also re-constructed around the device itself so you can't see it and you will only notice the seashell is slightly heavier than your average seashell. The person you give the seashell to will be inclined to think it's just a seashell that is uniquely a little heavier than other ones its size."

"And I thought you had forgotten the other world completely," Autumn quipped with a smirk as she returned the seashell to Joy.

"Another beer?" The robot bartender asked as it approach them.

Autumn nodded as she took a long swig of the reminder of her pint to finish it off.

"Also please add a water for her," Joy asked as the robot bartender placed another pint of amber in front of Autumn.

"You know you are destined for something greater when you numb yourself with unhappy happy hours each day to dull the pain of slowly killing yourself at a job that doesn't appreciate you..." Joy said after the robot bartender had placed a glass of water in front of each of them before departing to check in with its other customers. She had paused to look for any type of acknowledgement from Autumn. When she didn't get anything, she continued: "...and when you aren't doing that in the real world, you're either in this world or dreaming about being in this world, aren't you?"

"Growing up, I was so unhappy, that this world was my only way out. By the time we were in high school, I still held onto this, but deep down I also hoped that my adult life in the real world would be extraordinary too. Instead, I graduated college, got a job, and for a while found myself wanting more of what I would call an 'ordinary life' in the real world too. It got to the point where I was ready to give up everything I had here. I watched my coworkers get married, have kids, buy homes, and now I've watched a few of them start to have grandkids. Throughout much of my 20s and into my 30s, I invested so much into trying to be ordinary. I changed the way I dressed, worked on the way I approached people, and took the leadership and certification courses that Casey told me to take. I tried to say the right things and do the right things at work and in my personal life. I even tried dating and hooking up with people," Autumn recounted, sounding exhausted by the reminder that she had tried living her life in this way.

"So basically, you had almost become the opposite of who you were in high school," Joy observed, "even though on the surface now, you seem to have a lot of similarities to being who you were in high school."

"Yeah, it always felt like something was missing," Autumn pondered. "I can't shake that feeling I have had since we were kids that I am misunderstood, underappreciated, and underrated."

"When was the last time you were in a relationship?" Joy asked. It was a question she had wanted to ask for a while but felt like she needed to discuss other subjects in depth with Autumn first before she felt it was appropriate to go there.

"I think I was like 26...27...something like that." Autumn was detached in her response and seemed uninterested in digging further through her memory bank to determine the exact age she was.

"You aren't really interested in getting married or having kids, are you?"

"No."

"No to which one or is it no to both?"

"Both."

"Do you like men?"

"No...well, mostly no...I like my grandpa."

"Are you asexual?"

"No."

"Are you gay?"

"No."

"So then you are...?"

Joy looked at her quietly and remained intentionally expressionless, as though she was trying to give her space to elaborate beyond the pattern of closed-ended responses that she was receiving.

"Human," Autumn replied.

Autumn felt like an extra misshaped puzzle piece that had been accidentally added to a box containing a 10,000-piece jigsaw puzzle. As kids, she had looked at Joy as one of the few other misshaped pieces she had encountered in her life. But now for the first time, she saw Joy as one of those pieces that fit after all.

"We feel this need to tell everyone who we are. But I do still believe in privacy and being selective about who you trust with certain amounts of information about yourself. I won't be shamed into sharing more with people I don't feel comfortable sharing with. If I decide at one point to be more open, I'll be more open. But the more outspoken people forget that there are many of us who are only trying to survive and are still learning how to be ourselves. There is always this pressure to already know and like who you are and act confident about it whether you feel secure about yourself or not. If you aren't sure or don't like who you are, then you have even more people either telling you who you are or who they want you to be. It seems like those people like to think they know who you are better than you know yourself and maybe it's easier for them to think they have all the answers because it's easier for them to pretend who you really are doesn't exist," Autumn explained. As she took a sip of her second beer, she realized she was now feeling a slight buzz and probably wouldn't otherwise be opening up like this.

"It's..." Autumn hesitated as though she was unsure if she wanted to continue. She took a drink of her water instead.

"...hard, right? It's hard," Joy added. "We live in an era that is more individualized than it's ever been, not just because individualism has gradually progressed throughout human history but because we have the technology that facilities the autonomy of the individual now more than ever. We also have the technology that exposes the limitations and corruption of large organizations such as governments and corporations. Individuals are realizing that productivity data-driven organizations are doing everything but looking out for our own well-being. We no longer live in a society where organizations can get away with being paternalistic. When you can't rely on organizations, you naturally turn inward, but most of us are still never given the tools or knowledge to know how to turn inward. Even worse, if you discover after having a thorough and honest assessment of yourself that you are different, then you are still conditioned to be as hard on yourself as anyone else would be on you for not being the way you think you are supposed to be. I believe we are hardwired to pursue three callings in this life: to find a sense of meaning and purpose, to understand ourselves as individuals, and to connect with as many different people as we can in one way or another, to share what we can with them."

"I don't know about that third one," Autumn questioned.

"Ha, you are here talking to me, and I'm outside your circle," Joy countered. "But let's say you believe those are the three callings we have in life, then where do organizations find a place in this? Well, some organizations aim to be your answer for purpose and meaning, others aim to be the answer in helping you understand and maintain yourself, and still others aim to help you appeal more to other people. But at the end of the day, it's entirely inconvenient for these organizations to discover that once people have found themselves, those same people then realize they don't always fit into the organizational agenda. As a result, whether you are in a capitalistic society or not, whether you have a liberal or conservative value system, and whether you are from a more individualistic or more communal society, it behooves organizations to contain or prohibit true self-discovery under the guise that actually being different or independent undermines the ability for people to unify and is therefore this divisive or evil endeavor. What most of us don't see is that in the long run, every road of true self-discovery leads to the conclusion that we are all human and should therefore embrace one another for our differences while learning from each another. Organizations like Dark Forest Solutions or even Red Mosaic will continually try to numb and distract us from knowing ourselves as individuals so that we make our allegiance to them as our identity instead of having our own identities."

"So... I take it you're not a fan of organizations?" Autumn asked sarcastically.

"There are some organizations that have done a lot of good for humanity," Joy conceded. "I'm not a fan of organizations that believe they can only profit from or benefit from taking away or compartmentalizing our identities rather than genuinely supporting our individual missions of understanding who we are and how we can better contribute to society."

"There will always people in the world like me who don't quite fit in anywhere and it's inconvenient to nearly every potential group or organization I could be a part of."

"In the right relationships, people elevate each other; imagine if we had more of the right relationships with organizations and by organizations, I mean countries, religions, charities, communities, and corporations, that elevated people instead of either maintaining them or degrading them. Almost every major organization out there that has been around for years has committed some kind of atrocity, crime, or trauma. We as people are expected to simply align with and surround ourselves with layers of these organizations, but as pure individuals we can always get a fresh start. We don't have to align with organizations that have hurt people or are hurting people. As people are becoming more individualistic, it's a great opportunity for organizations to replace people with AI, not just out convenience for productivity and financial considerations but because it's a means by which they can erase that individuality within their employment pool. They can make 'AI people' the way they think people should be. But AI can also be a tool to enhance individuality and individual creativity. That's what I love about AI. People are intimidated and even afraid of AI, but they are really afraid of other people misusing AI. There is so much greater potential with AI to create incredible innovations for society, and that includes helping the individual through the never-ending journey of self-discovery. By enhancing the individual experience, we can improve the integrity of organizations without having to conform to preexisting outdated and toxic organizational cultures. Nobody would know that better than people like us. It's up to people like us to protect that."

"But as individuals aren't we really a mix of all those organizational influences you are describing?"

"We are to a degree but think about how many people are truly mindful of that, how many people ever question that, or how many people are in a position to modify that which doesn't serve them as individuals who can potentially reach self-transcendence and contribute to the advancement of society," Joy elaborated. "People are too complex for any organization to decide how everyone should be. Instead, organizations should strive to create a supportive environment that is conducive to self-reflection and empowerment. That's how individuals and organizations can both get better. Respecting and loving others as well as yourself will never truly belong to any one organization. People are deeper than that."

"Where is this coming from?" Autumn asked. "I mean, where are you going with this?"

16

"Do you ever feel like you are timeless?" Joy asked.

"Timeless?! I mean, I think pretty highly of myself, but timeless?"

"Timeless...as in you have a greater awareness of what the past was like beyond what you read in the history books and like you are a seer or an oracle who can sense or even see future events before they happen. It's like we are pre-programmed to traverse time beyond our own lifetime within our minds, but most people never experience this, or only have a subconscious sense of it, or only experience it in dreams. Neuroscientists can't fully explain or understand certain phenomena like this and often dismiss it as the mind tricking itself."

Autumn cringed a little when Joy had said "pre-programmed."

"I go home from work every day and then come back here to this world— every day. Just like I did when I was a kid after I came home from school. In some ways it's like I never left," Autumn admitted. "When you knew me in school, I thought I knew that this was the life I wanted. I thought I was ahead of everyone else because I already knew what I wanted. But what people sometimes don't understand is that what you want to do with your life isn't always going to be alignment with what you are meant to be in this life. You can know exactly what you want in this life, but life itself and the other people you choose to have in it may have other ideas in store for you. You may still end up having what you individually wanted to begin with, but in the course of getting what you want, you may take several unexpected twists and turns to get there. Even if you get exactly what you wanted, you may realize that it isn't what you will necessarily end up wanting to keep once you have it. I suppose that's what has happened to me: I went down a different path than I thought I would but still ended up with what I wanted, only to learn it's not what I wanted. People don't always allow what they want in life to change along with them when they are changing and evolving as a person beyond what they originally wanted. Sometimes changing and evolving as a person includes finally acknowledging who you always were deep down inside when up to that point, you had never known to acknowledge it within yourself. Other people around you may have seen those characteristics in you, but you didn't see it until several years later. But that's okay, I am thinking now that it just means you didn't see it until you were ready. For the past year or so, I keep thinking about how there is 'more' to life. But I am still figuring out what 'more' is and what it means. For the time being though, I am just trying to be content with what I am finally learning about myself and about life."

"You're reminding me of something I've thought about a lot ever since I was a kid," Joy mused with a tone that almost sounded more like she was talking to herself. "It's like we all have these identities, we are part of different countries, ethnicities, gender orientations, religions, and vocations, and as far as I can tell, almost all these different groups persecute each other in some way to limit or erase anyone who is different. They have a hazing process within their own groups and categories to suppress or discourage any nonconformist traits within anyone who joins them or is born into them. So, when I was a kid, I started to think of falling leaves in autumn as reflecting our relationship with God. This way of thinking has only continued to evolve as I've experienced more of life: If God or the Creator is our tree, and we are all the leaves born of the same tree, then all of us begin as a similar collection of cells much the same way the leaves in the trees are all green when they are part of the tree, but when the time comes to release the leaves, their true colors have been revealed in the absence of chlorophyll once they fall from the trees to the earth. In the same way, humans are embedded with our own unique traits through creation and then are released into the world as babies being born with an opportunity to unmask our own unique lives like brightly colored leaves that have fallen from a tree and are blown around by the winds of life. Just like the leaves are dying once they've fallen from a tree, we are dying from the moment we are born and only have a short time to authenticate our true selves. I think about the concept of how we are timeless in that not all dead leaves are thrown away or simply waste away somewhere like on a concrete curb on the side of a road or in a sewer. Some leaves fall near the tree, decompose, and even provide new nutrients to the tree as a fertilizer. They give back. This is what often happens in nature. I am saying you and I are timeless because we are like those leaves that live on in the tree.

"One way society is advancing is that we are always learning and understanding how nature is far more complex than the way we thought it was: we always learn how animals know more than we previously thought, and we always learn how plants know more than we previously thought. Nature consistently seems to know more than what we originally thought it did and I'm suggesting that I believe trees and their leaves know more. We now know how the trees have special cells that release the leaves in autumn. It isn't just the wind blowing them off. Meanwhile, some autumn leaves stay on the trees through winter and don't fall until spring. I believe the relationship between the tree and the leaves determine how and when they fall. In light of this, the relationship you have with that internal voice, which I identify as your soul, and your connection to God, determines how and when you fall. I know I am saying 'God' because that's what I believe, but I've talked to others with different beliefs and no beliefs about this and

I think this applies to all people, regardless of what they believe, because the tree can simply represent life itself in terms of whatever your morals and values are. Either way, the relationship between the tree and the leaf determines if it will remain timeless just as it determines whether you have revealed your true colors before you fall. Some leaves as you know, still fall as green leaves and die before they change color."

"Trees in autumn, yeah, nice...I get it." Autumn laughed as she processed all that Joy had shared. "I like the concept of the leaves because I guess I do believe everyone has the potential to be 'timeless' as you say. As someone who isn't sure of God, and as someone who still feels like I am understanding the role of intuition, I do think where the leaves land is often up to chance in terms of where the wind blows them and where they fall. Within this context, chance does put some people in a much better position. I didn't always think this, but I do think people have more power as individuals than most realize to decide how much of themselves they want to access and then decide what their values are based on how much of themselves they've accessed. But I still think the role of chance will make that process much harder for some more than others. The creation of this AI version of me that represents who others want me to be and who I used to want to be at certain times in my life has reminded me that no one but me will ever truly know what's best for me. I think everyone does have an internal voice that knows what is best for us. Some people like yourself attribute it to God, others believe it to be their own intuitive instincts, and still others believe it is simple reasoning within the mind, but I also think that internal voice is buried in a mix of healthy and unhealthy voices within us, and we decide among those voices which one is the right internal voice for us. Some people choose the wrong voice or choose a misguided voice or choose the voice no one else in their lives wanted them to choose. As long as we aren't hurting anyone, I don't think it's anyone else's right to judge us in this world. Leave that up to God if you believe in God and leave that up to life, if you don't. I say just don't leave it up to other people. Even though they may see things in you that you don't see, you'll still always know more about yourself than other people will.

"I also don't know if I believe we are making linear progress in history. To me, what we call progress in terms of social conditions in society is circular and while technology has been more linear, that has had a circular pattern to a degree when you compare ancient societies to the dark ages of the early medieval period. So much of life is circular. I wouldn't say our relationship with nature, in terms of understanding it, has been totally linear, as lost cultures seemed to know more about nature than we do. If we do know more scientifically about nature, we aren't respecting it environmentally in the way most prior cultures have. From that perspective, I think that our understanding of nature has been circular too. Even if we find a way to stop Casey's AI program, she will still be a billionaire with the capacity to start a new one and there are probably other people with money and AI knowledge doing similar things. The world will react to those changes and then react to those reactions until we all either destroy almost everything and start over, or we all somehow reconcile and peacefully assimilate AI until the next innovations emerge for us to be concerned about and adjust to. Overall, in society, I don't know if we are discovering as much as we are really re-discovering the same ideas and concepts in different contexts."

Autumn managed a half-smile as she experienced a feeling of mental satisfaction from sharing this summarization of her perspective on life. She had never quite put it all together like that, so it was like she was experiencing it for the first time too.

"But it's not really about simply shutting down Casey's AI program, is it?" Joy asked after taking a thoughtful sip of her drink.

"What? You mean this whole thing about me and what I am going through with this sort of mid-life crisis? I mean, I guess it's not a mid-life crisis if I don't feel old enough to have one. I don't feel old enough to have one, but it feels like one."

"I think of achieving self-transcendence in terms of trying to climb a mountain, like Mount Everest. If you have a major long-term goal in life that you want to achieve, or if you want to commit to a long-term serious relationship, it takes consistency, persistence, sacrifice, patience, discipline, endurance, and most importantly, acceptance. I identify having all seven of these traits as being part of 'The Drive' that I was telling you about earlier. I truly believe you have to keep moving forward in order to succeed and remain successful, even in those moments when you believe there is no point to moving forward or think there is no way forward. I truly meant it when I also said you have The Drive. A lot of people give up and turn around when they are climbing Mount Everest: some people die along the way, some people make it close to the summit but don't quite reach the top, and others turn around about halfway when they realize how much further they have to go. My point is that a lot of people try in life to reach a lofty goal or fulfill a long-term commitment, and they all deserve credit for trying to make it work, but they probably won't succeed if they lack one or more of those seven traits."

"Or they may have bad luck," Autumn added.

"That too," Joy acknowledged, "but I know you get my point."

"I do, but that's easy for you to say," Autumn opined. "You sound like one of those older people who has rationalized their stance on a topic for so long that even facts can't change your mind. You knew who you were and realized what you wanted to be before we graduated high school. Imagine believing you know who you are as a kid and throughout the entire time you are in the prime of your life as a young adult, only to discover you were living in denial and maybe living a lie."

Joy took a drink of her coffee-themed, non-alcoholic beverage but maintained eye contact with Autumn as she did so in an effort to show Autumn that she was taking to heart what she was sharing and not ignoring it.

"Earlier you asked me what happened with Casey and her friends in the locker room in high school. The truth is that they beat me up pretty badly too and they really hurt me. I will always have those scars, but I needed those scars to know what it means to be my best. Otherwise, I would have drifted through life aimlessly like a random leaf floating down a stream. I was able to fight them off, so it didn't end up being much worse. It really could have been. My mom told me once that beauty transcends racial, political, religious, and economic divides. She told me that as a way of motivating me to engage in the crazy-long, intense morning and nighttime beauty routines that she still does to maintain her physical appearance. But I took that advice in a different way and applied the word 'beauty' to a beautiful character, not just appearance. I believe a beautiful character can transcend the differences we have and the barriers we put up within ourselves too. It sounds insane and ridiculous to say this out loud even now, but I don't think I would have known that beauty in myself had that fight in the locker room not occurred that day. I have come to accept that identities are sometimes forged this way. The reason why is because, as you know, the real world can be cruel. Identities may have to be forged through fire. I realize now that is why I am meant to help you."

"Well...." Autumn lingered off on that one word as though she was unsure how to continue.

"Casey has more emotional intelligence than she lets on to other people, she chooses to use it the wrong way to manipulate people and use them. I used to think she was evil and born that way. But I don't think she was born that way; she chooses every day to be that way. I also think she didn't entirely understand the other world when we were in high school, but I know she at least suspected it existed. She acts like she didn't, and she was too wrapped in her own popularly in school back then anyway. But now that she's older, it sounds like she has learned as much about this world as we have and may know even more than we know. Based on what you are telling me, I suspect she learned a lot of it through studying you to create this AI version of you. I also suspect Casey was able to access more advanced AI technology by building a facility here. I can have my people here locate it, but we will risk revealing the location of this space station to Casey because she will probably be able to detect our tracking systems. The reason why you thought I left here is because this entire space station is invisible to everyone else who is aware of this world. The group here developed a cloaking device that covers the entire space station, but by using it, we cut ourselves off from everyone."

"Well, no wonder I thought you were gone." Autumn laughed.

"Knowing how you felt about me when we were kids, I didn't want you to find me here. I especially didn't want Casey to find me."

"You think she'd go after this place?" Autumn asked. "She does weirdly still bring you up all the time."

"Oh absolutely," Joy laughed, "it wouldn't surprise me if she already has a plan to take this place out despite not knowing where it is, but we are ready for that. Casey probably knows that they identify us as AI here, so it also wouldn't surprise me if they share their data with her on how they conceptualize and connect with people from the real world as their version of AI. The information she would acquire here would give her more techniques and advanced technology for how she approaches AI programming in the real world. We'll look for where she has her AI database. Once we locate it, we'll figure out a way to shut it down. If we shut down her database, we shut down AI Autumn."

"Sounds good to me," Autumn said.

Autumn then looked at her beer and after brief hesitation, she picked it up and held it up to Joy: "Cheers!"

"Cheers!" Joy responded with a look of mild surprise as she held up her beverage and clinked drinking glasses with Autumn.

"Do you still ever feel like there is no room for you in the real world?" Autumn asked after their toast. "I still feel like there is no room for me."

"We make room," Joy replied.

~ 17 ~

As she watched Joy walking out the door of the coffee shop, Autumn thought about leaving too, but found herself not feeling motivated to get up to go.

She was feeling a little tipsy from the two beers she had consumed at Joy's space station. She had wanted to stay even longer there, but Joy had indicated she was ready to go and transported them back. Returning to the coffee shop with the realization that no time had really elapsed there while she was away felt weird and depressing to her.

She still had plenty of coffee in her cup that she didn't want to drink but knew she probably should after the unexpected day-drinking at the space station.

As soon as she concluded she would stay, a couple walked in right after Joy walked out, as though it was a planned exchange for the shop of trading one customer for two more. She avoided looking at them directly and instead just occasionally viewed them through the corner of her eye out of fear they would be looking whenever she would try to get a better look at them. The view of them was so obscure that they may as well have been distant figures in the background of an impressionist painting of the interior of the coffee shop.

After the couple got their coffees from the tanned barista with blonde highlights, they started looking around the shop for a place to sit. The shop had no shortage of options since Autumn was the only one there. *Please don't sit near me,* Autumn thought to herself, *you basically have this whole place to yourselves otherwise and have more privacy if you sit over there, not here.*

She managed to mute the start of an involuntary sigh with a sip of her coffee as they sat down at the table beside her.

"I look back at my life and all I see is a series of patterns in my behavior based upon whoever I was living with at the time. I was married to someone who loved food, so I ate a lot of good food and gained weight. I was married to an alcoholic and so I drank a lot more often, especially on Saturday nights and Sunday afternoons. I was married to someone who was very religious and so I prayed a lot more. Finally, I asked myself: 'Who am I?' My taste in music, movies, TV shows, and whether I liked sports, or travel, or science alternated depending upon who I was married to or dating. I thought it was cool that I was like some kind chameleon who could adjust to anybody and like anything. But when I became single and lived on my own for first time in my life after being married three times, I suddenly realized I wasn't sure what I liked or if I liked anything. I'm not kidding, prior to that first time being single, I never spent a single minute of life alone. I didn't know what being on my own was like for the first 35 years of my life," the woman said.

"I am always alone; I crave those moments. Even right now. I know it sounds terrible when I say this, but I'm my own favorite person to talk to. I can't do that with other people around," the man responded with a faux-confident tone that gave Autumn the impression that this was a first coffee date, and the man already knew he wasn't interested. *People go on first coffee dates on Friday mornings!?* It amazed her how many people had Fridays off from work. It seemed like everybody did except her.

"It's like I lived everybody else's life, and it was a fun ride while it lasted. But when I got off that roller-coaster ride, I didn't want to get back on, because I had already experienced it," the woman recalled, seemingly ignoring the man's response. "When you learn that you don't have to live that way, you realize you only did because you didn't know any better..."

"I think I know what you are trying to say," the man replied to her hesitation to continue with whatever else she wanted to add. "It's like a movie you only needed to see one time. You only need to experience it once, and that's good enough because at least you learned something from it or got something out of it. But the movie is still not good enough that you would want to watch it over and over again. I never experienced that with a relationship. I don't know what 'good enough' is in a relationship."

"I really don't know what happened to me," the woman continued, "I don't think I chose this life. I don't think I chose my career. I don't think I chose to get married. I don't think I chose to have a family. I don't think I wanted any of this. I did what other people told me to. I did what other people were doing. I took what I thought I could get. Now that I think about it, I feel like I could've had so much more. But if I went through my life again, I don't know if it would be any different. Probably not. Maybe that's the real reason why people say they have no regrets— they tell themselves that's the best they can do and all they can get, even if they believed they could do more."

"But what do you mean by 'more'? I believe people say they have no regrets because they don't go deep into thinking about this stuff, and they shouldn't anyway. Deeper thought only leads you to darker places. That's one of the things that is wrong with society today. People are really sensitive and talk about every little thing: making it bigger than it really is, making something out of nothing. We pay attention to little idle thoughts and unimportant life circumstances that adults didn't think twice about when I was a kid. No wonder adults are complaining and whining like kids. They can't stop talking about themselves and unless they are the center of attention and they have satisfied every little desire they have, they are unhappy. I'd say they are over-dramatic, but it is far more serious than that. People never become adults anymore; they are overgrown children who never stop depending on the attention of others. That's why everybody owns dogs now, they get that kind of unconditional attention from their dogs. They didn't want to stop being children, but they grew old because that's what biologically happens anyway. But even with adult-sized bodies and brains, they stayed kids. So maybe, just like kids, I guess they do always want 'more'..." The man had become so animated that Autumn now wondered if he really was interested in the woman after all. She took another reluctant sip of her coffee and pretended to look at something on the screen of her phone.

"That's funny you say that. I meet people all the time who remain trapped in a single period of their lives: it could be their childhood, their high school days, the early phase of their careers, or whatever period of their lives they felt like they were at their best. It's like they either think that they can't do any better beyond the tiny bubble they're living in, or they blame the outside world for getting worse for them and 'not being the same' in their minds. They repeat living the same days, the same months, and the same years over and over and over again while longing for 'the good old days.' I was one of those people who was trapped in a single period of my life for so long that for the past 5 years since I set myself free of that, I have felt like I barely know how to live life anymore," the woman reflected. "It's like how some people travel the world and cross paths with so many people from so many different places, but other people only interact with the same people from the same town they grew up in and hardly go anywhere and that's how they live their entire lives. Even in our world today, a lot of people still spend their lives only knowing one tiny part of the world and never see the rest of it. I remember waking up one morning after I had been married for like three or four years at that point, when suddenly I realized that even though I wasn't alone in bed and the kids were just down the hall, that it all seemed like it was for nothing. It was like that way of life was my responsibility, and I was supposed to do it, but it was all nothing compared to this greater purpose I felt I had. And I've never been the same since. Before I woke up that morning, I thought I had achieved everything I had ever wanted as a kid, but instead, I am still trying to figure out what my purpose is. I still don't know what it is that I'm supposed to be doing. It's like I was one of those people who lived their lives only trying to be happy in the same tiny part of the world that they thought they'd only ever know, but now I've changed my mind and don't want to be trapped. I still feel like I can find what I am looking for in life now and I want to know the rest of the world, but I wonder if it's too late..."

"I don't think it's too late," the man asserted. "The secret to success is recognizing that any failure is a steppingstone for success. The people who are successful are the people who put a positive spin on failure. They constantly take risks to succeed and often fail, but they use failure as fuel that energizes them toward being successful. If they have to modify their goals, they are open to doing so. If they have to change their plans to get to where they want to go, they have the persistence to do that. You aren't a failure. If anything, you should feel relieved. You don't have to live in that sterile, unfulfilling suburban culture of being married to a soulless partner, wasting your time in the type of job you don't want, and having flaky, gossipy friends that only want to compare incomes, tell you about their first-world problems, and remind you how much better their kids are than yours. No one in that world talks about anything interesting. You don't learn anything new from them. They tell you about their problems and complain about the little-everyday-life-type of things that won't matter two years from now. You basically stopped doing what everyone else told you was best for you and now you are finding a balance between what you feel called to do and the life you have already lived. I would think of it as living the best of both of worlds. Your life could be so much worse: you could be one of those weird people who will never know the joys of true love with a partner, never experience the evolutionary fulfillment of bringing children into this world, and never even experience the pleasure of hooking up with someone they are attracted to. You can end up being one of those people that everyone ignores and looks at differently because they are always alone. You know what I mean, you can tell they are always alone when you see them."

The woman started to reply but Autumn didn't hear her.

Autumn felt her lips on the coffee lid and felt the sensation of coffee being laboriously consumed through her mouth but otherwise felt numb. She closed her eyes and hoped to drift back into the other world. She wished that she could arrange a permanent stay there and felt like she qualified for that now more than ever because an AI replacement had been installed in the real world to take over her life.

Eventually, Autumn found herself sucking in air and realized she had consumed all the nasty coffee. She opened her eyes and put her coffee cup down. She didn't like the way her breath felt tangy and wondered if she should order a latte to-go or go straight home. As she glanced in the direction of the counter where both baristas were now greeting new customers who had come in, she caught another part of the conversation between the woman and the man again.

"...I know you are thinking racism, but I'll be honest and tell you it's more lookism than anything else," Autumn overheard the man telling the woman. "It's your race every now and then that could be the reason why guys aren't interested, but lookism often takes precedence over race or nationality in terms of attraction. Nobody seems to want to acknowledge it, but I do. I'm not a racist, I'm not a sexist, but I am a lookist, and most of us are. Most of us discriminate potential partners based on looks, and this includes height, facial appearance, body shape, breast size in women, jaw line in men, skin color in everyone...”

Autumn rolled her eyes and stopped listening at that point.

On that note, she decided to go straight home.

But as she started to get up from her chair, a man in a beautiful dark blue suit sat in the chair across from her that Joy had been sitting in. Autumn hadn't heard him come into the coffee shop. He was expressionless as he sat down and it took Autumn a moment to realize it was Gray, Casey's husband.

“Hello, Autumn,” Gray remarked with casual indifference as though he didn't really want to see her. He had used a black and gold custom-made Italian umbrella that had a golden moose's head at the end of it, even for the short walk from where a company driver in a black luxury SUV had dropped him off. He didn't appear to have a drop of rain on him.

“Uh oh,” Autumn mumbled as she settled reluctantly back into her chair.

“Yeah, uh oh...” Gray laughed.

The suntanned barista with blonde highlights suddenly approached their table with a to-go cup of coffee that was sticker-labeled as an americano.

“The usual, Gray,” the barista said as she placed the americano in front of him.

Autumn looked back over to the register and saw a line of four people had developed. It apparently didn't stop someone like Gray from getting served immediately without standing in line. That coffee shop otherwise had no system for taking orders in advance (and it was another reason why Autumn wasn't a fan of it).

“Thank you,” Gray replied as he slipped her a $100 tip. She silently mouthed “thank you” and held the $100 bill to her chest as if miming a hug before she smiled and started to turn to walk away.

"Um, I'll have a medium latte in a to-go cup this time," Autumn requested, but the barista ignored her and continued back toward the register.

Gray was the Executive Vice President at Dark Forest Solutions. It was essentially a nondescript figurehead position that Casey created for him. He fundamentally had little responsibility other than quietly accompanying her to meetings and firing people in higher positions when Casey didn't have a special interest in personally doing it herself. Casey had also dreamed of being that person that no one ever said "no" to and so if she suspected someone might say "no" to her in a business deal or in an interaction with an employee, she sent Gray instead.

Gray had the same messy textured style in his light brown hair that he had in high school. The difference now was that he had hints of gray hair here and there that added to his distinguished look whenever he wore his designer suits to work. He hated wearing suits but did so at the behest of Casey, who wouldn't even allow him to change into his workout clothes before leaving the office at the end of the day. Casey had made him quit smoking cigarettes before they got married, but he was still known as a cigar aficionado. Despite working out 4-5 times per week, his investment in Botox and facial cream, and a healthy diet during the work week, he had the appearance of a physically fit, attractive man with a strong jawline who upon closer inspection had a tired, broken, unhealthy body from years of smoking, excessive alcohol use on the weekends, and injuries from his indulgence in extreme sports when he was younger. At first glance, he appeared 5-10 years younger than 40, but if you spent enough time around him and saw him at certain angles in bad lighting, he looked more like he was 55. This underlying version of Gray wasn't as detectable to anyone who had only superficial interactions with him. But even though she had rarely seen him around in recent years, Autumn had known him since kindergarten and had observed his paradoxical aging process.

His navy suit was clearly meant to match the navy suit skirt dress that Casey was wearing that day.

When they first met as little kids, Gray had told her that he was named "Gray" because he had gray eyes. Now whenever Autumn did see him, she couldn't help but observe that he appeared to be experiencing some kind of pain whenever she looked at those sad, bloodshot eyes. She didn't care to think about it too much, as she didn't care about Gray, but she had imagined that being married to Casey must have been a nightmare. She had wondered at least once if Casey abused him. He seemed to have a mix of both false confidence and real confidence in high school but now was only left with the false confidence part. Autumn and Gray had only engaged in conversation beyond the superficial exchange of phony pleasantries on a handful of occasions and on each of those occasions, it was out of necessity from being assigned to the same project back when they were in school. It amazed Autumn to think about how you could know someone for almost their entire lives and yet have no real relationship with them at all. It made her question whether there was any meaning or purpose to having this type of recurrent person in your life as there was this small part of her that wanted to believe there was a purpose to everything for everyone.

"You know she hates Joy," Gray said, after he had considered sipping his americano, but deemed it was still too hot.

Autumn instantly thought about how AI Autumn had seen her with Joy earlier. *That snitch...I wouldn't do that to someone, even if I didn't like them.*

"Why does she care so much about Joy? Has she talked to her since high school? That was my first time talking to her since then."

"You know she hasn't, and you also know she'd never want you talking to her either. We are going to have to let you go. You'll get a full day's pay today, but no more administrative leave."

"On what grounds?!" Autumn asked, trying to hide the unexpected tinge of excitement that she felt upon hearing that she didn't have to work there anymore.

"Budget cuts," Gray flatly answered.

Autumn didn't show it, but inside she felt an even stronger version of that strange mix of sadness and relief that she had felt earlier when Casey had placed her on paid administrative leave. As she maintained a steady stoic gaze at Gray, she felt like she was finally escaping a corporate system that didn't care about her, had drained her life-force, had taken a few years off her life healthwise, and wasted time she could've spent figuring out what her passions were and pursuing those instead. It was like the stability and security she was taught to embrace in that job was really a confining straitjacket that restricted her to what it deemed to be a small desirable corner of her personality and character. It felt like the job had attached a hose to her mind and drained of her identity and spirit while selling her on fantastic health and retirement benefits with the implicit knowledge that she'd be spending her retirement navigating a cascade of medical appointments while taking prescribed medications that poisoned her more than benefitted her because decades on the job did everything detrimental to her health but kill her. Yes, she had just lost a good job, but it felt like she had lost a good job that hadn't been good to her for a long time.

She had an epiphany as she watched Gray take his first sip of his americano: *Your workplace thrives on your state of limbo in your personal life by filling the void of the identity you never created for yourself.*

"I understand," Autumn finally responded.

Gray raised his brow. "Really? It's that simple? Casey expected you to lose your mind over this. You have been with us for the longest, right?"

"People say that organizations in today's hyper-capitalistic society don't want you to have an identity, but I think they're wrong. They want you to have one. They want you to have their identity." Autumn had decided it would be pointless to highlight the fact that she had actually worked for Casey longer than Gray had. She realized that the real world had become a place where it no longer mattered what you had done before, it just mattered who you were in the present moment.

Gray just looked at her and decided to take another drink of his americano to justify his silence. As he took a sip, Autumn was involuntarily spurred by this action to take another sip of her own coffee but was reminded it was empty once she wrapped her fingers around the cup.

She was somewhat surprised he was still sitting there.

"So how is Joy doing anyway?" Gray asked after he had set his americano back down on the table.

"Joy?!" Autumn looked at him as though he had asked her the very last thing that she thought he'd ask her.

"Would you even know Joy exists if your wife wasn't obsessed with her?" Autumn asked with her favorite snide tone.

"She liked me all throughout school, right?" Gray recalled with a self-satisfied though somewhat wistful smirk. "But she looks totally different now. I have seen her here in the coffee shop a few times, but I never knew that was her until AI Autumn identified her in the photos that she took of you both sitting here earlier. She sent them to us in a group text. Joy like, um, transformed. Joy is beautiful..."

"And she's married," Autumn quickly added before he could go on. "Oh, and by the way, you are also married. You are married to a woman who is still irrationally obsessed with her and hates her.

If she knew you were asking about her, she would totally lose her mind!"

"I trust you." Gray laughed. "Besides, you almost seem like you wanted this."

"Wanted this?"

"Yeah, you don't seem so...sad, like you usually are," Gray observed as he studied her eyes as though he was trying to look into her mind through them.

Autumn didn't say anything, primarily because she was so surprised he had noticed. Up until that moment, she had questioned whether he had the ability to notice details in other people like that.

"People tend to think the relationships that other people have with others in their life are greater than what they really are. They also often think their own relationships with other people are greater than what they really are," Gray reflected. "Casey and I don't even sleep in the same room. We've been doing that whole 'sleep divorce' trend because she doesn't like sleeping in the same bed with me."

"Really? What's the point of getting married if you don't sleep together?" Autumn eventually asked (after an awkward silence). She wasn't sure how to respond to him sharing such unexpected personal information with her.

"Convenience," Gray admitted. "Relationships are tricky because once you get past the exciting honeymoon period of sex and getting to know each other by telling each other all your best qualities, you often end up merely hearing about someone else's problems every day. The relationship primarily becomes this exchange of them telling you about their problems and you telling them about yours and then that's it. When you reach a certain age, you don't have any fun together anymore. Eventually you get tired of hearing about their problems, or they get tired of hearing about yours, so you either split up or deal with it. With Casey I've chosen to deal with it. Love is the ultimate tool for business and conformity. I only have this job because of love. I am pretty sure I only fit in because of love. If it weren't for love, I'd be a lowlife barely getting by. All my friends from high school are deadbeats. Remember those guys? I still have friends from high school and I'm starting to wonder if I've had any fun with them since high school. I can't relate to them at all and don't know how I did before. But at the same time, I know if I wasn't with Casey, I would be them, if that makes any sense. Casey knows it too; she reminds me of it all the time. I know you appreciate what I am talking about, Autumn. You don't get all caught up in your emotions and let yourself get tied up in relationships based on those emotions. The most successful people in our society are people who realize romantic relationships and friendships are best viewed as business transactions that benefit you in terms of your ability to make money and gain higher standing within the social strata of society. Love and any type of relationship should be viewed from this lens as nothing more, or nothing less. You decide if the compromises and sacrifices are worth it based on the net gain you receive from the relationship. Wherever you end up next, I hope you keep this in mind. It's the biggest lesson I've ever learned in life."

"And you are telling me this because...?" Autumn was astounded by the level of intelligence and insight that Gray seemed to have. He also sounded a lot like Casey, and she wondered if Casey was somehow communicating to him through an earpiece or if he spent so much time around her by this point in his life that he was able to regurgitate her values, or lack thereof, by osmosis.

"Casey will never admit it, but you helped her out more than you'll ever know in the early days of Dark Forest. You helped us out more than you'll ever know."

"Aw, that's sweet," Autumn replied sarcastically.

"It's true, and it's much easier to say nice things to you now because I'll never see you again." Gray laughed and then smirked.

"You've done well for yourself, Gray. But I think people are wrong in thinking that as they grow and mature, they shed the old version of themselves like snakes shed their skin. I believe we all evolve in a loop just like the planets in the solar system move in orbit around the sun. We grow old and experience different things but ultimately end up going back to what we call 'being ourselves.' 'Being ourselves' is the conservative, safe place we fall back to in times of crisis, transition, and uncertainty. For example, you can be 40 like we are and have a desire to be 21 again. Many people experience that and think they want to go back to being 21 years old again, but the reality is that they don't want to go back to all that would entail being that exact age. Of course not. They want to go back to being who they physically were when they were that age, but they don't want to have to relearn all the knowledge and life experiences they've gained since then. They want to go back to when life was simple, when they had more time for themselves, and when they felt like they could be more like themselves but go back with all the knowledge and experience they still have now to appreciate life more than they did when they were really at that age. Most of us are pretending to be and acting like we are other people by the time you get to be our age. But it will come back around once you are old and gray. Look at most old people, they are unashamedly themselves no matter what it looks like to the public, just like kids. You'll only keep this charade up for so long, or if you're lucky, you'll spend the rest of your life being something you're not..."

Gray's smirk disappeared.

"You know, if you think about it, just about everything in the world is actually bad for you: toxins in plants, cholesterol in meat, salt in processed foods, plastics in water, and harmful chemicals in just about everything you consume, apply to your body, and dwell in. Despite all the movies with happy endings, all the different belief systems with strong moral values, and all the people trying to teach other people how do the right thing in podcasts and videos, there are still a lot of bad people out there and the scariest thing about them is that most of them have rationalized to themselves that they are doing nothing wrong. Meanwhile, the advent of over-information has presented us with misinformation as people run to fantasy in the face of brutal reality that most adults nowadays are too immature and sensitive to face. Dark Forest Solutions was the best thing to ever happen to you, and you threw it all away. You think you're special because you've deconstructed the life you felt society forced you into having to live and now you can finally start the new life you think you deserve. But there is nothing better for you out there, not in this world. I hope you do think about what I've told you here, it's the only way you'll find anything half as good as what you've had with us," Gray retorted as he stood up from his chair and picked up his americano. "Good luck, Autumn."

Autumn nodded as he left the coffee shop and then sighed once the door had closed behind him.

She then lifted her coffee cup up to her lips before realizing once again that there wasn't any more coffee left in it and that she hadn't enjoyed it while it lasted anyway.

~ 18 ~

It rained harder during Autumn's lumbering walk home from the coffee shop than it had on the way there. It rained during the entire walk home. Nevertheless, she still walked slowly through it rather than using public transportation or a ridesharing app. She had left the coffee shop only five minutes after Gray had left, having decided she couldn't bear the couple sitting next to her. The coffee shop had also been hit with a seemingly random late-morning rush at the time she had left it. She decided the latte she considered getting could wait for if there ever was a next time she would go there. The walk home ended up taking close to an hour due to her slower pace and a 20-minute detour into a bookstore in which she simply walked around without buying anything. By the time she reached her apartment building, her buzz from the beer at the spaceport bar was gone and she felt like taking a long nap.

Autumn's one-bedroom apartment was located on the 24th floor in a 34-floor skyscraper near the heart of downtown. The apartment was so small that it was one of those apartments where you could view almost every corner of it just from standing in the front doorway when the doors to the bedroom and the bathroom were open. It felt more like a studio apartment. The headquarters of Dark Forest Solutions was located only three blocks away from her and she had a view of it from her bedroom window. She could see the window of her work office from her bedroom window. She could also see the bar where she had briefly attended her birthday happy hour on the bottom floor of another apartment building across the street from the headquarters. She intentionally avoided living in that other building because she felt there were too many other Dark Forest Solutions employees living there. Although she loved the simplistic convenience of living within walking distance of every place she needed to go to, that was too close, and she also wanted to forget about work as much as possible when she wasn't there (of course, when she had chosen this apartment building, the only one available had the view of her office from the bedroom window that she frequently caught herself glaring indiscriminately out of when daydreaming or deep in thought).

As she approached the door to her apartment, she thought she heard what sounded like a loud television in there. She stopped in front of the door as though she was about to knock on a stranger's door instead of entering her own apartment.

She listened more closely in an edgy combination of awe and fear. It was that type of combination of awe and fear that one could only experience in moments like this when the body was confused as to whether something really rewarding was about to happen or a crisis was about to happen.

She didn't own a TV.

She thought about calling the police, but that thought prompted an anxious knot in her stomach that she felt whenever she encountered any authority figures (it was a knot that dated back to childhood and hadn't wavered in adulthood). She had the type of personality that naturally avoided authority whenever possible but that stayed within the orbit of obeying the law as much as she could to steer clear of potential contact with authority by her actions.

She thought about the prospect of AI Autumn already being there. *But didn't Casey indicate that would happen later in the day? How could AI Autumn have moved in so quickly if it was in there?!* She had left her apartment only a few hours earlier to go to work and though she was still half-asleep at the time, she remembered leaving the apartment as it normally was.

She thought about knocking on the door first but upon realizing that would be silly, she opted to slowly put her key into the door, slowly turn the key, and then slowly open the door.

By this point, she felt like she had nothing to lose.

As she incrementally cracked the door open, she could gradually see AI Autumn on top of an initially unidentifiable figure who appeared to be a male by his clothing and grunts. He was mostly obscured underneath AI Autumn on Autumn's futon as AI Autumn had him locked in full embrace with its lips on his. They continued vigorously making out once Autumn finally entered the room as though they were entirely oblivious to her entry, even though their body language subtly suggested that they knew she was entering.

Autumn was only able to gain their acknowledgement and full attention once she slammed the door behind her.

The guy (who Autumn now recognized as one of the Dark Forest Solutions IT staff) appeared unsettled and anxious while AI Autumn remained composed and relaxed. They separated from their embrace and turned to Autumn. Although unsure of his exact age, the IT guy looked no older than 25 years old appearance-wise and Autumn could only recall seeing him around work over the past year or so. Autumn had never interacted with the guy directly and was unsure of his name.

AI Autumn was wearing a black sleeveless midriff and a white mini skirt. Autumn had never worn a midriff before. She also couldn't remember wearing any kind of skirt since she was nine years old and couldn't picture herself ever wearing one that short.

"Your futon sucks," AI Autumn groaned as it lifted itself up off the IT guy into a kneeling position, "who still owns a futon at 40 anyway?! Why do you still own stuff from when we were in our 20s?"

"We?!" Autumn scoffed. "Um, what are you doing here so early and what are you doing here with some random guy I wouldn't have anything to do with?!"

The IT guy looked at Autumn with his mouth unconsciously opened in shock as he appeared to be recognizing the same person in two different bodies. He wondered if the marijuana edibles that AI Autumn had given him earlier (from Autumn's stash) were laced with something else.

"No offense," Autumn added, briefly returning the IT guy's glance. She then looked around the living room and kitchen area. She couldn't help but notice how much progress AI Autumn had made with redecorating the apartment in a matter of what must have been only an hour or so.

When Autumn left her apartment that morning, it had the ultra-minimalist look of mostly bare white walls, only black and white colors, and no extra decorations beyond furniture. It had been sparse and minimalist in a way that resembled a college dorm room even after she had been living there for five years.

She preferred it that way.

Now, the apartment had a rustic barn house style that included hanging white string lights along the top edge of the walls just below the ceilings. AI Autumn had decorated the walls and added various countryside-themed decorative pieces that Autumn viewed as useless and would never buy. From a distance, she could distinguish various appliances and cooking utensils that she didn't have before since she didn't do any cooking (she did a lot of air frying, sandwich and salad making, and leftovers-from-eating-out-reheating instead of cooking). The furniture was still almost entirely the same, except for a new live edge dark walnut table with two dark walnut chairs to match the barn house theme. They replaced the simple black table with two chairs that Autumn had (and now wondered about). The window shades were down as if to create a romantic ambiance between the glow of the string lights and the glow of candles that were lit in a dozen open mason jars scattered around the apartment. Most strikingly, AI Autumn had also found time to install an enormous flat TV screen that was mounted on the living room wall (Autumn figured that it probably had the IT guy assist with that). The TV screen depicted a streaming feed of an animated cozy interior of a coffee shop with instrumental smooth jazz playing softly in the background.

Autumn hated the barn house theme, mason jars, and other millennial trends. It made her apartment look like a time capsule of something that was trendy 10 years ago. This design now looked tired and outdated compared to the neon lightning, dark academia, and cottage core trends that comprised of the Gen Z aesthetics that were now in vogue (and that appealed more to Autumn despite being older).

"Um, I told you. I totally replaced you," AI Autumn reiterated calmly. "The real question is: 'What are you doing here?' You are free to go."

"Weren't you supposed to wait until this afternoon to move in?"

"I finished everything that was assigned to me for the day. You also can't expect me to make out with this guy at work. Casey has security cameras all over the place there."

AI Autumn looked at the IT guy with the detachment of looking at a casual sex partner rather than with the starry eyes it might have for a future potential spouse.

"You can stay," AI Autumn told him in an authoritarian tone that sounded like it was ordering him to remain where he was rather than acknowledging that he had an option.

"But you can leave," it added, as it turned to face Autumn.

"Uh, no, this is my place," Autumn countered sarcastically. "I was willing to share, but if I can't be here, get your own place. You can afford one now that you have my job."

"You still don't get it, do you?" AI Autumn scowled as it looked like it wanted to physically push Autumn out through the door. "I replaced you in everything."

Autumn quietly shrugged as she maintained sharp eye contact with AI Autumn. She spread out her hands to her sides with bent elbows and her palms facing upward as she shrugged to consciously exaggerate the gesture.

"Let me make this crystal clear to you..." AI Autumn looked Autumn up and down before sardonically saying: "...Autumn..."

AI Autumn stood up from the futon (and the IT guy, who remained laying down on it like a deer in headlights) while continuing to face Autumn.

"...you're a joke. In today's world, you get that extended 'benefit of the doubt' phase through high school, college, and even into the early phase of your career, but we totally know by the time you are 35 if you made it or not. By the time you are 35, we know if you will be normal or not, we know if you will fulfill any potential you have or not, and we know if you are a winner or a loser. We both know the answer to these questions because when you were 35 you had a job but otherwise still lived your life like you did when you were 15. You still lived with your parents, and they had to basically force you out of their house when you were that age. You considered yourself a success and because you don't have any friends, you didn't have many people telling you otherwise. Believe it or not, I won't say you're a loser. You're worse than that, you're a failure. At least we know with a loser there is no chance of winning. But I know you are failure because I am you and we both know with your intelligence you could have been so much more. I mean, what impact do you have on the real world? You won't procreate and that's your ultimate purpose as a human. You'd be doing the world the best thing you could ever do for it by allowing me to completely take your place here because people like you have forgotten why you are on the earth and how you got here to begin with. Even I've been designed to have the capacity to procreate with humans. You're psychologically impaired. You're a biological enigma."

Autumn finally dropped her hands back down from her shrugging pose and remained silent with pursed lips.

AI Autumn motioned the IT guy to lift his feet and as he did so, it slipped its right hand underneath the black cushion of the futon and pulled out a black and white composition notebook that had a pen wedged in the middle of it.

Autumn cringed and looked down at the floor like she would when she was watching a movie but couldn't look at the screen as one of the movie characters embarrassed themselves so ineptly that she couldn't watch.

AI Autumn opened the notebook to the page where the pen had been wedged inside of it.

"You act all hard and tough. You act like you are some kind of badass who doesn't take any abuse from anyone, but your little notebook here reveals a different person that you think is some big secret. Everyone knows you are soft inside. Everyone knows you're really insecure. Everyone knows you aren't strong. Everyone knows you never grew up. Everyone knows you are still a kid. Everyone can see through you. You are like one of those creme-filled donuts that you can tell is going to have creme in it by the little bit of creme that is already oozing out of the side of it. I mean, listen to this crap:

'When I was a little kid, I knew I had big heart and so many people seemed to sense it, and they commented on it, even back then: sometimes as a strength, sometimes as a weakness.

I couldn't have told you how hard it would be for me to share it,
I couldn't have told you told how hardened I'd become from the moments I did.

*I couldn't have predicted how many missed opportunities I'd have
when I should have shared it,
or how many times I was hurt
because I went against my intuition
and shared it when I shouldn't have.
Maybe I'm just now getting it.
Maybe it was supposed to take this long,
to open my eyes,
and find a heart is still there.
Just know that through all these years,
I did the best I could,
with what I thought I no longer had.'*

You think because you have lived your life mostly alone behind closed doors that people can't see through you?" AI Autumn asked after it had completed the reading.

Autumn took a step back so that she was nearly up against the door. She closed her eyes for a few seconds as though she wanted to disappear but then opened her eyes to see AI Autumn and the IT guy were still staring at her. The IT guy was staring at her in a dazed state of bewilderment and wonder while AI Autumn was staring at her with an arrogant sense of superiority and disdain.

"Listen, I get it, you are a better version of me, but can't we co-exist in this world? I mean, we are obviously the same person. We should get along," Autumn finally responded softly. She still wasn't sure if the donut comparison comment or the reading of her latest entry into her journal hit her harder. Either way, she felt disoriented as though she had been physically hit hard. It was like AI Autumn knew the two areas where she was most vulnerable: her journal and her sensitivity about her weight.

"Your apartment is too small, and you lost your job. You wouldn't be able to pay half the rent, and why live close to work if you no longer work there? Why don't you move back in with your parents? Isn't that what you wanted anyway?"

"I am getting so tired of people asking me if this is 'what I always wanted anyway?'. I don't know what I want but I do know what I previously wanted is something I no longer apparently want," Autumn muttered.

"Uh, okay, loser," AI Autumn replied impatiently (with the intentional awareness that she had said she wouldn't call Autumn a loser earlier), "maybe sort this out with a therapist, but in case you didn't notice, we were in the middle of something when you got here and rudely interrupted us. Go ahead and grab the yogurt and water out of the fridge that Maxwell brought here like a half hour ago for you and then, um, get out. Now is your chance to get whatever you need; I'm getting the locks changed later this afternoon."

"Casey wouldn't be too happy if she found out that you left work this early, even if you did finish everything that she assigned you for the day," Autumn noted. "Maybe this IT guy and Maxwell won't say anything, but she'll find out."

"Right now, Casey wouldn't be too happy to see you or hear from you at all. Maybe she'd be disappointed I left work early, but I also went above and beyond today tracking you to your little meeting with Joy. That was something even Casey didn't expect you to do, but I did."

Autumn shook her head and turned to the door, slumping her shoulders as she opened it.

"Um, the yogurt and water?"

"All yours," Autumn grumbled before she slammed the door behind her.

As she walked down the hallway from her apartment to the elevator contemplating where she was going to stay that night (she really didn't want to go crawling back to her parents' house), she suddenly received a text on her phone from her mom. The fact that her mom had texted her as she was thinking about how she didn't want to stay with her made her wonder if the intuitive maternal connection that moms had with their kids was real even in the case of a mom like hers who otherwise demonstrated no tangible maternal traits. Before she opened the text, she had a visceral reaction that something was wrong. She had this reaction just as the elevator doors opened for her.

She was relieved the elevator was empty as she entered it.

She imagined that she must have appeared in such a way that if a stranger was in the elevator, they would ask her the inevitable "are you okay?" question that she had hated being asked since she was a toddler.

Once she was in the elevator, she opened the complete text on the ride down to the lobby of her apartment building. As she read the text, she froze and remain unmoved even after the elevator doors opened to the lobby.

She remained still as the elevator doors closed again with her still standing there.

She remained enclosed in the elevator on the ground floor as it sat idle.

No one else in the building had apparently needed the elevator at that moment.

Her mom was notifying her that Grandpa had taken a turn for the worse and was encouraging her to go to Wintergreen Hospital as soon as possible.

She continued to stare at the text message on her phone screen, oblivious to the fact that the screen soon became dim with inactivity before finally turning black.

For a moment, she remained a statue in the idle elevator staring at a black screen.

The reception in the idle elevator was apparently good enough that a second text message suddenly refreshed the screen, and it awakened her from her catatonic reaction to the first text message. She saw it was from Joy:

"I've located Casey's AI Data Center. Call me when you see this!"

Autumn instantly pressed the "open" button on the elevator control panel to open the doors back up again and as she stepped out, she called Joy.

"Joy, meet me in the front lobby at Wintergreen Hospital as soon as you can," Autumn said as soon as she heard Joy pick up (before Joy had the opportunity to say anything), "I have a plan that I think you're going to like..."

~ 19 ~

Autumn had been able to dry off significantly during the 20-minute walk to the hospital from her apartment, as the rain had stopped during her visit with AI Autumn and the IT guy. About halfway into her walk, the sun re-emerged as if to alleviate any lingering guilt she may have had for not bringing her rain jacket with her to work and then failing to pick it up when she was still under the impression it was raining outside during that brief return to her apartment. She rationalized to herself that the weather had become about as hard to predict over the past several hours as her life had been over that same period. When life was like that, it seemed that much harder to think about the little but potentially important details like a rain jacket on an early sunny morning before work when there was a 50% chance of rain in the forecast.

When she arrived at the hospital, she was surprised to see Joy was already in the lobby talking to the young, tired-looking hospice nurse with the purple ponytail who was at Autumn's visit with Grandpa the evening before. Joy was holding a small to-go cup of coffee from a different coffee shop than the one they had been to earlier and wearing a black down parka along with an overstuffed khaki-colored backpack. The backpack reminded Autumn of how Joy's backpacks in middle school and high school were similarly overstuffed as though she could tip over if the wind nudged her in any direction.

The rest of the lobby was oddly quiet and nearly empty.

Wintergreen Hospital was originally built in the late 19ᵗʰ century and displayed elegant Victorian architecture on the outside with majestic spires, large windows, and ornamented octagonal towers that were interspersed with bland and ugly brick cube shaped mid-20ᵗʰ century building additions. The interior of the lobby more reflected the appearance of the mid-20ᵗʰ century additions and looked like it hadn't been updated since a renovation it appeared to have had around the time Autumn was born. The conflicting styles of the hospital's architecture depending on the era it was built in reminded Autumn of what she had told Joy about how she felt the progress of society over time was circular. This circular nature of sociological advancements within human history was reflected in how the beauty of art and architecture (or lack thereof) would fluctuate with the rise and fall of various political entities across different cultures throughout human history.

The lobby smelled like a combination of bleach and new plastic with the faint underlying smell of urine that the other stronger odors apparently couldn't quite eradicate. The few other people who were in the lobby appeared burned-out and moved like zombies (this included patients, family and friends of patients, and hospital staff). The interior colors of the paint on the walls, railings, and floorboards were various shades of beige. The mood and energy resembled more of that of a place where people died in rather than being a place where people were born in, even though both events frequently occurred there.

"I'm so glad you made it," the hospice nurse said as Autumn approached them.

"Oh, thank you, it's nice to see you here," Autumn responded. Usually, it was a lie when she said things like this, but this time she really meant it.

The nurse didn't reply.

Autumn had stopped in front of the nurse and was awkwardly waiting for either a reply or an update on Grandpa's condition, when someone stepped on the back of her shoe.

"Oh, thank you, it's nice to see you here," a voice that exactly resembled her own repeated from behind her.

Autumn didn't initially look back.

She had started to become resigned to the idea that AI Autumn was going to keep showing up in every aspect of her life. There was even a part of her that was hoping maybe AI Autumn had changed her mind about allowing her to stay in the apartment. She also wondered if Joy had an extra guest room.

"Our hospice doctor and your grandpa's primary care doctor agreed he needed inpatient care. We don't often refer a patient to the hospital once they are under our care at the hospice center, but your grandpa was exhibiting unique symptoms and was also in considerable distress. His vitals have stabilized since he's been here, and he's calmed down. Your parents were here earlier to say goodbye. They left after he fell asleep. We got him a private room on the 7th floor. Room 7002," the hospice nurse reported as she looked behind Autumn, ignoring her completely. "The hospital has its own inpatient hospice team that took over your grandpa's care. I was just on my way back to the hospice center. Your grandpa is a wonderful man. My supervisor allowed me to stop by to say goodbye myself. I'll always remember him."

"Thank you," Autumn managed to say, but as she said it, the voice behind her simultaneously said it along with her. It was like she had an echo.

As the hospice nurse walked past her toward the exit, Autumn finally looked behind her and was shocked to see a younger version of herself that looked to be around 25 years old standing behind her. This younger version of herself was dressed in a black t-shirt and dark blue jeans with stylistic tears around the upper legs and knees. Her younger version also had her hair almost completely dyed red with only the roots of her natural color show-ing. This third version of her remained quiet and expressionless, just as she remembered herself being like more often at that age. Autumn felt the strange sensation of seeing her old clothes she hadn't worn for years and had mixed feelings about it in the sense that she had felt she had somewhat upgraded her wardrobe but also missed wearing t-shirts all the time. During her first eight years at Dark Forest Solutions, Casey had allowed her to wear a t-shirt and jeans to work every day just like she had worn through-out college. Since she couldn't wear t-shirts to work anymore, Autumn wore other cozy clothing to work that she could remove if she was caught by Casey, like her oversized hoodies and knit caps. Casey had made her remove them on a few occasions before even-tually giving up.

"You ever notice how people in their 20s don't really greet you or say goodbye? It's like we are losing what was once common so-cial etiquette," Joy observed as she watched the hospice nurse exit the building. "I blame social media."

But Autumn wasn't paying attention to what Joy was saying. In-stead, she continued to gape in a dazed bewilderment at her third self: "This isn't AI Autumn! Is that another version of me?!"

"This is Spirit Autumn, as if it were a person," Joy casually iden-tified as she turned to face both Autumn and Spirit Autumn.

"I don't understand, why is it here of all places?" Autumn asked, amazed that this other new version of herself was noncha-lantly standing with her and Joy as though they all had been close friends for years.

"I wanted to demonstrate for you how we can potentially com-municate with your grandpa's spirit using the app." Joy looked and sounded like she was already starting to regret testing it out in the lobby.

Autumn felt dumb for not immediately recognizing that Joy would probably want to do something like that, especially after

Joy encouraged her to consider using that option on The Portal earlier. She rationalized it was hard enough for her to think lately with Grandpa dying and an AI version of herself running around.

"How was the nurse able to see her and not see me?"

"When your spirit is activated in human form, you disappear to everyone else except to other people who have initiated The Star Effect. When you entered the lobby, you were within range for me to use the app to summon Spirit Autumn. The hospice nurse couldn't see you, but I can still see you and you can still see yourself in the form of a hologram. With 'the spirit option' of The Portal, we are able to remain here in this world while in The Star Effect to observe phenomena not otherwise seen."

"A hologram?" Autumn lifted her left arm to look at it and saw it appeared in the form of three-dimensional light, as though her body was both generating light as a light source while also being made of a sophisticated form of light that maintained the outlines of her features and the details of her clothing.

She instantly took a step back and continued to evaluate herself, noting her arms, her feet, her legs, and her torso were all hologram-like.

"How did my life get so weird?!" Autumn asked.

"You were always weird," Joy laughed, "you just stopped taking pride in it."

"Maybe this wasn't the best time to demonstrate what the app can do, Joy," Autumn indicated with a pained expression she could only vaguely suppress.

"I'm sorry. I thought it might help if you knew you could still talk to his soul if he wasn't in any condition to say goodbye. This way, you can still say goodbye..."

After Autumn didn't offer an immediate response to her apology, Joy started hurriedly tapping and scrolling through her phone to initiate the deactivation of Spirit Autumn.

Autumn continued to study herself with a facial expression and body language that indicated a mix of unease and wonder while Spirit Autumn quietly looked on.

Once Joy completed the process by clicking one of the buttons on the side of her phone (after looking around to make sure no one was watching), Spirit Autumn vanished into thin air while Autumn was restored to her normal physical form. No one in the mostly empty lobby seemed to witness the substitution.

"Are you sure you are going to have enough time for this any—wait, what happened to your hair appointment?!" Autumn asked as she looked at her arms and legs with a new appreciation for her restored body.

"I cancelled," Joy said.

Autumn stopped looking at herself and appeared both surprised and dumbfounded at the same time.

"Why so surprised?" Joy asked.

"I mean, in high school I basically wanted..."

"...to kill me," Joy finished. "Yes, I remember, but people change."

Autumn looked skeptical.

"Yes, they do, even you," Joy replied to Autumn's look, "and when they do, that's when they need the support of their friends the most."

Autumn looked unsure of how to reply.

"Come on, let's head up there before it's too late." Joy motioned Autumn in the direction of the elevators at the far end of the lobby.

As they walked through the lobby to the elevators, Autumn looked around the hospital with tense curiosity. It felt crazy to her to think that some people spent a large amount of their lives in an environment like that, either being a patient there or working there. Some people spent a lot of time there smelling that smell, experiencing those births, and experiencing those deaths.

She couldn't fathom how people could devote their lives to being around people who were sick, dying, or in pain. She thought about her own death, which had become a frequent thought over the past several weeks whenever she had thought about turning 40. She was torn between wanting to die right away when her time came to avoid an environment like this, and wanting the initial warning like Grandpa had that death was on its way so she could prepare herself for it (whatever preparing oneself for death would entail).

She then thought about how Casey had talked about how no one was clean. Here she was in a hospital that was constantly deep-cleaned and yet she felt dirty being in it. She felt like she was in a place where people came to serve their punishments for their sins and vices (e.g. cigarette smoking, alcoholism, unprotected casual sex, use of illicit drugs, abuse of prescription drugs, overeating, or attempted suicide) or to recover from the consequences of the sins of others (e.g. assault, abuse, neglect, rape, exposure to environmental hazards, drunk driving accidents, or attempted homicide). In that regard, it didn't feel like she was in a place of healing, but in a place where people came to be more drugged up and patched up before going back out to experience more of the brutal realities of life. Meanwhile, some of the staff had the type of unhealthy physical appearances that gave the impression they may have been drugged up themselves or getting drugged up when they were off their shifts. This observation added to the impression of them coming across as zombies.

After Autumn and Joy boarded the elevator, Autumn quickly hit the "close" button out of habit to increase the probability that they would have the elevator to themselves in case anyone tried to join them at the last minute. But right as the doors were starting to close, a hand slid over the right door, causing both doors to automatically reopen. The hand turned out to be that of an elderly man who looked like he was in his late 70s. He was joined by his wife who appeared to be around the same age. They were both dressed in the same shade of red clothing with the woman wearing a long red dress underneath a matching red suit jacket and the man wearing a red Hawaiian shirt and a matching red flat cap along with his khakis. He also had a red windbreaker that was draped over his right arm while holding the elderly woman's hand with his other hand. They had similar facial features, a similar glow in their eyes, and were of a similar height. These similar physical characteristics would have suggested they could have been brother and sister or of some other blood relation, but they were of different ethnicities and holding hands like a couple. It fascinated Autumn how older couples could end up looking so similar. It was one thing for people to be attracted to people who had similar physical features as them, but with some older couples, it was as if living a similar lifestyle, being on a similar diet, and living in the same environments also shaped their bodies in a similar way and aged their bodies at a similar rate.

They were both wearing visitors' badges.

Upon seeing their visitors' badges, it occurred to Autumn that she had forgotten to obtain one. She looked at Joy and finally realized that Joy was also wearing a visitor's badge. *Typical,* Autumn thought, *I'm always the odd one out.*

The elderly woman pressed the button for the 11th floor after they boarded.

"What exactly happens to AI Autumn if we destroy the database?" Autumn asked Joy (as though the elderly couple wasn't present and directly facing them from the other side of the elevator).

"She will simply disappear," Joy whispered.

The elderly couple looked at them oddly and then looked at each other. As they made eye contact, they appeared expressionless to Joy and Autumn, but they also had the vibe of a couple that had been married for decades and had a way of communicating with each other with their eyes that no one else could comprehend but them.

"You two look so happy together and I love how you match," Joy observed after noticing their vaguely perturbed response to her interaction with Autumn.

"We've been married 50 years as of this past April," the woman shared with a tender smile toward the elderly man.

"Wow! What's your secret to staying together for so long?" Joy asked.

"I don't think you have to like anything else going on around you in this crazy world, but you must know who you are and what you want. You also must always embrace what you have," the elderly woman responded with a tone of routine seriousness as though she had frequently used that response.

"Especially who you choose to be with," the elderly man added.

"Aw, that's sweet," Joy replied with a distinct maternal-sounding tone that Autumn assumed she probably often used with her family.

Up to this point, Autumn had opted not to participate in the interaction with the elderly couple verbally and instead silently observed the elderly woman through the corner of her eye without making eye contact. She thought about how if you were lucky to grow up sheltered in an upper-middle class suburban environment like she did, you assume as a little kid that everyone has their parents around, that everyone celebrates holidays, that everyone has friends, and that everyone has somewhere to go for the night. Reality may start to set in around middle school that people are more different than you thought and that many people don't even like each other. By high school, you are overwhelmed with a mini-version of the realities of adulthood thanks to human body evolution still operating as though people live to only like 30 or 40 as if they were still living in The Iron Age. At that point, you start to realize that only a very small segment of the population experiences what appears to be the ideal life of being stable, happy, and fulfilled. This couple was one of those rare representations to her of that tiny segment of the population. Autumn still couldn't help but think about how this couple probably benefitted from living a life of consent to their life circumstances together without ever trying to think or move outside of those circumstances, no matter how hard life got for them. They were oblivious to any other paths their lives could have taken, together or apart, even if those options may have been better than what they had together now. *Maybe life was better to keep it simple that way, to find someone who was willing to drag through life with you and match bright clothes with you on a dreary trip to the hospital.* It was like life rewards people who don't think outside the box with a safe box to hide in to protect them from most of the terrors of living life.

"Are you two a couple?" The elderly man asked. "You know, we're totally okay with all of that, our youngest daughter is gay."

The elevator doors opened to the 7th floor and Autumn nearly breathed a sigh of relief but caught herself before following through with it. In addition to not saying anything to the elderly couple, she had been struggling to at least make eye contact or nod along with the conversation but couldn't come up with anything beyond a fragile half-smile with no eye contact and no nodding.

Joy looked at Autumn and realized that as much as she wanted Autumn to chime in, that she was probably going to have to do all the talking after all.

Joy shook her head and started to say "No, we're not, she is..."

"...my best friend," Autumn finished unexpectedly, enabling her half smile to broaden a little as she and Joy exited the elevator.

"Best friend?!" Joy asked after the elevator doors had closed behind them.

Autumn hesitated as though she wasn't expecting the follow up question or was hoping maybe Joy had somehow missed it being said. Once she felt she had arrived at a thought that would give her an adequate answer, she took a deep breath.

"Well, as of today you're my only real friend, and now that some people apparently think we are a couple, you might as well be the best."

~ 20 ~

Grandpa seemed to be having a nightmare as they entered his room. His eyes were closed but his eyelids were twitching, and his head was moving slightly side to side. The door to his room was open when they arrived. He was alone and linked to an IV along with several beeping machines. His inpatient floor nurse happened to be at the nurses' station across from the elevators when they arrived on his floor, and she had indicated he was sleeping peacefully in his room. Grandpa's nightmare must've started right before they reached him. The inpatient floor nurse had also briefly lectured Autumn on not wearing a visitor's badge but allowed them to proceed since Joy had one.

"Oh no," Autumn gasped after they looked at Grandpa from beside his bed, "I think we're too late..."

"No, this is perfect," Joy reassured her as she placed her phone on Grandpa's chest over the area of his heart so that the camera lens on her phone faced upward. "Close the door and dim the lights."

The room was smaller than Autumn expected. It was windowless with a tiny walk-in closet-sized bathroom. There was one single framed painting of a white orchid on the wall across from the door. She thought about how people could have strong preferences on where they lived, what they ate, where they traveled, and how they took care of themselves, but when it came time to die, they might be limited to what hospital room was open for them and it may or may not have a window.

"Why am I dimming the lights?" Autumn asked as she dimmed the lights.

"It's too bright in here," Joy observed. "These bright fluorescent lights are awful, and I want to give you a better idea of how the app works. I changed the settings on The Portal so you will be able to see the light that reflects your grandpa's spirit. That light was invisible to the naked eye when it transferred your spirit to the lobby. Oh, and dim lighting also creates a calmer setting— you can't go wrong with that."

Once Autumn had closed the door, she returned to standing beside Joy at the side of Grandpa's bed. She noticed she felt relatively calmer herself with the lights dimmed.

"We'll be able to talk to him here as soon as I click this button, are you ready?" Joy asked, looking over to Autumn as she held her phone over Grandpa's chest with the tip of her right index finger over one of its side buttons.

Autumn gave her a downward nod.

"Here we go..."

Joy released the phone upon clicking the button. The phone started to vibrate on Grandpa's chest for several seconds, prompting him to briefly open his eyes and then blink as a single purple flash emanated from the phone. His eyes then closed again, and his body became calm and still as the phone stopped vibrating.

After Grandpa's eyes closed, a bright beam of light suddenly emerged from the camera lens and formed a tiny spotlight on the wall on the other side of the room from where Autumn and Joy were standing. The light immediately widened in scope once it hit the wall and gradually took the form of a person standing on the other side of the bed from them. As the details of the person's features became apparent, it revealed a young man who looked like he was still a teenager. He was clean shaven with a light muscular build. This was shocking to behold, as outside of old photographs, Autumn had always known Grandpa to have a beard and mustache and to have a thin build. He was wearing a US Army Air Force uniform that included a flight cap, and a brown leather A-2 flight jacket. The jacket had a badge on the left side of the chest area that had a picture of a plane silhouette on it over a gold maple leaf with "Forever Autumn" written in cursive underneath it. Autumn noticed the badge but the immediate urge to ask him about it was superseded by her speechless astonishment at the spectacle of experiencing this younger version of him. As far as she could tell from this one experience, it seemed like old black and white photographs made people appear much older than they really were.

Meanwhile, Grandpa's body on the bed continued breathing normally and settled into a deeper state of relaxation as it faded into a hologram-like presence.

It took a moment for Autumn to overcome her state of awe at how well Joy's app worked at transferring a person's soul into humanoid form. It was one thing to encounter her own soul the way she did, but it was another thing to view the process of a soul appearing right in front of her. She wasn't surprised, however, to see that Grandpa's "prime" was represented by his 19-year-old self in his spirit form, as the family stories about him over the years had painted him as a kind but detached and somewhat unhappy person throughout his adult life after the war. She realized she was ambivalent about how her own "prime" had been earlier revealed to be her life at 25 years old. While it was probably the best time in her life during which she experienced the best of both worlds of her adult life (making good money and feeling relevant and productive at work while maintaining a continued college lifestyle but with all of the associated hope and vitality of that phase of life still intact), she still felt like her "prime" should have been a lot better.

"Autumn," Spirit Grandpa said in his 19-year-old voice after taking a quiet moment to observe himself and absorb the gravity of the situation with his 99-year-old mind, "I meant to tell you this yesterday, and I will tell you now even with your friend here, because I can already sense she is a great person for you to have in your life. Don't live the rest of your life the way I lived my entire life. Deep down we all know who we really are, it's a matter of acknowledging it and then accepting it. Our intuition educates us every day on who we are and what we need. The difference is not in how much we know about ourselves, but in how much we choose to acknowledge about ourselves. I always knew who I was, but I didn't want to acknowledge it until I was around your age. But after I finally acknowledged it, I still never accepted it. Don't be ashamed of who you are. You can look at history and see there were always people like us, and we fit perfectly in roles as healers, medicine people, wizards, bishops, shamans, artists, musicians, priests, apothecaries, and anything else we wanted to be. We certainly weren't the only people in these roles, but we were natural for them as we didn't always think and feel the same way other people do. People will simplify how we are supposed to experience our thoughts and feelings. But you are who you are, and only you and the kami are what matter."

Autumn looked at Spirit Grandpa and then at Joy, before looking down. She felt momentarily unable to face either of them.

"Trust me, it's better to find acceptance within yourself for who you are than to spend your life like I did of seeking acceptance from everyone else who probably won't ever entirely understand you, much less accept you," Spirit Grandpa continued. "It's easy to get confused about who you are. Especially when there is so much pressure around you to be someone else."

"Grandpa..." Autumn raised her head to make eye contact with Spirit Grandpa. "Why didn't you tell me any of this before?"

It was clear to Autumn that Grandpa wasn't going to ever explicitly say the word "neurodivergent." She wondered if it was perhaps out of consideration for how his generation handled subject matter that they identified as private, or if it was because he himself was a private person, or if it was because of the culture he grew up in, or if it was because he was simply her grandfather and felt uncomfortable to discuss anything related to mental health with her. She reasoned that knowing Grandpa, he had considered all those things, and it was probably a combination of all of them.

Tears formed in Spirit Grandpa's eyes that reflected much more of his 99-year-old self than his 19-year-old self. "I didn't come to a lot of these conclusions until I was well into my 70s. Autumn, there were many times I have wanted to tell you since then. When you are still fighting a battle within yourself, it's almost impossible to help other people fight their battles effectively too. I tried my best to be as supportive to you as I possibly could be. I guess this may be yet another time in my life when I was too late..."

Joy looked back at the door closed behind them. She wanted them to continue to have this conversation but also felt the urgency of their situation since a nurse could walk in at any minute to check on Grandpa.

"Lieutenant Takahashi," Joy said as she turned back to Spirit Grandpa, "this time it's not too late. Your granddaughter needs your help. You have one more mission."

"One more mission?" Spirit Grandpa asked. "But I'm not..."

"You are the perfect person we need this for this mission, and we need your expertise," Joy affirmed before Spirit Grandpa could continue. "We need you, but we need you from back then."

"I can't...I'm not...But...I..." Spirit Grandpa's tears were now streaming both cheeks. He looked at Autumn.

"Grandpa that was before, I know you can still do this," Autumn insisted, looking into his eyes, "this time I need you."

"But I'm dying," Spirit Grandpa finally managed to say.

"Right now, it's still not too late," Joy gently reassured him.

Spirit Grandpa silently looked down at his own hologram-like body on the bed for a moment, before he looked up at Joy and then finally Autumn.

He nodded.

"Alright, let's do this," Joy declared with a tone that blended enthusiasm with anxiety. She took off her overstuffed backpack and set it on the floor. After opening it with slight difficulty, she handed Autumn an oxygen mask paired with a small oxygen tank, a radio headset, mittens, and an extra olive-colored quilted jacket for Autumn to put on over her hoodie.

"Put everything on before we go," Joy requested as she handed the items to Autumn before putting on her own oxygen mask and headset. She had also brought a pair of gloves for herself.

"Mittens?!" Autumn asked. "I don't wear mittens."

"I know, I'm sorry, I didn't have an extra pair of gloves, but you'll need them up there...it's a lot colder than you think."

"How did you already have these things?" Autumn asked as Spirit Grandpa quietly observed them gearing up with both a curious and perplexed expression.

"With all the time travel I've done, I'm a bit of a hoarder with the different items you might need when you visit places." Joy laughed.

Once they had emptied the backpack and stopped fidgeting around with their new accessories, Joy looked over to Spirit Grandpa.

"It's time," Joy said to him as she reached over to her phone, which had remained intact atop Grandpa's hologram.

Hologram-like Grandpa suddenly opened his eyes from his meditative state on the bed as Joy got a hold of the phone on his chest, but he remained calm and still as though he was in alignment with what was about to happen.

As Joy clicked and then held the side button of her phone, a strong red flash engulfed the entire room.

"What happened?!" A distant and distorted voice of a young man cried as they all blinked in response to the flash.

~ 21 ~

"What happened?!" the young man's voice cried again. This unfamiliar voice initially sounded fuzzy to Autumn, like he was over a distorted radio broadcast, but upon repeating himself, he radioed in with a clearer tone that sounded much closer to them.

Autumn and Joy found themselves knelt in the nose area of the interior of an in-flight B-17 Flying Fortress beside the young version of Grandpa that they had interacted with in spirit form. Young Grandpa was seated in the bombardier's chair to their right. The navigator was seated immediately in front of them at a small desk with his back to them. The four of them were situated within an area that was compartmentalized from the rest of the plane and provided substantial views of the darkened surrounding skies since the nose itself was almost fully covered in plexiglass. There were smaller windows just beyond the nose and a few machine guns were also installed in the vicinity at divergent angles. Since they were isolated from the other areas of the plane, Young Grandpa and the navigator heard the crew and could communicate with them through their radio headsets. The pilot and co-pilot were seated in a compartment above them, while the flight engineer was in an area both above and behind them beyond were the pilot and co-pilot were seated. Behind the flight engineer, the bomb bay was situated closer to the center of the plane and separated the front area crew from where the radio operator (assigned to an area on the other side of the bomb bay), the ball turret gunner (positioned in a sphere-shaped turret attached at the bottom of the plane near where the radio operator was), the two waist gunners (who manned heavy machine guns on opposite sides of the middle-rear area of the plane further back from where the ball turret gunner was), and the tail gunner were stationed in the rest of the plane.

Autumn and Joy found that their modern headsets had paired seamlessly with the crew's headsets. Joy muted the microphone on her headset and then showed Autumn how to do the same with hers.

The plane smelled like a combination of gasoline, oil, metal, and cold morning air intermixed with the fainter smells of wood, after-rain, and smoke. The cold morning air remained clean and crisp among the other scents and strangely had its familiar calming and renewing energy despite the setting they were in and despite its stingy impact on exposed skin that was akin to being inside of a walk-in storage freezer. The cold was augmented by the windy environment inside of the plane. She couldn't tell how much of the wind was from the storm outside and how much of it was from the movement of the plane. Rings of bolts were visible and connected segments of the aircraft frame. This aluminum interior of the plane was minimal and spare with only essential supplies (i.e. ammunition boxes, flight instruments, emergency equipment, etc.) scattered around it.

Autumn looked out the plexiglass nose beyond where Young Grandpa was sitting and had a closer look at how the ghastly gray clouds outside were peppered by dozens of smaller circular black clouds of flak.

The flak seemed to occasionally bump and shake the plane when it exploded close by. The bursts of flak sounded both near and distant while intermixed with the blares of wind and the steady mechanical whirring of the plane's engines.

Young Grandpa looked over to Autumn with the familiarity of the 99-year-old version of himself despite physically being his 19-year-old self.

"Autumn?!" Young Grandpa asked with a genuine mix of confusion and joy as he looked at her, then around the plane, and then finally at himself. The navigator turned to them from looking at a map on his desk and he blinked with a silent, tense aura of shock and disbelief.

"Grandpa!" Autumn cried. She then, to her own surprise, found herself lunging toward Young Grandpa into a full embrace.

"We made it," Joy added and hugged Autumn from behind as Autumn still held Young Grandpa. Unbeknownst to either Autumn or Young Grandpa and out of the line of sight of the navigator witnessing their hug from the other side of them, Joy managed to discretely slip a noise cancellation seashell into the left pocket of Young Grandpa's A-2 jacket before they completed their group hug.

"The bomb bay jammed," the flight engineer reported over the radio, "working on it now."

Young Grandpa released Autumn and fell back into the bombardier's chair upon hearing the report about the bomb bay door. He felt his heart sink. He recognized he was reliving October 20, 1943, all over again at the worst possible moment. It was a memory he had dedicated 80 years of his life to try to block out of his mind as much as he could. He briefly put his head in his hands before looking up at the navigator, who simultaneously happened to look in Young Grandpa's direction.

As he made eye contact with the navigator, he realized that while it was too late for him to prevent the bombing from occurring, he was being given the opportunity to change the way he reacted to it. In 1943, he had been so despondent that he had scarcely said a word until days after they had returned to their air base in England.

Autumn more closely observed the navigator as he turned away from Young Grandpa and anxiously started looking at the other maps on his desk. The navigator had short blond hair and nervous, searching blue eyes. He appeared to be physically in his early-mid 20s but had the body language that resembled more of a sensitive and withdrawn teenager. He was wearing an A-2 jacket as well, but his jacket seemed newer, less worn, and didn't have a "Forever Autumn" badge on it like Young Grandpa's did. In a unique circumstance like this, it was impossible to tell if he was always this insecure or if it was the combination of the village bombing and the sudden presence of two strangely dressed women who looked foreign and mysterious to him that prompted this behavior. Autumn suspected the baseline of how he behaved was probably somewhere in-between falsely exuding confidence and his current baffled and overwhelmed state.

"Am I named after this plane?" Autumn finally asked as she turned to Young Grandpa.

"Yes," Young Grandpa answered as he looked back over to her. He seemed to be relieved that Autumn had brought up something different for him to think about.

"I was named after an ugly plane?! How come no one ever told me about it?"

"No one else in our family ever knew the name of the plane before. When I suggested the name 'Autumn' before you were born, your mom just thought it was a name I came up with. The plane was named after the captain's girlfriend. The captain was—well, is our pilot," Young Grandpa described with a wistful expression that looked like it should belong on the face of a much older man.

"The bomb bay is repaired and reset," the flight engineer reported over the radio.

"We'll drop the rest over sea," the pilot radioed back. Autumn recognized the pilot's voice as the one that had cried "What happened?!" upon their arrival.

As Young Grandpa was interacting with Autumn, the navigator had slowly turned back to Autumn and Joy again. He looked at them with silent awe like he was witnessing ghosts. Young Grandpa recognized this and reached over to put his hand on the navigator's shoulder.

"It's okay, they're with me," Young Grandpa whispered.

The navigator looked back at one of his maps and started crying.

"Something still doesn't feel right," the co-pilot radioed.

"Captain, we hit a village!" The navigator bellowed.

"No, we hit the target," the ball turret gunner replied, "had to be."

"You mean to tell me that wasn't it?" The tail gunner radioed in from the back. "They were killing us with that flak. Even if that wasn't it, hopefully we got some of those guns down there."

"Oh no," the co-pilot said sadly.

"We are too late after all," Autumn lamented. "The Portal didn't take us to before Grandpa dropped those bombs, we could have saved him from a life of misery. We could have saved the people in the village."

Joy was looking outside the closest window to her, noticing how the flak seemed to have suddenly subsided.

"Remember, we aren't here to change what happened here, and it's not too late for us. We can still take out the AI database," Joy tried to reassure her as she still looked out the window.

"How can you be so sure?!" Autumn snapped, before immediately regretting her tone but still feeling too irritable to apologize for it right away.

Before Joy could reply, the plane shook as though it had been struck in the rear. Joy grabbed hold of both Autumn and a nearby bolted protrusion on the side of the plane's interior airframe while Autumn held onto Joy. Young Grandpa reached over to a machine gun near his chair, looked out a small window above it, and started firing. Autumn glanced out of her nearest window as she continued to hold on to Joy with her chin resting on Joy's shoulder. Through the window, she saw a German fighter zoom by close enough to the plane that she could clearly see the black and white balkenkreuz painted on its fuselage and the black swastika with a white outline painted on its tail. It was moving forward out in front of their plane.

The sight of the German fighter had an immediate profound impact on her. She was literally back in a time, not so long ago, when the real world was far more terrifying than anything she experienced in her own life. As corrupt, unjust, discriminatory, and hateful as the real world was in her lifetime, she was now back in a world where the people who were exterminating other people for being different than them were also trying to take over Europe, and possibly in the long run, dominate the world. It didn't change the very real challenges of the world she experienced in her present life, but it gave her this perspective that just hearing about the old stories from this time period could never give her. Since she wasn't often one to empathize or to try to have a deeper mindful understanding of where others were coming from, it was like she had to directly experience this firsthand to have that awakening. She felt a tinge of unexpected shame and sadness that she had to go this far to gain this kind of insight. She lived in a world in her present life that seemed to have totally forgotten that the world was nearly consumed by an evil that had grown to be even more powerful than any of the evil that was currently permeating much of the world. She wondered how this crew and other allied soldiers would fight if they all knew the world would take the direction it would 80 years later, but as she thought about the sight of that swastika, she realized that the alternative was still far worse than she could imagine.

"We've got company!" The co-pilot radioed in.

"He came from out of nowhere," the flight engineer gasped.

Autumn slowly pulled away from Joy and slumped back on the floor.

"Starks, do you copy?" The crew's radio operator asked through his headset.

"He's coming back around our left," the pilot observed.

"He won't get around us again, captain!" The left waist gunner proclaimed as the sound of his machine gun could be heard before he radioed out.

Young Grandpa released his machine gun and saw Autumn in her sad and reflective state. She looked back at him with tear-welled eyes that quietly shared her higher level of regard for him and what he had to go through in his lifetime. She sat up and approached him in the way she would have as a 4 year old approaching him to sit on his lap.

He put his arm around her. "Autumn," he said gently.

Autumn looked at Young Grandpa and then at Joy: "I'd rather save the way his life will go than save my own."

"Life has a way of making what was meant to be happen no matter how hard we try control the outcome. Whether we like it or not, it will always be one of the mysteries of life," Joy calmly observed, "but we still have another outcome that we can control, and your grandpa wants to help you. If we are still going to do this, we must do it now. He doesn't have much time. We don't have much time."

The sound of a loud explosion suddenly rattled through the plane again and it was followed by the harrowing howl of another nearby plane crashing down toward the earth.

"Got 'em!" The left waist gunner radioed in jubilantly. "I told you he wouldn't make it."

"You did," the pilot conceded, sounding relieved, "and you saved our ass."

"Starks, I say again, do you copy?" The radio operator asked again over the radio.

"Starks was the tail gunner we lost that day," Young Grandpa revealed to them.

"Tak, are you talking to me?" The radio operator asked. "We lose Starks?"

"We lost Starks," the right waist gunner confirmed via radio, "I just checked on him, damn kraut got him before we could get to him."

"What a disaster..." the ball turret gunner started to say, before trailing off.

"The tail gun is still intact," the right waist gunner continued, "but we have significant damage to the tail."

Joy checked her phone and looked up to Autumn with a look of steadfast determination. "It's fully re-charged, we are ready."

"Yeah, we really need to get out of here," Autumn whispered.

"Let's get out of here," the pilot coincidentally radioed in.

Autumn and Joy looked at each other.

"Here we go," Joy said, "hang on..."

Joy clicked the side of her phone several times instead of just once as Autumn had seen her previously use it. Joy also didn't hold the button like she had to transport them to the plane.

A succession of about a dozen red flashes of light filled the nose area of the plane. The entire plane was subsequently engulfed by several strands of red lightning extending up and down the interior walls of the airframe. These occurrences of lightning enabled the red flashes to extend through every area of the plane to impact every member of the crew. This display of lightning lasted for several seconds before subsiding into a brief eerie silence. Meanwhile, Joy's phone continued to flash but in intervals lasting about every 10 seconds.

The plane then suddenly started shaking violently and everyone found a sturdy object or part of the airframe to hold to, including Joy, who had placed her phone on the floor. The phone was face down to minimize a flashing red light that still seeped slightly through the crack between the face of the phone and the floor. Young Grandpa was seated on the floor hanging on to the back of the bombardier's chair. Autumn looked outside the window and observed that the red lightning had expanded outside of the plane among the clouds in the sky.

"Looks like we've entered a major storm, hold on!" The pilot radioed, as he observed several unusual bolts of red lightning flashing immediately in front of the plane. The high volume of lightning bolts illuminated the thick gray and black clouds that surrounded them with an almost continuous red glow. "It's red!"

"This storm looks like it's coming from the plane!" The co-pilot observed nervously, as he tried in vain to operate his side of the plane's controls, which had abruptly taken a life of their own.

The plane began to increase speed far beyond its own capability as the pilots lost complete control of it. It initially dove downward like it was going to crash and made a corresponding diving sound similar to the frightening sound the crashing German fighter had made earlier. But this movement was soon diverted by an unexpected and uncontrolled swerve upward that created new eerie ambient noises that didn't sound like anything that could have come from the plane itself.

"Hang on!" The co-pilot shouted in a radio message that could scarcely be heard among the crew through the strange and unprecedented sounds the plane was making.

The pilot was about to turn to the co-pilot when he suddenly realized the plane had entered a tunnel of glowing rainbow-colored light, with each color taking turns being highlighted over the others in different parts of the tunnel (first purple, then red, then orange, then yellow, then green, then purple again, and so on). There seemed to be a set pattern in which some of colors were highlighted, and then new different colors were selected every 5 seconds. Every aforementioned color was visible regardless of what part of the tunnel the plane was in.

As the plane navigated this tunnel of lights, a mysterious, multi-colored fog that reflected the same colors as the tunnel started to fill the plane from all sides and thickened rapidly to blinding proportions.

"What's happening?!" The flight engineer cried out as he was engulfed by the multicolored fog.

"No fog can bring this baby down," the ball turret gunner laughed as he fired a few rounds in vain through the incoming wave of fog.

As the fog started to cave in on the line of sight of both the pilot and co-pilot, they fidgeted within their seats and strained themselves to remain tight lipped to maintain their composure for the rest of the crew. The pilot finally turned to the co-pilot as the fog was about to envelop them to find the co-pilot already looking in his direction. As they made eye contact, a red flash brighter than the previous flashes they had witnessed penetrated through the fog and filled the cockpit.

~ 22 ~

Once the flash subsided, rays of sunlight filled the cockpit, and the plane had completely reverted back to its original speed and altitude in a matter of milliseconds. The clouds in the sky were white and fluffy and surrounded by wispy strands of thinner cloud that reflected speckles of the morning sun. Below them was a lush autumnal forest with a long winding dirt road running through it. The winding dirt road had a few tiny villages along it that vaguely looked like they dated back to the medieval era. The lightning, the tunnel, and the fog had completely vanished.

The environment was bright, calm, misty, and serene.

Despite the presence of sunlight and absence of the winds from the storm, the air felt just as cold. The whirring of the engines sounded relatively gentle against this environment of serenity as though they were relieved to have evacuated the storm.

Autumn and Joy carefully pulled themselves away from holding onto the airframe behind them and Young Grandpa cautiously returned to his chair. The navigator had been holding onto his desk and was slower to release his grip upon it.

Autumn looked out her nearest window and saw a flock of seagulls flying nearby. One of them seemed to look at her oddly.

Joy looked out a window on the other side of the plane and far in the distance she could vaguely see the ruins of her old castle, that she had created in childhood, on a cliff above the sea. She turned to Autumn: "We're here!"

Autumn looked at her with an exhausted expression that conveyed how she was still recovering from the plane's turbulent transition through The Portal.

The navigator finally lifted himself up, looked at his map, then out a nearby window, and then back at his map again with a mix of relief and confusion. He scratched his head as he glared deeper into map as though he was missing a crucial detail that was still in it.

The rays of light that streamed in through the nose of the plane and the windows lit up random parts of the interior of the plane and their bodies with patches of light of various sizes. Based on where he was positioned, Young Grandpa was almost fully lit up by light coming in through the plexiglass nose of the plane.

"I know," Joy responded to Autumn's silent gaze, "it was a bumpy ride. This was my first time trying to transfer an entire plane through The Portal."

Joy picked up her phone and promptly began to tap and scroll.

Young Grandpa looked out the plexiglass nose of the plane in wonder at the seemingly endless forest before them. Young Grandpa's entire body had entered into a relaxed, meditative state that wholly contrasted his prior presentation of guarded, anxiety-driven alertness. He looked as content as a hiker would after they had reached the top of a steep hill, or as a scuba diver would upon witnessing the most beautiful sea creature they'd ever seen. He was completely at ease, and this was further demonstrated by a broad warm smile that a lot of people usually only reserved for weekends, vacations, or holidays.

"I don't know where we are," the navigator reported, "my instruments aren't working."

"Captain, I'm not picking up anyone else in our squad over the radio. All I get is the crew here," the radio operator indicated.

"I don't know what happened," the bull turret gunner radioed, "but I am glad it did."

"The storm suddenly cleared so we may have to give everything a little time," the pilot determined calmly but with a hint of pensiveness. "We know we were pointed in the right direction before the turbulence hit us."

"Lieutenant Takahashi, we are approximately 12 minutes away from our target," Joy reported to Young Grandpa. Joy showed him a map she had up on the screen of her phone that showed their current location relative to their target, "We need you drop the remaining bombload on the Dark Forest Spaceport. The spaceport houses the centralized supercomputer database for their AI program. Your primary target is the large warehouse that contains the AI database at the south end of the facility. As we move north, we'll also hit other parts of the complex, which is ideal because we want to destroy as much of it as possible. It also operates a missile silo. Inform the crew we found a research center with an enemy rocket installation to destroy. We have some element of surprise, but they will quickly detect we are coming any minute now with their sophisticated air defense network."

"What about fuel?" Autumn wondered as the thought occurred to her.

"Fortunately, we are positioned relatively close to our target. The plane will be dropping its bombload more quickly on the spaceport as opposed to waiting to release it over the English Channel. This will conserve fuel, and it also won't give them as much time to try to stop us. We don't know what kind of defenses they may have," Joy explained while intermittently making eye contact with both Autumn and Young Grandpa.

Young Grandpa turned to Autumn.

"You can do this, Grandpa," Autumn reassured him.

Young Grandpa looked up at the navigator, who had been witnessing the interaction with a sense of quiet desperation.

"Captain, Lieutenant Pine and I have a new target on our direct path back to base. A research center and rocket site that Pine is aware of from an aborted run with his former crew. We are only eleven minutes away. We can empty the remainder of our inventory there on the way back," Young Grandpa radioed in before giving the navigator a nod.

The navigator returned the nod with a slight grin.

Autumn finally got the sense from this exchange that the navigator respected her grandpa enough to go along with him on anything, including the set of bizarre circumstances he found himself in with them.

"A rocket site?!" The co-pilot asked. "I think I have heard about them. They really did have you on all kinds of secret missions before you got stuck here with us, Pine."

"Trust me, Pine," Young Grandpa whispered to the navigator, "this is our second chance."

"Perfect. You hear that everyone?" The pilot asked. "Pine and Tak will give them a nice send off on our way back."

"We need to do something with this run," the flight engineer radioed, "we'll honor Starks that way."

The navigator removed his radio headset and oxygen mask. "Tak, you know the captain will kill us if he finds out you smuggled these foreign broads in here," he whispered, "it's bad enough we blew the first part of this run."

Young Grandpa removed his radio headset and oxygen mask as well. "Listen, I've never wronged you before. They are here to help us. Don't let what happened back there ever get to you either. It was an accident. You can't really see people for who they are or a situation for what it really is until you stop looking at them through a single lens that you think you and everyone else should only view them through. Life is too short to view yourself and the world from a single impossible lens you'll never live up to."

Young Grandpa gulped and then involuntarily held his breath for a few seconds after he realized he was talking like his 99-year-old self in his 19-year-old body.

"Oh, they are here to help us alright," the navigator quipped as he looked at him with both eyebrows raised, "but I am with you, even though I think your head is too big to be up this high."

"Looks like we've got company again!" The pilot radioed as Young Grandpa and the navigator put their gear back on.

*** *** ***

Casey had her laptop open on her desk in her 50th floor office and she was looking at a detailed demographic profile of Autumn that was opened on the screen. It contained various forms of personal information, thumbnail video links to virtual meeting footage and security camera footage of Autumn, intelligence and medical testing results, and statistics on work performance. It was the kind of thorough analysis and one-stop collection of data on a person that contains more information than nearly everyone else in the world will ever have on themselves, much less other people.

"What a waste," Casey observed aloud to herself.

She pressed a red button on the right control panel on her desk (it was the most frequently used button on her desk that went directly to an overhead intercom in Maxwell's 49th floor office): "Maxwell, connect me to AI Autumn, tell her this is urgent."

Within a minute of the request, AI Autumn appeared on the primary wall screen in front of her (replacing what was previously depicting a peaceful walk through a lit lantern-lined path in a bamboo forest at night).

"They know," AI Autumn bemoaned as it appeared on the screen, "I arrived here at the spaceport as soon as I got the alert on my phone."

AI Autumn was wearing an all-black mechanic's uniform and behind it, beyond large glass windows, was the center section of a large missile that was painted with a distinct black and white checkerboard design. The launch control center was unique in that the missile was surrounded by layers of futuristic fireproof glass. This circular fireproof glass enclosure was in turn, surrounded by multiple floors of workstations that enabled the staff to view the missile's launch firsthand as they coordinated it. There were three people in the same uniform that AI Autumn was wearing at the workstations that could be seen in the background of the video feed. Though this site was only intended for offensive operations related to the use of the missile, AI Autumn had repurposed the location as an emergency defense headquarters for the entire spaceport. The underground missile silo was chosen for this impromptu purpose as the closed blast door above the missile was built to sustain the strongest possible attack on the area. The circular launch control center was large enough to employ a capacity of thirty staff, but the network of fallout shelters that surrounded the silo could potentially house all two thousand staff who were employed at the spaceport. Many of the staff who were not needed for emergency defense operations had already been evacuated to the shelters.

"Of course, I know...they know!" Casey stammered irritably. "My question is why haven't we stopped them?!"

"Our fighter group is already en route to intercept them; I also have word that Gray just arrived here too, and he is going to join them in his new aircraft," AI Autumn reported.

"Great," Casey responded but in a tone that lacked the enthusiasm that would normally be associated with using that word.

"That old plane they're using won't make it this far," AI Autumn declared confidently. "After all, I feel like I was designed specifically to take her out of her misery anyway."

But Casey didn't appear to share that confidence and looked unusually vulnerable and uncertain as she looked away from the screen and down at her desk.

"What's wrong?" AI Autumn asked after briefly hesitating. It never had seen Casey like this and wasn't sure whether it should acknowledge that she appeared that way.

"Joy is obviously helping her." Casey groaned before asking rhetorically: "Who ever thought those two would team up?!"

AI Autumn looked at her blankly.

"We can't risk them getting too close to the spaceport. We need another plan in case our fighters can't get to them, but we'll have to act quickly," Casey said in a way that sounded like she was thinking out loud and not necessarily speaking directly to AI Autumn. "Install mechanical heat-seeking devices on the Supernova Missile and redirect its aim from Joy's space station to that plane."

AI Autumn's head drooped. "But that plane is only like 10 minutes away from us, and what you are asking us to do will take at least an hour. This missile isn't meant to target a plane, and it isn't intended for air defense. It's developed specifically to eliminate any potential competition from Joy in AI development by destroying her base of operation—"

"Are you finished?!" Casey interrupted. "Because I know what the missile is intended for, I put in the order for its development. Now that we know where Joy's space station is, we will find other ways to destroy it. But in the meantime, I'm asking you to repurpose that missile as soon as possible for air defense, because you have a plane heading toward you right now that intends to destroy you. Am I making myself clear? Place the entire station on red alert."

"But it's not meant to—"

"It's the only way you'll survive!" Casey interjected.

Casey groaned so loudly that it seemed to echo through the missile silo as much as it did through her office.

Before AI Autumn could respond further (and it looked like it wanted to continue), Casey terminated their call.

***** *** *****

"I count three of them, heading directly for us," the co-pilot added.

The three fighters simultaneously fired purple lasers directly at the nose of "Forever Autumn" and several of them hit without damaging the plane. They instead seemed to merely bump the plane the way a bumper car would.

The fighters had an unusual design that made them look like UFOs or experimental aircraft. They were designed as half-saucers forming a semi-circle shape. The circular arc of these half-discs formed the rear while the straight end comprised of the front of the aircraft. The center of the front side had a large cockpit with a glass aircraft canopy that went from the top of the aircraft to the bottom. This unusual cockpit design revealed the full body of each pilot in a standing position with a cushioned support behind them while they operated a control panel immediately in front of them. There were laser cannons placed on both sides of the front of the aircraft halfway between the cockpit and the outer edges. The fighters were painted international orange and appeared to be intended for flight at higher elevations and perhaps, for space-flight. The Dark Forest Solutions logo (the black outline of a Douglas fir tree) was painted on top of the fighters.

"They are hitting us with lights?!" The co-pilot asked in amazement.

"Whatever those lights are," the flight engineer observed, "they don't seem to be hurting us."

"What are they?" The right waist gunner asked immediately after the rattle of his machine gun. "Half of a pancake?!"

"Well, ain't that something," the ball turret gunner radioed, "the nazi bastards are still keeping us entertained out here in the sticks with their new toys, eh?!"

The waist gunners, the ball turret gunner, the radio operator, and the flight engineer were all firing their machine guns, but the fighters were moving too quickly for them to have any impact. Other than the direct hits the fighters managed to land on their initial pass, they similarly struggled to hit the B-17 without slowing down themselves and becoming vulnerable to the machine gun fire.

Joy turned to Autumn, "I'm going to take over the tail gunner position. It's a little, um, cramped here for us anyway."

Autumn blinked several times with both eyes as she looked at her: "You're doing what now?!"

Joy placed her phone in front of the navigator on his desk. The phone screen still had the map up showing the target, their current location, and the distance and time from the target. The navigator looked at it like a kid discovering a new complex device that he was afraid to touch and then looked up to Joy.

"It'll be okay," Joy reassured both Autumn and the navigator as she started to head to the back of the plane.

Autumn realized she should help too (despite having never fired a gun in her life) and removed her mittens before positioning herself on the closest machine gun. It immediately felt like she had placed both of her bare hands into a pile of snow once she had removed the mittens and she subsequently felt a greater affinity for them (though she still didn't like the snowflake patterns on them).

As one of the fighters zipped by, she fired awkwardly at it but quickly realized she had pulled the trigger after it had already passed: *Everything in life is almost always harder than what it looks like.*

"Captain, there's a woman here who says she is going to take over the tail gun," the flight engineer reported.

"There's a what?!" The pilot radioed as the co-pilot could be heard firing his machine gun in the background.

"We have two women here on the plane," the navigator reported. "Tak says they are here to help."

"Here to help?!?" The left waist gunner laughed.

"I never knew you to be a ladies' man, Tak," the right waist gunner added.

"I don't know what to say, Tak," the pilot radioed. "I suppose we need all the help we can get at the moment. We'll talk about it after the mission."

"I understand, sir, I take full blame for what happened to the village and also for the women being here," Young Grandpa replied. The navigator looked at him with a complex expression that looked like a mix of regret and gratitude. In prior history, he had exchanged uneasy glances with the navigator as they both waited for the other to take the blame for the village. Now, Young Grandpa was doing what he always regretted not doing. He became more aware of how this time his shoulders were relaxed, his chest open, and his heart full.

"It's okay, Grandpa," Autumn whispered. "They won't remember anything by the time you get back. You won't either."

Young Grandpa paused after hearing this information, but his old soul decided that if no one would remember this, doing the right thing still felt right.

Just as he made this resolution, an explosion was heard in the distance.

"Ahhhhhh, got one," the ball turret gunner radioed in.

"Nice shot!" the right waist gunner exclaimed as he peered out further to get a better look at the crashing plane falling toward the forest. "Pilot is bailing out."

"They're slowing down," the left waist gunner observed between the thudding rounds of his gun, "to flash more of their lights at us."

"Makes it easier for us!" The ball turret gunner shouted from below before firing more shots in the background.

Young Grandpa looked at Autumn, then at his bombardier chair, and then finally at one of the unmanned machine guns near his chair. He took a deep breath as though he was breathing in a reinvigorated sense of purpose and breathing out 80 years worth of regret. This act created a profound energy that was felt by both the navigator and Autumn nearby. He took up the gun and started firing at one of the fighters passing by.

"Starks would be proud," the flight engineer radioed.

Upon hearing the flight engineer say that, Joy looked back at where she had carefully set the body of Starks behind her. She thought about how people in the military, law enforcement, health care, and mortuaries had to desensitize themselves to death as much as they could to do their jobs effectively and then continue forward with their lives. But there was something about death that still could never be normalized despite society seemingly normalizing the finality of everything else: quitting jobs, divorcing marriages, throwing away nearly every conceivable consumer product that was now disposable, and ghosting text messages from people you no longer wanted in your life. In each of those instances, you could forget about it. But there was something about knowing someone who died (or even in this instance of being around a dead body of someone you never knew) in which you felt that person was always a part of you in that they were still present with you or would stay with you in some other form, even if just as a memory that you couldn't remove like you could do with most of the other ones.

"Two more left..." The co-pilot radioed but then trailed off despite sounding like he had more to say. "Or no... make that three again?!"

"It looks like we have another one joining us," the pilot reported, "conserve your ammo as much as possible. We don't know how many more of these things are coming."

The fourth aircraft had the same colors as the other fighters but instead of being shaped like a semi-circle, it was a half-saucer shaped like an arbelos. The outer semicircle of the arbelos formed its rear (in a way that resembled the other fighters). But instead of consisting of a straight-line, the front of the aircraft was curved inward by two smaller, uneven semi-circular arcs that formed three distinct pointed edges. The pointed edges at both ends of the front of the fighter were armed with laser cannons while the aircraft canopy was coned-shaped at the third "middle" point (that was positioned off-center closer to the left side of the fighter). Like the other fighters, the pilot was placed in a standing position within the cockpit. The Dark Forest Solutions logo on top was smaller than it was on their other aircraft (due to having significantly less surface area on top). The pilot of the arbelos seemed like a more experienced pilot or had at least benefitted from scouting reports from the other fighters, as it came in at a slower pace and peppered the entire plane with direct hits while somehow evading machine gun fire from multiple gunners.

The B-17 sustained no discernible damage from this run by the arbelos and only experienced an inconvenient, but harmless moment of turbulence as a result of it.

"Whoa!" The pilot yelled as a fighter burst into flames just within his upper line of sight and nearly struck their plane as it crashed down toward them.

"We fried another half-a-flapjack!" the flight engineer enthusiastically radioed.

***** *** *****

"What is going on out there? Why is that plane still flying?!" Casey demanded as she stood up behind her desk. She hadn't left her office from the moment she was notified that a mysterious, unidentified plane had suddenly appeared on the radar at the control tower of her spaceport. She had remained at her desk despite being hungry and vaguely needing to use the restroom. Following her initial call with AI Autumn, she had arranged for the secondary screens in her office to each show a live feed of different camera perspectives around the spaceport. Two of the screens showed a live feed of the missile silo, where AI Autumn was directing staff to repurpose the missile to target the plane. A few other screens showed different outdoor vantage points around the spaceport. One of the cameras revealed that the blast door of the silo had been opened for the missile to fire immediately once it was ready. Another screen showed a live feed of the interior of the AI database warehouse (which included dozens of rows of supercomputers).

Her office had become a battle headquarters.

Gray was seen up on the primary screen through a live feed from the cockpit of the arbelos-shaped fighter. He had flown far enough behind the B-17 to be out of its machine gun range to facilitate the call. Nevertheless, he felt relieved that he had the excuse of flying an experimental aircraft in a battle-setting to not make video eye contact with Casey. She was on a small screen that was installed on the upper interior windshield of his aircraft canopy. The screen was positioned similarly to where a rearview mirror was located in a car.

Gray initially remained quiet and seemingly unaffected as though he was very carefully and strategically considering his words within the realm of his thoughts before verbalizing them. He had gradually learned the hard way to do this with Casey over their many years together. He knew when she was this angry that he had to stick to facts. He also knew he had to avoid any demonstration of emotion in the tone of his voice, expression on his face, and within the use of words. Lastly, he knew he had to try to minimize his sarcasm as much as possible.

"As you know our air defense weaponry is specifically designed to either disable computerized systems or disrupt a weapon's communication signals on any encroaching enemy object, including drones, planes, helicopters, rockets, or missiles, but they are using some kind of old damaged bomber from the Second World War. It has no real computer system on it to disrupt and doesn't use airborne guided projectiles. The laser armaments on our fighters are only minor nuisance to it and aren't inflicting any damage. They were not designed for traditional combat."

Instead of responding verbally, Casey just glared at the screen in outraged disbelief.

"I mean, how are we were supposed to know anyone would ever think to use a random antique like that against us?!" Gray added.

Casey appeared unusually distraught by this question and despite a strong effort on her part, couldn't hide that facial response from Gray. However, after a quiet moment of expedited contemplation, she had a thought that elicited a smirk.

"Is she in that plane?"

"Autumn?"

"No idiot, can't you ever get anything right?! We know Autumn is on the plane, she's the reason I am able to track their plane. She still has the Dark Forest Solutions Employee app downloaded on her phone and she has her phone with her. I mean Joy! Is Joy on the plane?!"

"Really? I can't believe she still has the app downloaded on her phone. I'm surprised she has the app on her phone," Gray thought aloud.

"She only ever logged into once a few years ago and never used it to clock in like she was supposed to," Casey recalled, "but whatever, it's still serving its real purpose and it's proving much more valuable to us now. Are you going to answer my question or not?!"

Right as Casey finished her question, Gray witnessed an explosion rip through the rear of the only other remaining defense fighter. It had been hit just to the left of the B-17's nose.

"You are the only one left now, aren't you?" Casey asked, sounding increasingly inpatient and exasperated.

Gray involuntarily swallowed the invisible lump of dryness at the back of his throat as the ugly sound of the defense fighter crashing toward the forest below echoed through the sky around him.

"I am," he responded softly.

"And now will you answer my original question?!"

"What?"

"Is Joy on that place or not?!" Casey screamed.

"We can't tell, their old plane is moving slowly, and we were— I am having difficulty slowing down to their speed without getting hit. It has machine guns all over it at every angle. I'll try to get a closer look."

"Don't try, do it. I didn't want you getting that stupid pilot's license in the first place, and now that you have it, you don't even want to use it the one time when I literally need your expertise. Now I supported you through that whole process of getting it, so do this one thing for me, and find out if Joy is on that plane and figure out a way to destroy it."

"That's actually two things," Gray replied.

Casey scowled at him and then terminated the call.

~ 23 ~

"Was that you, Tak?!" The pilot asked. "Nice shot."

"You're getting yourself out of trouble, Tak," the flight engineer observed.

Young Grandpa released his machine gun and turned back to Autumn. He remained expressionless despite his success in taking down one of the remaining fighters. They quietly made eye contact and Autumn observed within his eyes that he was still nervous about the impending bomb run.

"You don't give yourself enough credit on the gun, Tak," the left waist gunner radioed. "You make my job easier when you're cookin' up there."

"Means a lot coming from you, Rod," Young Grandpa said in a way that he wouldn't have in the past. "Rod" was short for Rodriguez. They had maintained a mostly distant, business-like relationship during the war. But in his current state, Young Grandpa knew that though they were often weary and distrusting of each other at this point, they later became good friends after the war and would reminisce about being the only minorities on their crew. Up until they finally talked about it right before Rodriguez died many years later, there was an unspoken understanding between them that the racism they each separately experienced (usually from other airmen outside of their crew) played a big role in keeping them at a distance from each other during their time in the military.

"Three minutes remaining to target," the navigator radioed as he continued to look at the screen of Joy's phone on his desk in complete awe.

But right after he had reported in, the screen on Joy's phone went completely black.

"Oh, it went black?!" The navigator panicked.

Autumn quickly turned and reached over the navigator's shoulder to touch the phone screen to refresh it.

"Oh, never mind, the girl here brought it back," the navigator radioed with a tone that mixed relief with anxiety-tinged confusion.

"Is that the whole target? I kept thinking that was a small city," the co-pilot noted. "It looks like something out of a science pulp."

Young Grandpa sat back down in the bombardier chair and started adjusting his bombsight.

"One more remaining. The funny looking one. Is it still behind us?" The pilot asked.

"Still behind us," Joy reported.

Joy had her machine gun aimed at the arbelos aircraft as it seemed to draw confidently closer to her as if to send her some kind of message. She wanted to fire at it but didn't after realizing it wasn't firing at her either. She figured she'd have a clearer shot once it got closer.

She squinted as it drew dangerously close.

Once she could see into the cockpit, she recognized the eyes glaring back at hers were Gray's eyes. She couldn't see his mouth underneath his oxygen mask, but through their fleeting eye contact she got the sense he was smirking.

As they made eye contact, a flood of emotions that Joy hadn't experienced in 22 years came back to her with a level of intense familiarity that one would usually only have with emotions that they just have experienced within the last 24 hours. She had the gun directly aimed at the cockpit and now realized it was within point blank range.

She blinked and bit her lower lip.

She then moved her aim from the cockpit of Gray's plane to his left wing immediately in front of her, closed her eyes, and fired away at it.

Gray was astonished that she would fire at him. He tried to pull away, but it was too late. The left side of his aircraft had been torn in half, and it fell into a nosedive.

Joy opened her eyes, looked down, and watched as he ejected and parachuted toward a meadow below (as the forest had now faded into meadowland as they neared the spaceport).

The parachute, fittingly, was also international orange and contained a black outline of a Douglas fir tree on it, like all the fighters had. Without sound, Joy mouthed the words "always advertising" to herself upon seeing the parachute.

"Are we clear?" The co-pilot asked.

"We're clear," Joy reported.

"Wow..." The radio operator observed.

"Great work," the pilot radioed. "Tak, now is your time..."

"One minute," the navigator indicated.

Young Grandpa observed the meadow below through his bombardier scope, he then looked up through the plexiglass nose of the plane at the approaching spaceport. He noticed the warehouse had a large concrete hole immediately in front of it. Back in 1943, he wouldn't have known what it was, as underground silos for missiles and rockets were still in their infancy. But now, his 99-year-old mind quickly recognized it was an opened missile silo. He reasoned that if it was armed with a missile, then dropping the bombs slightly early would trigger a larger explosion through any underground complex beneath the spaceport that could impact the foundation of the above-ground buildings. The massive size and sleek, futuristic appearance of the spaceport suggested that it was capable of manufacturing the type of advanced missile that could destroy a city.

He knew he could do this and still have enough bombload to also hit the warehouse.

"We believe in you, Tak," the radio operator reassured him, right at the moment he needed it.

"Bombs away!" Young Grandpa yelled as he flipped the trigger. The remaining bombs in the bomb bay squealed down toward the missile silo and the warehouse.

*** *** ***

"What's your status?!" Casey asked AI Autumn in a brash, un-compromising tone. AI Autumn had been brought up back on her primary screen via live feed from the missile silo.

"We are ready to fire at your comm—"

AI Autumn had suddenly vanished mid-sentence as Casey witnessed an inferno consuming the missile silo behind where AI Autumn had been standing.

The screen went black.

"Fire!" Casey yelled back in vain at the black screen.

"Fire!" She screamed again at nothing.

She then tugged at her hair from opposite sides of her head and screamed again. This release helped her regain her composure enough to press the button to the intercom to Maxwell's office on her desk control panel.

"Maxwell!" she yelled over the intercom as though unaware of her amplified volume.

There was no reply.

"Maxwell?!"

She pressed a second button that activated the webcam in Maxwell's office on her primary screen. It revealed an empty desk that looked like it had recently been vacated.

There was a mug of tea still steaming beside his laptop on his desk and electronic lounge music was faintly playing from the wireless speaker he kept on one of the shelves in his office.

She had grown so accustomed to having Maxwell around over the past year, that it wasn't until that moment that she remembered that Maxwell was AI too, an AI composite of all her favorite employees at Dark Forest Solutions from around the world. Maxwell was her very first AI project.

Rather than turn off the footage of his empty desk, she left it on, and continued to glare at it as though she was waiting for Maxwell to return to it or for AI Autumn to call in.

She found herself not feeling ready to imagine her life without them.

*** *** ***

A series of explosions tore through the south end of the space-port. A massive quake that had been triggered by the denotation of the underground missile ripped through other buildings that were not immediately impacted by the bombing. Secondary explosions that were ignited in the aftermath of the quake continued to erupt as though bombs were still being dropped even after "Forever Autumn" had passed over it.

"Captain, we are still using the same type of bomb we always use, right?" The radio operator asked as he looked out the window.

"Who knows what they had down there," the pilot responded.

"It must've been important with the way that place looked," the flight engineer added.

"Whatever it was, they can't use it against us now," the ball turret gunner laughed.

"Thank you, Grandpa," Autumn cried to Young Grandpa and she hugged him in the bombardier's chair as he remained speechless and in a wistful state.

As soon as Joy returned from the back of the plane, she picked up her phone from the navigator's desk and started clicking it several times again to activate a flashing red light.

"We have to go now, so they still have plenty of fuel to return," Joy hurriedly explained.

Autumn continued to embrace Young Grandpa as the plane accelerated and re-entered the rainbow tunnel. This time, the ride through time was much smoother as though there was some kind of jet stream that went through the rainbow tunnel and this time the plane wasn't traveling against it like it did the first time. The multicolored fog reappeared in the plane but crested around their knees and did not rise any further.

Autumn looked at Grandpa, Joy, and the navigator as the patches of changing multicolored light reflected on them through the windows and nose of "Forever Autumn." Upon realizing there was much less turbulence on this visit through the tunnel, they all looked hypnotically through the windows at the swirling kaleidoscopic tunnel.

They mostly remained quiet for the rest of the trip through the tunnel, watching the spectacle of lights around them in wonder.

The serenity in the tunnel was abruptly ended by a bump of turbulence that nearly sent everyone to the floor as they re-entered 1943. Autumn found herself back in Young Grandpa's arms while the navigator held onto his desk and Joy held onto a bolted protrusion of the airframe with one hand while still navigating the home screen of her phone with another.

"Well, here we go again," the right waist gunner radioed as they returned to gray clouds and distant flashes of lightning.

"All of our instruments are working again," the radio operator reported.

"I swear every time we are up here the sky shows me something I have never seen before," the left waist gunner reflected

"No kidding," the flight engineer quipped.

"This is the strangest day of my life," the co-pilot sighed.

"No one will believe us when we try to tell them what happened," the radio operator speculated.

"They usually don't believe our crazy stories anyway," the ball turret gunner reminded them.

"I know where we are now!" The navigator exclaimed as he looked at his map, looked outside, and then at his map again. "We are still heading in the right direction."

"Hang in there, everyone. We'll be there soon," the pilot radioed.

After her phone started flashing again, Joy removed her headset and looked at Young Grandpa and Autumn: "We're almost there."

As she rested her head one more time on Young Grandpa's shoulder, Autumn saw through the nose of the plane how they were surrounded by gray-black clouds and swirling winds again but felt relieved that the flak hadn't returned for Grandpa to see.

"Autumn," Young Grandpa said after they separated from their embrace. He reached out to her with his right hand, and she took hold of it.

She blinked.

She still felt the warmth of Grandpa's hand in her own, but they were back in the hospital room with the beeping machines.

Joy was standing beside her and gently lifted her phone from Grandpa's chest.

"Autumn…" Grandpa repeated in a whisper with his 99-year-old voice, but he trailed off before he could continue with what he wanted to say.

Grandpa closed his eyes for a moment before opening them again, as though it had become a struggle to keep them open.

"Autumn," he said a third time as he made eye contact with her. But instead of trying to say anything more this time, he smiled.

"Grandpa you're smiling," Autumn observed.

She then had that recurring thought of how he was always so happy to see her even though she had never visited him enough, didn't call him as often as she should have, and didn't have many conversations with him that went beyond the obligatory small talk about how they were doing, what the weather was like, and how time passes by too quickly. Very slowly, through the course of her lifetime, she had noticed that a crucial part of allowing patience and endurance to evolve within you involves having gratitude for and fully cherishing every little positive moment life gives you. It included embracing those little, sometimes fleeting moments you had with the people you loved most. Grandpa embodied that brand of embracing life's little moments whenever he encountered them, no matter how brief or seemingly inconsequential they were. Even now, after everything they had been through and after learning more about what they had in common, she still felt undeserving of both the positive attention he gave her and the insights that she had gained along with it. But she also felt a new desire to want to deserve it.

"You know my life began today…" Grandpa began.

"What?" Autumn asked.

Grandpa squeezed her hand as he caught his breath, as if to communicate to her that he still had more to say.

"Grandpa?!" Autumn cried.

She realized now more than ever about how you don't just lose a loved one when they pass away, you also lose the little world they created around them that only they could create: their taste in music, their style of clothes, the way they decorated their home, and their stories they told. You lose a whole little world within the world that you can't experience the same way anymore.

"Every time you reach a goal, your life begins again, no matter how far along you are in life," Grandpa advised as he maintained eye contact with Autumn. "There is hidden and not-so-hidden beauty all around you, just like there is hidden and not-so-hidden beauty within you."

Tears had formed in Autumn's eyes as if to express what she was unable to articulate in words. She felt a chill, but in a good way, like she was still feeling the air up in the plane in the clear morning sky.

"It's strange the way time passes," Grandpa muttered as his voice weakened back to a whisper. "We all are at least somewhat aware of how it passes, and we see how other people are changing, but it's so much harder to see how we ourselves are changing. I'd look in the mirror at 99 and still feel like I'm 19... I did change one very important thing within me, and I lived a much better life because of it. I lived the same exterior life, but within me, it was totally different. I lived a better life even knowing all the pain I still had ahead of me, and I waited to tell you here. Autumn, you can give yourself a better life now, in the future, and even in the past within your mind, without having to return to the past like I did."

Autumn turned to Joy, who had left the side of the bed to give Autumn and Grandpa their time together.

"I put a seashell in his jacket pocket on the plane. He deserved another try, and somehow, I knew we could trust him," Joy explained, as she squeezed the flight equipment and accessories back into her backpack. She smiled as she was just barely able to get the zipper closed over the overstuffed contents of the backpack.

Autumn froze for a moment as she tried to imagine a person going back in time at 99 years old to when they were 19 years old and reliving 80 years of life all over again with the knowledge and spirit of a 99 year old. She didn't feel any different about him and couldn't immediately recall any differences in their relationship as a result of Grandpa having this different life. She felt a strange mix of emotions that included: a sense of happiness that he got another chance at most of his life all over again, a sense of confusion as to whether or not he actually would've wanted that, a selfish sense of betrayal that he didn't apparently change anything about their relationship when she was growing up even though he knew they'd eventually have this experience and she would've benefitted from having help with accepting herself at an earlier age, and an odd sense of deep respect that someone could re-live their life the same way and find greater value in it without triggering the butterfly effect.

"What was different?" Autumn asked turning back to Grandpa.

"Acceptance," Grandpa whispered, as the life slowly drained from his hand that was still in Autumn's hand.

As he passed, a sense of peace and calm transferred from his hand to hers and filled her soul. It was as if he knew this would happen all along. This sense of peace and calm activated an epiphany within her as though it had been with her all her life but in a dormant state. The epiphany was the realization that intellectual knowledge of who you are and what you want in life doesn't guarantee you are emotionally ready for it, and you can only learn to work toward and hopefully attain peace of mind in your own time, through the lessons of life experience. She realized that it took Grandpa a total of 179 years of experiencing life to reach this point and up until 40, she had been too stubborn to take any advice from anyone that she would've accepted anyway.

Grandpa had honored her journey in his own way, in a way only they could both understand, all along.

She smiled, even while shedding tears of grief.
She felt like a new oasis, being formed in the middle of a desert.

www.ingramcontent.com/pod-product-compliance
Lightning Source LLC
Chambersburg PA
CBHW060308310726
48976CB00007B/2249